VULTURE'S KISS

THE IBIS PROPHECY: BOOK TWO

What Reviewers Say About BOLD STROKES Authors

KIM BALDWIN
"*Force of Nature* is filled with nonstop, fast paced action. Tornadoes, raging fire blazes, heroic and daring rescues…Baldwin does a fine job of describing the fast-paced scenes and inspiring the reader to keep on turning the pages." – L-word.com Literature

ROSE BEECHAM
"…her characters seem fully capable of walking away from the particulars of whodunit and engaging the reader in other aspects of their lives." – *Lambda Book Report*

GEORGIA BEERS
"Beers weaves a tale of yearning, love, lust, and conflict resolution. She has constructed a believable plot, with strong characters in a charming setting." – *JustAboutWrite*

RONICA BLACK
"*Wild Abandon* tells how these two women come to realize that 'life was too precious to be ruled by…fears, by…demons.' While these two women struggle with their issues, there is some very, very hot sex. If you enjoy complex characters and passionate sex scenes, you'll love *Wild Abandon*." – *MegaScene*

GUN BROOKE
"*Course of Action* is a romance…populated with a host of captivating and amiable characters. The glimpses into the lifestyles of the rich and beautiful people are rather like guilty pleasures…a most satisfying and entertaining reading experience." – *Midwest Book Review*

CATE CULPEPPER
"…an exceptional storyteller who has taken on a very difficult subject …and turned it into a spellbinding novel. As an author, she understands well that fiction can teach us our own history." – *JustAboutWrite*

JANE FLETCHER
"*The Exile and the Sorcerer* is a mesmerizing read, a tour-de-force packed with adventure, ordeals, complex twists and turns, and the internal introspection of appealing characters." – *Midwest Book Review*

JD GLASS

"*Punk Like Me*…is different. It is engaging. It is life-affirming. Frankly, it is genius. This is a rare book in that it has a soul; one that is laid bare for all to see." – *JustAboutWrite*

GRACE LENNOX

"*Chance* is refreshing…Every nuance is powerful and succinct. *Chance* is not a novel about the music industry; it is about a woman discovering herself as she muddles through all the trappings of fame." – *Midwest Book Review*

LEE LYNCH

"Lynch, with a dozen novels to her credit dating back to the early days of Naiad Press, has earned her stripes as a writerly elder. She was contributing stories to the lesbian magazine *The Ladder* four decades ago. But this latest is sublimely in tune with the times." – *Q-Syndicate*

JLEE MEYER

"*Forever Found*…neatly combines hot sex scenes, humor, engaging characters, and an exciting story." – *MegaScene*

RADCLYFFE

"…well-plotted…lovely romance…I couldn't turn the pages fast enough!" – Ann Bannon, author of *The Beebo Brinker Chronicles*

SUSAN SMITH

"This disparate duo's lush rush of a romance - which incorporates reincarnation, a grounded transman and his peppy daughter, and the dark moods of a troubled witch - pays wonderful homage to Leslie Feinberg's classic gender-bending novel, *Stone Butch Blues*." – *Q-Syndicate*

ALI VALI

"Rich in character portrayal, *The Devil Inside* by Ali Vali is an unusual, unpredictable, and thought-provoking love story that will have the reader questioning the definition of right and wrong long after she finishes the book." – *JustAboutWrite*

VULTURE'S KISS

THE IBIS PROPHECY: BOOK TWO

by

Justine Saracen

2007

VULTURE'S KISS
THE IBIS PROPHECY: BOOK TWO

© 2007 BY JUSTINE SARACEN. ALL RIGHTS RESERVED.

ISBN10: 1-933110-87-2
ISBN13: 978-1-933110-87-5

THIS TRADE PAPERBACK IS PUBLISHED BY
BOLD STROKES BOOKS; INC.
NEW YORK, USA

FIRST EDITION, AUGUST 2007

CREDITS
EDITORS: JENNIFER KNIGHT, SHELLEY THRASHER, AND J. B. GREYSTONE
PRODUCTION DESIGN: J. B. GREYSTONE
COVER GRAPHIC: SHERI (graphicartist2020@hotmail.com)

By the Author

The 100th Generation—The Ibis Prophecy: Book One

Acknowledgments

So much to learn, it takes your breath away. I want to thank Thomas Behr for sharing his knowledge of the First Crusade, Yoni Debel for information on the Church of the Holy Sepulchre, and Tim at DeHLTA for explaining how to blow things up. I am greatly indebted to Inga Horwood, who read the rough manuscript and critiqued me gently. Special thanks is due to gifted editors Shelley Thrasher and Jennifer Knight who, when you think you're flying, get rid of the hot air without taking the wind out of your sails (and would for example NEVER stand for a hideous mixed metaphor like that.) Thanks also to Sheri for a beautiful and insightful cover, to Julie Greystone for nipping and tucking in all the right places, to Ruth Sternglantz for Hebrew instruction, and above all to the awesome Radclyffe who keeps this whole enterprise going.

DEDICATION

To Dr. Angelique Corthals, who brought me to Egypt,
and to the Jewish-American Medical Project that brought
me to Jerusalem.

DISCLAIMER

This story deals with religion, monotheisms and polytheisms. Judaism, Christianity, and Islam have all made their contribution to art, learning, and the formation of cultural ideas. Each has a core of goodwill and an attempt at a just moral code. But at their fringes are the dogmatists and absolutists whose otherworldly doctrines threaten the secular values of tolerance and basic human rights.

On the hard Christian right stands the politically powerful evangelist John Hagee and his 18,000-strong congregation, who argue that, to fulfill God's plan for the Rapture and the Second Coming of Christ, the US must join Israel in a preemptive strike against the Arab world. Judaism, which traditionally looks to Israel as its spiritual home, has its most militant proponents among the settlers who—supported by the Israeli military—pursue what they believe is God's plan to make all of Palestine Jewish and, in doing so, perpetuate conflict in Israel and in the Middle East. Islam, it will surprise no one to learn, has Al Qaeda and other violent fundamentalist sects that see the West as satanic and seek to do it grave harm. In all cases, the mix of religion and politics is lethal.

This story, though fictional, suggests that religion be returned to where it started, in the reverence for the majestic, and sometimes vulnerable, elements of nature.

Prologue

*I*t was of a Friday, the very day and hour of Our Lord's crucifixion, that the city of Jerusalem was taken. The valiant duke, the knights, and the other men of arms descended from the walls into the city. All of them that they met they slew in God's name, men, women, and children, sparing none. No prayer nor supplication could avail them. They slew so many in the streets that one might not pass but climb upon them that lay dead. The men went in bands, holding in their hands great poleaxes, swords, mallets, slaying all the heathen until the channels and gutters ran with their blood, and the streets were covered with the dead. Truly it were a lamentable thing, had these not been of the enemies of our Lord Jesus Christ, and misbelievers, who had defiled the place with their foul law of Mohammed.

William of Tyre (c.1181) trans. from Latin: William Caxton (1481)

*W*hile the Frankish armies went rapine through the city, on the high platform the noble emir surrendered. He came with our women and his guard and laid down his sword before the Frankish prince. The emir was courteously met and granted mercy. Yet a knight coveted one of the women and sought to take hold of her. Strangely, a vulture came upon him suddenly and lit upon his chest, catching its talons in his garment and striking him in the face. The knight fell back, covering his eyes. An armbruster shot it through with a bolt from his crossbow and it flew off. The knight was sorely vexed and snatched the woman's child into the air. A cry seemed to go out from the very wind to stay his hand.

Sharif al Kitab (fragment: c.1102) trans. from Arabic: Saïd Khoury (1998)

1

Haunted

Valerie Foret remembered when the vultures came the day she died. Lying supine on the rocky dune, she saw them through dead eyes as they descended on her murderer.

The sandstorm stopped him from fleeing, blinding him and choking the motor of his jeep. The wind ripped away the handkerchief that covered half his face as he jerked to a halt. He crawled beneath the dash on the passenger's side and tried uselessly to pull his shirt up over his head. But the tiny particles of the desert crept into his nostrils and along his throat. When he began to cough, he was already doomed, for each cough required an inhalation, and every inhalation forced more cutting sand into his lungs. He thrashed wildly, inhaling fire and coughing out pieces of his lungs until the desert finally stilled him.

Abruptly the sandstorm stopped and left him staring sightlessly at her, his face a powder-caked *kabuki* grimace.

The vultures appeared next, a dozen of them, descending all at once around the jeep. One or two fluttered near him, heads bobbing, and pecked tentatively at him. Others joined them, tearing through the fabric of his shirt to reach the tender flesh. The rest gathered then, squabbling, displacing one another on the ground, in the vehicle, and on the still-warm cadaver.

Valerie watched the roiling mass of feathers through her own dead eyes, wondering if she was next, wondering how it would feel to be torn apart. Even if they did not devour her, she knew something would. He was carrion for vultures, she for microbes; it made no difference in the end. All that mattered were the people who were left, the ones who would mourn or be outraged.

Sated, the flock of scavengers calmed and they withdrew from the hideous remains. They did not leave but seemed to wait for something, forming a rough circle on the ground. And then it happened. At the center the largest of them elongated vertically and assumed a new shape. The narrow vulturine head broadened, the reptilian neck withdrew into itself, and empty eyes began to reveal expression. Wide wings drooped to the fluttering tatters of a black abaya, and beneath the tatters a woman appeared. The croaking birds drew away from her with gobbets of flesh still hanging from their beaks.

The apparition stood for a moment, gazing out over the desolate landscape, the last of the storm wind playing with loose strands of her long black hair. Finally she noticed the dead woman who stared at her, and she neared, moving mysteriously, with feet that did not quite touch the ground.

She was enveloped in a strange light, a bright darkness that seemed the residue of some unworldly place. Severe and powerful, she was stunning, in the perfect uncompromised way of a predator, with eyes as savage as the scavengers behind her and black as eternity.

The iridescent darkness around her expanded, both ominous and inviting. She extended one arm, clothed in the fluttering thin black cloth, and the slender limb seemed to oscillate, now woman's arm, now blood-smeared vulture's wing. She beckoned, compellingly, but with eyes that offered nothing but abyss. That was the choice, Valerie knew. To stay and decay into the desert sand or embrace the alien thing.

Dead, yet still she ached. *Don't leave me here,* she thought as the lovely monster loomed over her.

The shrill buzz of the three o'clock bell jolted her from her reverie.

Oh, right. Her last class. Damn. She had been staring out her office window, lost in memory again, a frightening habit that had gotten worse in the last few months. How much was real memory and how much was the imagery of her feverish longing?

She shook her head. No time to brood on the question now. A classroom full of dullards waited for her to explain Egyptian theology.

She laughed inwardly. If they only knew.

2

Trouble

August 28. Brussels University, Department of Archaeology

"Vulture worship. That's a little disgusting." The well-developed young man who stood at the back of the classroom hooked his thumb over the belt of his jeans, causing his bicep to bulge slightly under the sleeve of his spotless white T-shirt.

Why did stupidity so often house in such robust bodies? Valerie wondered. Well, it was the last day of a summer review class for students with credit deficiencies. What did she expect?

"But you are missing the point here." She circled to the front of the podium. "The animals had conquered the desert long before humans, and people had every reason to be in awe of them. The two goddesses, Nekhbet the vulture and Wadjet the cobra, could survive in the desert without water, and for the Egyptians, they symbolized a tenacious life force." She smiled at his simple masculinity. "Besides, Nekhbet appeared to mortals as a beautiful woman. You would have found her irresistible." She set the chalk down below her blackboard drawing of the vulture-form hieroglyph for "protection."

The young man slid the fingers of both his hands into his jeans pockets. "You think so? But what if in the middle of a hot kiss she popped back into a vulture? Not to mention in the middle of doing, you know, the other thing." The other students laughed openly and he sat down, smirking.

Only one student seemed unamused. A sleek, raven-haired woman sat in the front row and watched intently as the lesson continued, never lowering her eyes. She leaned back slightly, crossing and uncrossing blue-jeaned legs. Her dark blue blouse was a fraction too tight and unbuttoned a fraction too far down for classroom dress. A wave of black hair spilled over the slender shoulder into the visible cleavage. She took no notes, but ran her fingertip back and forth over closed lips.

Valerie directed her gaze elsewhere, though she kept returning to the disturbing anomaly, the dark shimmering spot that reduced everything else in the room to dullness. Her unrelenting stare made it hard for Valerie to concentrate.

She forced her attention back to the young man. "If you find the vulture goddess disgusting, Monsieur Vernaud, then you'll really have trouble with Khepre, the dung beetle who created the world by rolling up a ball of cow feces." The class murmured appreciation. "But never forget, we are talking about one of the first great cultures of humankind, and their divinities were their way of dealing with nature. When the gods were revered, nature was revered. Rather more reasonable than having to placate a vengeful father-god, don't you think?"

The four o'clock bell spared her any further youthful disdain. The students stood up murmuring their private conversations and gathering their things, all but the dark-haired one, who was suddenly beside the podium.

"Do you have a question, Mlle...uh...?" She couldn't remember the girl's name, couldn't actually remember seeing her in class before. The student hunched her shoulders slightly as her male counterpart had done and slid her fingers into the two front pockets of her jeans. What was it about blue jeans that lent them so easily to sexual posing?

"Belle Cather." The student shrugged for no apparent reason, drawing up her shirt in a curve under her perfect breasts. "I'd like to talk to you privately, if that's possible." She glanced toward the other students who were going through the door or who hung back waiting their turn to talk to the professor.

Valerie was taken aback. Asking for a private conference usually meant the student wanted an exam postponement. In this case, there was no exam. What was going on?

"Uh, well, yes, certainly, Mlle Cather." To her surprise, she found herself stammering. "I'm tied up with conferences the rest of the afternoon, however. Can you tell me what you need to talk about?" Five or six other students were closing in from the periphery, each one with a question.

The young woman dropped her eyes. "Something important that I need to discuss in private. If you don't mind." She pressed her lips together as if stifling the rest of what she had to say.

"Perhaps after the other conferences. In my office. I have a few minutes before a dinner meeting with the dean."

"No." The lovely creature looked at her through long lashes that were the same jet black color as her hair. "It will take more than a few minutes. I will come after dinner. Will eight o'clock be late enough?"

Valerie glanced at the other students who were already within earshot. Her inner alarm was beginning to sound. *Student flirtation. Danger here. Frivolous, unethical, reckless. Twenty-one, too much makeup, too much libido, too little intellect, nothing to offer but one brief thrill. Danger. Run away.*

"Yes. Eight will be fine," she answered quickly and directed her attention to the next student in line.

❖

Valerie stayed in the empty classroom for a moment and stared at the vulture hieroglyph. What the hell had just happened? More to the point, what was going to happen? Was it the sex-charged air of the young students that weighted everything toward the carnal? She didn't know, but something about the black-haired girl had affected her. Whatever the discussion at eight o'clock that evening, it was unlikely to be about Egyptology, or even meaningful. Well, no matter. She had given up the thought of having anything meaningful with women.

The last time she had found "meaning" was in a Bedouin tent somewhere in the vast Egyptian desert. By the flickering light of an oil lamp, she had poured out her secrets to a mysterious woman and given herself to someone—to something—about which she knew nothing.

Yet when their lips had finally met, the Bedouin had not given back desire, but revelation, a staggering apocalyptic vision. It had changed the meaning of everything Valerie knew. Meaning in the place of passion. Enough meaning for her to lose her life over.

Since that night, Valerie had felt empty. No woman's kiss moved her beyond mere lust, and she sometimes wondered—half laughing at herself—if she had simply lost her taste for mortals.

She glanced through the open door where Belle Cather, full of promise, had disappeared.

Well, lust would do.

3

Gladius Dei

His hands were steady as he duct-taped the device against the thin metal wall that separated his compartment from the one in front. He added another strip, crisscrossing the others to hold the mechanism fast. Then he wedged his rock-filled suitcase against the explosive so it would blast forward.

He nodded, satisfied, and set the timer. Thirty minutes. That should put detonation somewhere around Qena.

The train slowed to a crawl as the porter announced the station. He slipped off his rubber gloves and dropped them on the floor where they would burn away. Some half dozen tourists shuffled along the corridor dragging their holiday luggage toward the door. When the train started again, at the last moment he opened the door and jumped out.

On the platform, he tugged the brim of his hat a bit lower and strode briskly out into the warm night air of Luxor.

Fifteen minutes later he pulled onto the highway that ran parallel to the railroad tracks. He could drive at top speed now; the night traffic was sparse. The train was well ahead of him, but he did not need to be in sight of it, only close enough to hear the explosion.

He checked his luminous watch. Ten minutes to go. The August night was hot, and he propped his arm on the car window to let the breeze blow into his shirt sleeve. Under the calm of his competence and resolve, he was excited. It felt good to be a lone soldier, fulfilling a complex and righteous mission that was both personal and for the greater good.

It had taken him a long while to surrender his will and to accept his duty. He bore the scars of harsh discipline. But he bore them with honor now as the signs of his identity. He was the heir to generations of piety and sacrifice of the most rigorous sort—a lineage of martyrs in a way. His father, who had so often laid the strap to him, would finally be proud.

The soft boom somewhere ahead of him and the orange glow in the distance spread warmth downward from his chest. *I am the arm of vengeance*, he thought. *I am the instrument of righteousness*. He felt, curiously, like both a victor and a martyr.

4

Caught

Valerie hummed a bit of Italian opera as she organized the chaos in her office. It had grown imperceptibly during the summer term, and now, before she went on leave again, she had to deal with it.

She reduced the towers of reference books, returning them to their places on the shelves, but the loose papers thwarted her. Each one required a decision: create a folder and file, or discard. And every one of them contained some vital piece of information. Defeated, she simply squared the piles, improving their appearance but obscuring further the location of any given article if she should need it.

Among the papers were some photos and she paused to study them. Ah, yes, the "family" photo Derek had insisted on taking just before they left Luxor two years ago. Valerie smiled at the memory. They had been hurrying to get the train back to Cairo, but he had run and bought a disposable camera and asked the merchant to snap the shot, in the middle of the Luxor street. Silly, sentimental, wonderful Derek.

She held the photo close. Auset, poor dear, looked exhausted, and no wonder, having endured childbirth on the floor of an Egyptian temple only two days earlier. Yussif, beaming, to the extent one could beam from behind a thick black beard that generally rendered him ferocious. Derek was grinning too, no doubt because he had just acted out a living opera of heroic sacrifice and triumph. Valerie, herself, looked a bit distracted. And in the middle, asleep in Auset's arms, lay the newborn Neferenepet, the Child of the New Year who had just been acclaimed by a few hundred Egyptian gods.

Valerie stared, bemused, at her own image and wondered what attracted students to her. No one would call her pretty, not in the girlie sense. Her oval face could occasionally look bony, especially after a few months on excavation when hard labor completely burned off the lentils and pita she consumed. She used to like her large, slightly slanted eyes until she learned they came from the paternal side of her family. She shuddered a little. Akhnaton eyes. Was that what appealed to students like Belle?

Maybe it was the scar. She ran her fingertips over the crescent-shaped ridge just in front of her left ear. The look of the adventurer, the veteran of mortal confrontations. She chuckled to herself. You could say that.

Someone tapped at the door.

❖

"You're right on time, Mlle Cather. Come on in."

"Call me Belle."

A thin sweater, too short to be tucked in, had replaced the blouse. She wore the same dark jeans, which hugged her narrow hips and left a line of exposed skin between pants and sweater. The flawless skin was caramel colored, and she was obviously not Belgian. Moroccan, perhaps? The last name gave no indication. The face was generic pretty, as if copied from a cover of one of the glamour magazines.

Valerie sat down on the narrow couch at the side of the office and motioned toward the armchair at the corner. "So. How can I help you?"

Belle ignored the chair and sat next to Valerie on the tiny office sofa, then shifted sideways, clasping her hands in her lap. "I'm sorry I missed some of your lectures," she began. "Did you talk much about the Egyptian gods? Did the students always react as they did today?"

Noting the proximity of their legs, Valerie smiled inwardly. She had no doubt where this was going. "Yes, and I'm afraid they did," she answered pleasantly. "The few who are religious take offense at polytheism altogether. They have their own supernatural beliefs and allow no room for any other perspective. The students who are not religious have no interest in the supernatural at all. And both groups are contemptuous of what they see as animal worship."

"They do seem resistant—and superficial." Belle rested one elbow on the back of the sofa. The sweater on that side of her waist lifted to reveal a handbreadth more skin.

Valerie's face began to warm with the realization that Belle's knee had somehow approached her own and now brushed lightly against it. "In a way, their skepticism is healthy, but they are also inflexible, unwilling to explore different ways of comprehending the world. But what was so important that you wanted to talk about?"

"I will get to that in a minute. First, please tell me about yourself. How did you become interested in Egyptian religion?"

Ah. The tell-me-about-yourself gambit. She had used it herself many times. Obviously Belle had nothing "important" to talk about, and the "conference" was pure flirtation. The pressure on her knee confirmed her suspicion. "That's a complicated story, and I don't think you want to hear the long version."

"Maybe I do. Maybe I care why. Do you teach this subject out of conviction, or just because it is entertaining?" Belle shifted closer so that they sat almost parallel, arms and legs lightly touching.

Valerie could smell the freshly shampooed hair now, and the pleasant fragrance of youthful skin. "Are you asking me whether I believe in the Egyptian religion?"

Belle laughed emotionlessly, tilting her head back with the feigned amusement of a fashion model. "Perhaps I am. Will you answer?"

Sitting so close, Valerie studied the well-formed lips and teeth. What stroke of luck or fate had brought such a delicious creature to her couch? She was almost too good to be true.

Valerie tried to move the focus away from herself. "Why did you take my class? Maybe your beliefs are more relevant than mine. That seems to be an issue with some of the students."

Suddenly Belle grew serious and leaned forward again. Her arm slid along the back of the sofa and her breast grazed the professorial shoulder. "You are evading my question. Tell me, first, what you believe."

Valerie was aroused by the challenge and the intimate touch. Already her mind jumped ahead to what was coming: the climb, step by delicious step, to shivering thrill. Familiar heat spread upward, urging her toward gratification. So easy to press the little vixen back against the sofa and get the whole thing started. "I'm a scientist. I believe what I can see, and…touch." She laid a fingertip lightly on the side of the fashion-model face.

"Is that so?" Belle murmured.

Her head was close now, the thin white line of her upper teeth just visible between parted lips. Valerie detected the smell of mint that in a moment she would taste firsthand. Oh, minty kisses were nice. In the precious heart-pounding seconds before the first touch of a new mouth, she slipped her hand between the young thighs. This little romp was going to be quick. Quick and very good. A millimeter from the inviting lips, she closed her eyes.

Thwack!

Valerie's head snapped back from the force of the slap.

5

Grim Tidings

V alerie blinked in disbelief.

Then she recognized the woman, and the noble epithets ran by her as if on a frieze: Mistress of the Desert, Lady of Elkab, Vulture of Upper Egypt, Protector of the King, Goddess of the White Crown. Nekhbet.

She was livid. "*This* is what you do? The Aton raises his hand against us once again, and this is what you do?"

Valerie rubbed the side of her face and looked up speechless at her accuser.

The Eurotrash clothing had disappeared along with Belle and her pretty pout. The goddess was clothed as she was portrayed in tombs and temples, in a simple black sheath dress from calf to bosom. Her sleek shoulders and arms were bare, and the swelling of her breasts was visible just above the sheath.

"Excuse me, but I could ask you exactly the same thing. Is this what *you* do? You glide into my classroom and my office looking like some nubile young thing, flutter your eyelashes, and entrap me."

"Entrap? I entered your world as one of your own, to see what you have accomplished at the end of two years. If you imagined other motives," Nekhbet gestured toward the sofa, "you are in error."

"Me?" Valerie was indignant. "What did you expect me to think? No student visits a professor at night for scholarly discussion. You said you had something 'important' to discuss, but it was just a ploy to get us together."

Nekhbet waved a dismissive hand. "Do not argue these subtleties with me. I have something important to tell you, and you have let your baser urges interfere."

"Baser urges?" Valerie was sputtering. "So I'm to blame for—"

"There have been disasters. Rekemheb has disappeared. His ba-bird no longer flies between the worlds."

Valerie's indignation abruptly became alarm.

"His ba-bird is gone?" Valerie knew that the soul took the form of a bird when it left the deceased. It flew between the living world and the next with its human face as long as the bodily form remained. Its disappearance was ominous.

"We left his mummy safely in his new tomb. You saw that. Is it possible that someone has found it?"

"Perhaps time has found it and the flesh crumbles. Whatever the reason, you must create a likeness to house his ka. If it is not too late."

"I understand the principle. But do you think I can create a likeness of him just from memory?"

"Foolish child, you have already forgotten. Wherefore was Derek born in the image of his ancestor? He will be the model. There is a man in Egypt who knows the craft. I will guide you to him. But you must hurry."

Valerie could not take her eyes from the divine mouth where an exquisite groove descended from between the nostrils to the bow of the lips. The suggestive upward curve at both corners of the mouth hinted at a smile. But Nekhbet never smiled.

The same solemnity, the same dark eyes, deep as history, that had mesmerized her two years before did so again. It was the face, faintly Greek as well as Egyptian, that haunted her dreams and reveries.

It had been two years since she had witnessed the stunning spectacle of the gods in the Temple of Dendara. Over that time, she had labored to write their chronicle and tell their glory, and all the while, the thought of Nekhbet had been with her like a heartbeat. Valerie wanted her again. She wanted her all the time.

"The summer term is already over," Valerie said, forcing her mind to the task at hand. "I can leave in two days. But if it's so urgent, wouldn't it be faster for Auset and Yussif to go? I mean, to arrange for the statue before we arrive?"

Nekhbet lowered her eyes. "That is the other disaster. Yussif is dead."

6

Mission Accomplished

A fter the orange light of his bomb faded from the night sky, he drove the rest of the way to Cairo at normal speed. With unfeigned nonchalance, he left the rented car at a garage in Giza. A television in the small office was tuned to the news station, and while the clerk did the paperwork, he watched impassively as the the explosion was reported. The young woman noted the news for a moment, shook her head at the familiar talk of terrorism, then resumed writing.

He tapped his fingers lightly while he waited, concealing satisfaction. The plan was successful so far, but would the bait work? If not, he had alternate plans. One way or another he would get them all together and move them into place for the final retribution.

He licked his lips, as if savoring the first taste of a banquet. To his surprise, the year-long mission had not sapped him as he had feared, but made him stronger, and he knew that strength showed in his demeanor. He had always been handsome, with light wavy hair, but now he exuded potency, and people responded to it.

By their deeds ye shall know them.

The clerk handed him his receipt and held his glance a fraction of a second longer than she needed to. Yes, it was the best thing he had ever done. He had sacrificed his normal life, yet he had never felt more virile and alive.

7

Summoned

Valerie dropped down on a chair. "Yussif is dead? When? How?"

"See for yourself." Nekhbet pointed to the small television atop the bookshelf, a device she seemed to accept but would not touch.

Valerie clicked it on and swept through the stations until she found a news broadcast. The tidy, attractive form of Worldnews correspondent Najya Khoury appeared, leaning toward the camera while behind her a fire raged. Explosion, derailment near Qena on the night train from Luxor, she reported. Fatalities unknown but terrorism suspected.

"He was on that train?" Valerie knew the answer.

"Yes. He lies on the ground and his ka is departed from him."

Valerie sat slack-jawed, remembering Yussif's scowling bearded face that would break into a radiant smile at the sight of his gorgeous wife or her infant daughter. She recalled their conversations on the long march through the desert, and the surprisingly deep intelligence of the man. Precious few Egyptian men would marry a woman with an illegitimate child by a black foreigner. "Does Derek know?"

"He does." She indicated the phone, which at that moment rang.

Valerie answered, still staring at the images on the television screen and at Najya Khoury, reporting in the scripted tones of the newscaster. "Derek? Is that you, dear?"

He answered breathlessly, his voice higher than usual, from the shock of the sudden tragedy. No time for a long conversation, no night for chitchat. They agreed to leave right away for Cairo on Thursday flights, he from Paris and she from Brussels. They could plan everything else once they were together.

"I'll call you with my flight information," Valerie said. "I'll telephone Auset too, first thing tomorrow morning." She set down the phone, her head swimming. "This will change everything."

"No. It changes very little."

Nekhbet's beautiful lips were pressed thin. "The same crisis looms as before. Your seas are dying, and the wild places are despoiled. The land and air are poisoned, and the Aton still whispers in the ears of the powerful. This is but a small tragedy."

"It is not small to Auset. I thought the gods were protecting us."

"We protect the Child above all, but we are not omnipotent. And Yussif…we never thought—"

"Because he was not part of the original plan. Yes, I know," Valerie said bitterly. She closed her eyes and forced the anger away. "All right. As you heard, I've made arrangements to leave Wednesday night."

Nekhbet did not move and merely raised her chin a little. "There is something else."

"Oh? Yet another disaster?"

Nekhbet ignored the sarcasm. "Where is our Book? The chronicle you were called to write two years ago. We have waited."

Valerie took a step toward her desk and yanked open the top drawer. "You mean this?" She lifted out a thick manuscript held together by rubber bands and dropped it with a thud on the desktop. "I finished your damned Book a year ago, and it's only now being published. By a small women's press. I don't imagine they see themselves as apostles of a new religion, though."

Valerie laid her hand on the printout. "This cost me a year's work and kept me from the professional articles I should have been writing. What about your side of the agreement? You were supposed to look after us. But for two years I have seen no sign of you."

"I made no agreement," Nekhbet said, aloof.

"Not in so many words, I suppose." Valerie fumed for a moment. "Damn it. I died for you. I went into the underworld because of you. The memory of it haunts me all the time."

"Many have died for us and in far worse ways. You can make no claim to martyrdom. You descended into the underworld and fled from it again." Nekhbet's glance swept around the office. "You have recovered from death quite well."

"Martyrdom is the last thing I would claim. I only want you to protect us a little. No one did that for Yussif. Is he in the underworld?"

The goddess would not meet her gaze. "It is complicated. We will talk later about that. First do as I tell you."

"Talk later? When will that be?" Valerie replaced the manuscript in its drawer, but when she glanced back, she was alone. She exhaled angrily, uselessly, and walked over to the office window, trying to sort her thoughts.

Below her, in what remained of the summer evening, students were emerging from the lab or the library. They had no idea this bizarre other world of ghosts and animal-headed gods waited just outside their own. That once again, after millennia, nature and their own jealous authoritarian god confronted one another. And that she, of all people, was chosen to be the one to tell them.

She felt uneasy about Cairo. If Islamists were blowing up trains, things had gotten very bad again. And dangerous for a white European. She unlocked her bottom desk drawer, lifted out a .38 revolver, and dropped it into her briefcase.

8

Brussels to Cairo

Gods, how she hated crowds. She had become an Egyptologist in order to spend time in the vast openness of the desert, and now here she was trapped in a tiny seat in an airplane. The tall man who sat next to her had been politely silent for the entire trip, for which she was grateful, but he blocked ready access to the aisle. Worse, the person in front of her had reclined his seat to nap and thus removed another third of her airspace. She was caged, and even when she escaped to walk in the aisle, which she had done repeatedly, she had always to return to her confinement.

She stared out the window into blue sky above and vaporous clouds below, starved for openness. Finally through a gap in the cloud she glimpsed land. The dun-colored patches told her they had crossed the Mediterranean and reached Africa. She guessed they were curving over the Libyan plateau and, mercifully, were only about half an hour from Cairo.

Seeing the desert from such a height called to mind the soaring vision that Nekhbet had once given her. Valerie smiled inwardly at the chain of events that had led up to that moment: the four of them wandering in the desert carrying a stolen mummy, the encounter with the Bedouins, the strange midnight invitation to the Bedouin tent, the tense, thrilling flirtation with the beautiful woman under the veil, and finally, the shattering kiss. The kiss she had craved her whole life, without knowing it.

She could not even find a word to describe the ecstasy that she had experienced. For the briefest moment she had been caught up in pure, scorching eroticism, but just when she feared she would die from it, her consciousness had slipped free of the physical and become pure thought and image. She had witnessed Egypt, all of it, throughout its history, complete with the desecration and destruction of its gods. The wonderful, terrible vision had told her that, in spite of the kiss, she was not so much loved as needed. That through the mummy they carried, she was tied to those gods and that she was called to bring them back to the world.

She sighed. Here she was again, still needed but not loved, on a mission to rescue a man who had been dead three thousand years. Not just any man, but her own distant ancestor, himself once martyred for the gods. She had grown to like him, this priest of Hathor, who had come into her life as a ghost. Now his ka, the spirit that could live as long as form and substance existed to house it, had disappeared, and she was ashamed that she had let it happen. Why had she not thought of making the statue when they entombed him?

Of course the whole point of the ka's appearance in the tomb had been to prepare them for his last descendant, the precious infant who was born finally at the end of their flight through the desert.

Nefi made it all worthwhile. Half black, half Egyptian, of parents who were Christian, Jewish, Muslim, and pagan, she was their hope. Born on the Egyptian New Year's morning, in the sanctuary of Hathor's temple, and welcomed by all the gods of Egypt, she was somehow the seed of both the new and old religion, though it was not clear how. Even the name the gods had given her, Neferenepet, which simply meant "The beautiful new year," only hinted of her destiny.

For that matter, Valerie had no idea what any of them were destined for. She had written the Book called for in the scribe god's prophecy, describing the gods' spectacular appearance in the night sky over the temple, yet she still had no idea how the gods would find their way into a world fraught with religious turmoil or what effect they would have. They seemed to have little interest in human affairs and no power to influence them. With their headpieces that marked them as wind, river, harmony, wrath, fertility, and countless animals, they were simply the powers—or fragilities—of nature. She found it somewhat endearing that they did not rule, or impose laws that commanded how humans should behave, dress, eat, and love.

On the other hand, on her more contentious days, the struggle of the Egyptian gods to be recognized seemed preposterous. If the gods did not reward or punish, or even provide any real guidance, what good were they? What was a god, anyway?

❖

The seat-belt light finally went off, and the passengers stood to retrieve luggage from the overhead compartments. Dulled by the half sleep she had fallen into, Valerie sat patiently, hating the crush of people worse than the confinement of her seat.

She peered drowsily at the passengers as they shuffled toward the exit, and for an instant, as if in a dream or nightmare, the man at the front of the line took on the snout and ears of a jackal before he ducked his head through the doorway and moved out of sight. *Anubis?* she thought, astonished. Behind him, the man who had sat next to her through the flight suddenly had a falcon's head. He seemed to stand taller for an instant; then, as Horus, he too passed through the doorway. The woman that followed presented Wadjet's cobra's head. Tasting the air with her forked tongue, she curled briefly toward the passenger behind her. Valerie wondered if the next one would be Nekhbet, but no, she sprouted the horns of the cow goddess Hathor, a sphere of light suspended between them.

A spark of divinity ignited in one passenger after another. Valerie named them to herself. Horus, Wadjet, Hathor, Amun, Shu, Nuut, Sekhmet, Ptah. Only the last one in the line, a man who bore an extraordinary resemblance to the actor John Gielgud, nodded toward her, his puckered mouth morphing into the long ibis beak of the scribe god Jehuti. Then he too exited the cabin and Valerie remained sitting, stupefied.

A hand touched her shoulder lightly. "Madame," a steward said, "I am sorry to wake you, but we have arrived. Can I assist you with your luggage?"

9

Cairo, Mother of the World

Valerie stared at the sky, watching a lone vulture glide in soundless arcs. She imagined what the airport must look like through its miraculous eyes as they surveyed the land from high above. Nothing but a wide strip of concrete in the middle of a sandy wasteland.

Derek's plane had been on the ground for half an hour, but customs was no doubt holding him up. He would not have had time to apply for a visitor's visa in Paris and would have to do it here before he could leave the airport. And so she waited, impatience sapping all other emotions, even the sorrow and dread she had carried with her for the past forty-eight hours.

She returned to the poorly air-conditioned terminal and paced for a few minutes, then stopped to look through the glass wall at the runway. Light struck her from somewhere at the side, and she could see her reflection in the glass. Rumpled clothing and disheveled hair. *Oh damn*, she thought. *I look terrible.* She stepped closer and studied her own tired face. Six months teaching in Brussels had left her pale again, and her sun-bleached hair had returned to its original light brown.

Yussif had once compared her oval face and visible cheekbones with those of Fairuz, the Lebanese singer. He had meant to compliment her, of course, since the young Fairuz was a beauty, but the aging star also became famous for her scowl. Valerie had tried to smile more, but it always felt fake. She had to laugh at the comparisons men were always making. Derek too had meant to compliment her by referring to her "Cleopatra eyes"—not realizing that Cleopatra was Greek, not Egyptian. She wondered if Fairuz—or Cleopatra—ever looked as puffy and tired as she did now.

Ah, there he was, finally. She watched him for a moment before they met and embraced. Usually ebullient, he was subdued. Then she realized he wasn't alone.

A large, slightly rumpled man in pale blue trousers strode beside him, carrying a matching suit jacket folded over his arm. Two others walked in step behind them. Their expressions, devoid of cheer or even interest in their surroundings, revealed they were not tourists. Their massive shoulders and set jaws gave them the demeanor of hit men.

"Valerie, dear." Derek kissed her lightly, then stepped back.

He was still heartbreakingly handsome. Large eyes rimmed with lashes of extraordinary length were set above cheeks a shade lighter than the rest of his dark face. As always, they gave him a sort of radiance, even when he mourned.

He took her hand, nervously, as if he knew his next remarks would be unwelcome, and indicated the blue-suited man. "Valerie, this is my stepfather, Reverend Harlan Carter. He's engaged to speak at the East-West synod in Cairo later this week, but he met me in Paris so we could fly together. He also wants to...uh...meet his granddaughter."

Valerie focused on the reverend, holding a weak smile. He was fleshy, from his wide, short neck and thick shoulders to the muscular roundness of his chest and belly, encased in an expensive white shirt. He wore suspenders, the stylish kind that bankers wore, and pinned to his shirt pocket was a small crimson metal cross. But most shocking of all was his color.

He was white, or had been white, before the Egyptian heat had rendered him an apoplectic pink.

Regaining her composure, she offered him her hand. He took it courteously, but cupped his own hand to prevent their palms from touching. Half a handshake. "So, you are the young lady who brought my son to the heathens. We finally meet."

Valerie supposed he intended his remark as a witticism, but no one smiled and he seemed not to notice.

"Oh, how nice," she said blandly, concealing annoyance. Auset would need a great deal in the coming weeks, but she did not need a Protestant clergyman.

She glanced toward the two cheerless men behind him, and a third she hadn't noticed before.

"This is Mr. Dredding, my lawyer and advisor." Reverend Carter laid a hand on the shoulder of the older man, the only one who wore a hat, a pale straw porkpie. "These other gentlemen are here to look after me." The bulky hit men nodded perfunctorily. "I am so sorry about your friend's death, Ms. Foret. God acts in mysterious ways, his wonders to unfold. Perhaps it is His way to bring the little girl back to her real father."

Speechless at the clergyman's tactlessness, Valerie glanced at Derek, who only gave a tiny shrug. Falling silent, the six of them moved on to Baggage Claim, where they spread out along the carousel.

Valerie stood beside Derek and jabbed him with her elbow. "You never told me he was white. All these years I've been imagining him as black."

He saw his luggage emerge from the bottom of the chute and yanked it off the treadmill with a single swing. "I didn't mention it? I thought I did. Well, what difference would it have made?"

"I don't know. None, I guess. I just imagined him as a sort of Martin Luther King, but he's more like Colonel Sanders. Anyhow, would you explain to me again why he came with you—at a time like this?"

"Frankly, I was a little put off myself when he told me. But he was already engaged for these sermons with the synod. I told him about Yussif being killed, and an hour later he called again to announce he'd changed his schedule to be here with me. What could I say?"

"You could have said this is a delicate private matter and you prefer to deal with it alone."

Derek looked pained. "Well, he's here now. He'll do his preaching thing and at some point pay his respects to Auset, inspect his granddaughter, and then leave."

"Fine, as long as he doesn't interfere. Oh, by the way, don't forget, tomorrow is Muslim Sabbath, so we have to get to the *souq* today and—"

The reverend appeared in front of them, all bags accounted for. After a few moments his ominous retinue arrived, each one with a single suitcase. Bodyguards, it seemed, traveled light.

❖

He stepped out of the shadows but kept a cautious distance, staying amidst the mass of people outside of customs. Well concealed, he watched the five Americans arrive and be met by her. He saw it coalesce, the little family that he would soon take apart with surgical precision.

It gave him a particular thrill to hear her voice, though they were too far away for him to make out what she said. All of those in the cult would have to be gotten rid of, but she was the worst. She was the source and cause of his mission.

At first he had thought she was simply one of those awful women that men had to endure in the professional world. But when he found out, through her own sickening account, what she did in her darkest moments and what went on in her filthy mind, he knew what he had to do.

Her physical presence revolted and confused him. He could barely stomach the fact that someone with her perversion enjoyed the authority of a university professor and the fame of a great discovery. That she had a boyish attractiveness simply added one more outrage. She ought to be disfigured, repugnant.

He stood within the mass of passengers around the baggage carousel, watching her, and made up his mind. He would do her last.

10

Father, Son, and Venus

I think we have it sorted now," Derek said. "Pa, you'll come with Val and me in this taxi, and Mr. Dredding and his...colleagues in the one behind it."

Reverend Carter frowned faintly at the black-and-white Ladas that pulled up in front of them, but Valerie didn't bother to explain the noisy, smoky Russian vehicles that dominated the Cairo streets.

Derek got in the front seat next to the driver, abandoning Valerie to the reverend in the back. As the taxi took off, Derek twisted around and broke the awkward silence. "I've got prezzies," he said tunefully and fluttered his eyelashes. In spite of the grim reason for their arrival, he was obviously trying to be his normal bright self. He opened a leather carry-on and withdrew a plastic bag. "I didn't have time to wrap them," he apologized, and fumbled for something at the bottom of the bag. "This is for you." He reached over the back of his seat and dropped a small white plaster thing into Valerie's hand.

"The Venus di Milo?" She peered perplexed at the armless figurine that had become the world's cliché for "statue" and examined it to see if there was anything special about it. Except for her name scribbled on the bottom, she found nothing.

"I know it's not a *real* gift, but you told me Venus is the Roman version of Hathor. I bought it for you in the Louvre as a sort of good-luck piece, you know...to meet someone." He raised one eyebrow.

"Ah, well, thank you for worrying about my social life, but it's not that bad. All right, maybe it is." She dropped the figurine into the knapsack at her foot. "What else have you got in there?"

"Let's see. I got this for Auset." He unfolded a bright orange scarf. "And these for Nefi." He held up pink leather shoes.

"Tap-dancing shoes? Derek! She's only two years old. I think she's just learned how to walk without waddling."

"They're not for real dancing. They just have this tiny tap on the toe. Like training wheels."

Harlan Carter had detached himself from their conversation and stared out the taxi window at the trash-strewn, drab gray landscape on his side of the road. For the first-time visitor, Valerie knew, it gave a sad introduction to the Egyptian desert.

"Look what they've done to this place," he grumbled. "It used to be the land of milk and honey."

"So, Reverend Carter…" Valerie said lightly, "what exactly will you be preaching on at this…uh…synod?"

The reverend smiled without warmth. "As Derek might have told you, our church is affiliated with the Mission for the Family organization based in Atlanta. It has sponsored me as a guest preacher here."

"Yes, he did mention that." Valerie clasped respectful hands over her knees and waited for wisdom.

"What my son has probably not told you, since he does not believe it, is that these are the End of Days. But I counsel you to believe. A great conflict is arising, far beyond your imaginings, that will determine who is saved and who is lost. I have taken up the burden of trying to save as many souls as possible."

"Even in a Muslim country?"

"God loves the Muslims too, Miss Foret. They do not murder their unborn children as we do in the West, and they punish promiscuity and homosexuality." He did not look at his stepson as he spoke. "Since they ceased to have four wives, Muslims cherish family the way God intended it to be. They are heathens only because they have not heard the rest of God's message. I am here to get them to listen to it."

Valerie raised her eyebrows slightly. "The 'God-intended family.' Interesting concept. And what would 'the rest' be?"

"That God loves them, but they have gone astray. It is true that they submit to God and they recognize Jesus Christ, for which I give them credit. But they have got to be made to recognize that Jesus is the one coming back to judge them, not Mohammed."

"I see."

"I am also here to look after my family."

Derek twisted around again. "It's my family, Pa, not yours, and that's why I'm here. You don't have to be involved at all. I'll do whatever Auset needs me to, including staying in Egypt."

"Staying in Egypt? That's ridiculous. Your child is part of our family, and you should be raising her in your own country. Lord knows, you've spent little enough time there. A Christian man takes care of his own." He shifted in his seat toward Valerie. "Don't you agree, Ms. Foret? Or are you of the Jewish faith?"

The overly delicate phrase "of the Jewish faith" irritated her. "Ahh, no. Lapsed Catholic, I'm afraid."

The reverend lowered his eyes. "A shame, to give up your faith. Jesus died for you, and He will soon call you before Him."

Derek winced. "Pa, please—"

Valerie felt the door creak open to her internal weapons locker. She licked her lips. "Not for me, he didn't. I wasn't born yet."

Derek inhaled, as if to speak, then stopped. Nothing he could say would prevent the duel that was coming.

Harlan Carter brushed dust off his jacket as if it were flakes of her blasphemy. "You didn't have to ask him, child. God loved you so much He let his son be crucified for the sins of *all* men. For yours too."

Valerie squinted, turning the idea in her head like a jeweler studying a crystal. "Let me see if I understand this, Reverend. You mean God created a son, perfect in virtue, to suffer the punishment for the rest of us, his other sinful children. And to show His love for the *guilty* ones, God let the *innocent* one be tortured to death on a Roman cross." Valerie looked at him directly. "That's pretty sadistic, don't you think?"

A plump pastoral hand went up between them, as if to project light from his palm into the darkness of her mind.

"Sadistic? Oh, child. You have no idea." He spoke in a rich baritone. "The creator of the universe is not warm and fuzzy. His plan for the world is a harsh one, but it is also full of mercy. When the Day comes, the Lord will descend from heaven in a robe that has been marked with blood. He will visit His wrath upon the sinful, and even the penitent will gnash their teeth. Salvation will be costly."

Valerie stifled the urge to smile. "This is the message you're going to preach in Cairo?"

"Not only that. The Egyptians must be told of the restoration of the nation of Israel and the rebuilding of the Temple of Solomon. All of Palestine must be reclaimed from the Mohammedans. It will be a hard pill to swallow, but it is God's will."

"I don't think they will welcome that message, Reverend."

"I know that. I have chosen the most difficult of all missions, and in the eleventh hour. Some will be obdurate."

Valerie looked back over her shoulder at the car behind them carrying the lawyer and bodyguards. "I think they will be *very* obdurate, Reverend Carter."

Just then the taxi drew up to the Hyatt hotel, and the reverend swung himself from his seat through the open door. He stood up and checked to see if his bodyguards had followed. They had. He leaned back down to speak.

"Do not think I didn't notice your sarcasm, Ms. Foret. Your soul is yours to save or lose, but I will not let you harm my granddaughter. A Christian man takes care of his family. Good day to you."

11

Always Home

"Well, I think that went rather well, don't you?" she said as Derek moved around to the back seat and the taxi pulled away.

"Please, Valerie. I need you to help me here, not fight with my stepfather. It's going to be hard enough to take care of Auset and Nefi, and keep him out of the way." He tapped on the back of the driver's seat. "Zamalek, please. Shari' al Zahir. Did I pronounce the street name correctly?" he asked Valerie.

"Perfect. Your Arabic is getting pretty good." She leaned forward and got the driver's attention again. "After Zamalek, please go on to the Shari al Hassan."

"You're not coming with me? I thought we both were going to Auset's."

"I decided I should give you two some private time together. After all, you need to discuss important things with her about your daughter. Don't worry about me. I still have the same room near the souq where I'm perfectly comfortable. Plus I need to call the museum. I'll join you at Auset's house later this morning. Then we can go together to the souq to order Rekemheb's statue."

He leaned back against the taxi seat for a moment, looking helpless. "What can I say? It must be so awful for her."

Valerie took his hand absentmindedly, comforting herself as well. "Yussif was her bulwark. Ours too, in a way. He wanted nothing but to be a good man and to have a happy family."

"I know. I spent two vacations at their house in El Kharga. Some people might have thought us a little weird, getting along that way, but Yussif was always easygoing. He was as much like a brother as I could ever imagine. So what happened on that train, anyway?"

"I don't know any more than what we both saw on the news. They think it was terrorists, but that's what they always say. They're mostly right, of course, but I don't see any context here. It's not like they killed a lot of foreigners like they did in the Valley of the Queens in '97."

Derek moved his jaw around, as if he were actually chewing on a thought. "Do you think Yussif's in the underworld? In the Hall of Judgment where I found you? I've been wondering about that for days."

The "Hallelujah Chorus" sounded suddenly from the vicinity of Derek's hip. Valerie looked around. "What's that?" The melody continued in dry, tinkly electronic tones.

"Sorry. Cell phone." He unhooked the palm-sized silver object from his belt and flipped it open with a deft flick of the thumb. "Hello? *Ach, Johannes. Nun, was ist?*" He lowered the phone for a moment. "Sorry, Sweetie. My agent in Germany. It'll just take a min."

Valerie stared out the window at the shabby apartment buildings being built along the Avenue of the Pyramids. Badly reinforced, they collapsed occasionally during Cairo's frequent tremors. She loved Cairo and the Cairenes, the fast-talking cynical city folk of Egypt, but she was glad she didn't have to stay in it for more than a few days at a time. Whether because of inefficiency, corruption, waste, or simply an exploding population, the quality of life in much of Cairo was poor, and the air in all of it was dreadful.

Three minutes later Derek clicked his cell phone shut with a flick of the hand. "Sorry about that. New engagement. Recital in March. Some castle in Provence."

"Weren't you just in Paris?"

He smiled, wan. "I was in six countries in the last four months. That's what's so crazy about my stepfather wanting me to bring Nefi 'home.' Home for me is all over the musical world."

"I know what you mean. I don't travel the way you do, but I feel just the same whether I wake up in Brussels, New York, or Cairo. Home's where my friends are."

"Tell me about it. Since last May, I've had goulash with Barenboim in Budapest..." He held up his fingers, wiggling each one as he enumerated. "Blinis with Rostropovitch in St. Petersberg, Sachertorte with Ozawa in Salzburg, croissants with a handsome baritone who shall remain unnamed in Paris, and in about fifteen minutes, Arab *chai* with Auset in Cairo."

"Do I detect a theme here?" Valerie teased. "Or a just a man with sugar 'issyews?'"

He grinned back. "My point is, I don't have a sense of place. You don't either. It's partly our careers, of course, but we also know from Rekemheb that our ancient ancestors were Egyptian. Who cares about Atlanta or Brussels? Our family," he made little quotation marks with his fingertips. "Our 'family' started here, then wandered all over Africa, the Middle East, and Europe. We're kind of world Bedouins."

"Nice way of putting it." She thought about the Belgian orphanage that had darkened her childhood. It was the last place she would call home.

He gazed up at the ceiling of the taxi for a moment. "Do you think they were like us, the ancestor Dereks and Valeries?"

"You mean smart, good-looking, and gay? Oh, I'm sure of it."

12

Northern Sinai Trade Route—1099

Desperately thirsty, Faaria brushed powdery sand from her lips. She glanced toward Sharif for comfort, but the way her brother was slouched over the saddle of his camel told her he was no better off. The afternoon sun baked them, and no one in the caravan had any more water. She had a single small mouthful left in the bottom of her goatskin. It wasn't enough to slake her thirst but she kept it, taking strange comfort in the knowledge that it was there, that she could drink it any time.

What fools they'd been to leave the trade route and venture into the Sinai desert on an insane pursuit, risking their lives for a few manuscripts. But Sharif was mad, and he had made the rest of them mad too, convincing Husaam al Noori that the books were worth it. Thieves had taken them, he said, but he was certain they could be bartered with, and he knew where they hid. Near a well, he said, where they could replenish their supply for the two-day trip back north to the village of El Arish.

What a shock to find the manuscripts but not the water. The well was dry. She chuckled bitterly at the irony. They came upon them dead, thieves murdered by other thieves. But, *Alhamdulillah*, they had been killed for the gold they carried, not for what they had hidden under the heaps of dung-smeared straw. The dead men could not have lain there long, for they had not yet attracted vultures, and the bundles of straw, of so little interest to the attackers, still protected their vellum treasures.

And here they were, Husaam al Noori, his scribe and companion Sharif al Kitab, his daughter Amhara, and herself. Cairo merchants who ought to have known better. They carried alabaster, ivory, flax, and now six manuscripts—and not a drop of water. They had been traveling, parched and by sheer force of will, for two days, and El Arish was nowhere in sight.

Faaria heard a soft whimper and looked over at the other camel where, in her panier, Amhara held her limp infant.

"My milk is dry. I have nothing left to give her," Amhara whispered hoarsely.

Faaria stared at her through sand-scraped eyes. The daughter of the caravan owner was still beautiful, even though windblown, parched, and in anguish for her child.

Amhara shook her head. "If the gods wish to punish me, I accept it, but please, not my baby."

Faaria understood. Amhara had no husband, and the dark-skinned, year-old infant had been sired—so said the camp gossip—by a Nubian camel driver who had run off to avoid being killed. Now the young mother was unmarriageable as long as she kept her child, the proof and outcome of her transgression.

"I am so afraid," Amhara whispered and held the precious bundle to her breast. "She doesn't even cry any more."

Faaria rode close enough to see the baby, limp fists closed on her chest. Her little bow lips were blistered like her mother's, and her head lolled back. It seemed unlikely that she would last much longer.

Faaria sighed inwardly and reached for her goatskin. "There is not much left, not enough for us. But maybe for her…" She handed the crumpled skin across to Amhara and watched hungrily as the precious water dribbled for a few seconds into the tiny mouth, then was gone.

Gone. For all of them now. She struck her camel with the goad and lurched forward, not wanting to be thanked. If she was going to die of thirst, she didn't want to have to make polite conversation while she did so.

Was this what dying was like, she wondered. A pity. They were all so young and—if they had made it to Damascus with their alabaster and ivory—they would have been rich. They were like a family, the four of them, though Husaam al Noori was in fact their employer.

How kind fate had been to set the two half families—the widowed father with his errant daughter and the misfit siblings—in each other's path. Life was hard after their parents' death by plague, though it was not all that promising before then either.

Sharif was delicate of form, attractive some would say, but for his deformed foot and the limp it caused him. Faaria was also somewhat fair, though her hair, red like his, made her suspect. But the fits of madness—at least they called it madness—set her apart from all the other women. She dreamed of birds and animals that spoke, and she mistakenly told the dreams to others. They called her demented and, worse, *shaytaneya*, possessed of the devil, and if Husaam al Noori had not taken them in she might have one day been killed for it.

But something akin to love had developed between the merchant and Sharif, his scribe, accountant, and companion. For the assistance and comfort Sharif gave him, Husaam tolerated his boyish sister as long as she made herself useful. Today, however, she was useless.

Let me die, she prayed silently to the indifferent sky. Not the baby, not Amhara, not Sharif. Take me. She swayed dangerously on her saddle, feverish and dizzy from exhaustion, no longer caring. She scarcely heard the voice of the drover at the forefront of the caravan call out, "*Shuff. Alhamdullilah.* The caravanserai!"

13

Intruders

Valerie trudged across the Midan al Hussein into the shabby and pungent butchers' souq where tourists were a rarity. She passed the chicken cages that were always piled up just before the cloth sellers' market and felt a moment of comfort when she came to the familiar entrance to Sammed's café.

Keeping the room and Sammed's goodwill on permanent retainer was one of the smartest things she had done. In the two years she had worked on cataloging the newly excavated "priest's tomb" it had been her home. It was always there when she returned from the desert, whether for supplies or a quick rendezvous with Jameela al Rashidi, wife of the Chairman of the Council of Antiquities.

Even after Jameela had lost interest and Valerie had begun to teach summers at the University of Brussels, she had held on to the room, paying the meager rent from afar. She always kept a few books, a change of clothes, and her other fedora there, just to come home to something familiar each time she was in Cairo.

"*Sabah el kheer*," she said to the young man who stood behind the tiny counter. "Is Sammed around?"

"*Sabah el noor.*" He gave the standard reply. "He's out for awhile. Business."

Valerie knew what that meant. Sammed was making some deal. For foreign cigarettes, probably, or whiskey, which enjoyed a surprisingly large market in Cairo, Islam notwithstanding. She would touch base with him later, maybe after a trip to the *hammam* for a bath.

She walked around to the side of the simple mud-brick and plaster building that blended in so well with every other house in the souq, and climbed the narrow brick staircase to the upper floor. As she reached for the door handle, she stopped, puzzled, at the deep buzzing sound that came from inside the room. Cautiously, she opened the door.

"What the hell?"

In the corner of the single room, nude except for boxer shorts, a man lay on the narrow bed. With his head thrown back like a defeated boxer, he snored vehemently. She stomped into the room.

A pair of cargo pants was folded over the back of a chair, and under it hiking boots stood side by side. At the foot of the bed, on the floor, an open rucksack lay on its side, its contents of folded clothing visible.

Valerie detected a faint odor of beer in the room. The bastard had apparently gotten drunk and fallen asleep, sweat and all, on her clean linen. Worst of all, a killing offense, he had covered his eyes against the light with her fedora!

Valerie let her knapsack drop onto the floor and strode over to the bed.

"Wake up!" She kicked the foot of the bed. "What the hell are you doing in my room?"

"Huh?" He woke with a start and sat up, befuddled. "What the fuck? What the hell are you doing in *my* room?" he echoed. As he swung around to sit on the edge of the bed, the fedora fell to the floor and she snatched it up.

"This *is* my room, so you will please take your..." she looked at his rucksack on the floor, "*things*, and get out."

"I don't know what the hell you're talking about, lady. We paid for this room already."

"Excuse me?" a faintly condescending voice said behind her. "Is there something we can do for you, Miss?"

Valerie spun around, as if she had been spat on.

A woman stood in the doorway, slightly shorter than herself. Late thirties, Arab or Indian, and her tailored Western clothing screamed "professional." She looked familiar, but from *where*? Anger shouldered out any further thought.

"What you can *do* for me is get out of my room."

"Come on, Najya, this dump isn't worth fighting for." The man had stood up and was pulling on his pants. "Let's just get a room in a real hotel." He zipped up his fly and buckled his belt but seemed to see no need to put on a shirt.

Valerie could smell the odor of his skin now, pungent and male.

Najya. Now she remembered. The newscaster. As the man grabbed his knapsack and began to stuff his clothing back into it, Valerie saw the camera case on the floor. She softened a little and backed toward the door. "Uh, sorry to evict you this way, but I keep the room on a permanent retainer. It's obvious Sammed has tried to slip one past both of us. I'll just go and get it all sorted."

She hurried down the outside staircase while they packed. Damn, she thought. This on top of everything else. She wondered who she could complain to if Sammed was still out. But when she rounded the corner to the street, she saw him, authoritative in spite of his short rotund form. Owl-like with his large curved nose punctuating his orders, he directed two muscular Sudanese who carried bulging burlap sacks. Obviously a recent large purchase.

"Sammed!"

He glanced toward her, his momentary surprise immediately replaced by congeniality, and waved the two Sudanese inside.

"Dr. Foret. What a pleasant surprise." He extended both hands.

"Yes, I bet it is. What are those two people doing in my room? You know we had an arrangement."

He clasped his hands in front of him, as if he had just applauded something. "Yes, yes, of course we did. And I have honored it, I can assure you. But this was an extraordinary situation, with a very special person. Najya Khoury. Surely you know this journalist."

"Yes, now that you tell me, but what is she doing in the souq with the riffraff?"

"I did not inquire, but please accept my profoundest apologies. I will see to their removal immediately."

"That doesn't seem to be necessary," Valerie remarked as the two intruders descended the stairs. The man had put his shirt on finally, hurriedly tucked in, and he struggled with a pole in one hand and a camera on a brace on the other shoulder. A battery pack strapped around his waist tugged at his trousers, exposing a strip of the undershorts Valerie had already seen.

Najya Khoury, unruffled, followed him carrying a trim black flight bag.

"I am sorry for this misunderstanding." Sammed was deferential. "May I offer you a cold beverage before you leave. On the house, of course."

"Thank you, no," the journalist said. She held up a blue cell phone. "We have made other arrangements. We'll come back later for our refund." She glanced at Valerie. "I wish I could say it has been a pleasure, Dr. Foret, but…" Without finishing her sentence, she marched down the narrow street toward the butchers' souq and the opening to the square.

Valerie pivoted around to Sammed. "How did she know my name?"

"Oh, Dr. Foret. Of course she knows you. She is a journalist, and you were big news when you found the priest's tomb. The papers ran the story for weeks."

"Umm." She watched the two turn the corner to the butchers' souq. "I suppose I was a little brusque, wasn't I?"

"Oh, certainly not." He changed the subject. "Are you here to work again on the tomb, *Duktura*? Will you be staying with us for awhile?"

"I don't know, really. I'm here for an emergency, family business. But I expect I'll also need to spend some time at the museum."

She glanced again toward the narrow street where the two journalists had gone and felt a twinge of embarrassment. They were probably perfectly nice people.

14

Auset

Valerie approached Mahmoud al Fakhir's house, curious to see what sort of life the widowed Auset had returned to. It was a good one. Her father was clearly a prosperous man. His large house combined his business and his family life in a congenial way, at least architecturally. His high-end antiques shop and his household were at once separated and deftly joined in a style of building that had housed the prosperous since the Greeks. The ryad, two stories high and built in a quadrangle around a central courtyard, nestled inconspicuously among the apartment buildings in the Zamalak section of Cairo.

As she walked around the periphery of the quadrangle, she noticed that one full side held the showrooms and commercial space of the antiques business. Two of the sides, with windows only on the second floor, clearly housed the family. The fourth wall, where the tops of trees and rose bushes were visible, revealed a garden at the center. Valerie thought, absurdly, of a tale of Scheherezade.

She arrived again at the west side at the private entrance, as discreet as the antiques business was public, and knocked on the door. An elderly man opened it and stepped back, bowing slightly. Of course Mahmoud al Fakhir would have a houseman.

"*As salaamu 'alaykum,*" she greeted him formally.

"*Wa 'alaykum as salaam,*" he replied and led her down a corridor to the central garden.

But for the recent tragedy, it would have been idyllic. The quadrangle was full of fruit trees and flowering shrubs. At the center, a stone fountain bubbled up a thin stream of water that fell into an upper, then a lower bowl. Where it dribbled softly over the rim, brightly colored birds fluttered and drank. Brick paths radiated out in four directions from the fountain and cut the garden into quarters. In the moist garden air, the fragrance of roses mixed with the stronger smell of jasmine. Directly across from where Valerie stood, Derek had one arm around Auset and held his daughter in the other.

Auset turned at the sound of her footfall and embraced her. The half-Arab, half-Jew had always had a certain voluptuous beauty, but today her face was simply swollen from weeping. "Thank you. Thank you for coming," she whispered hoarsely.

"Of course," Valerie answered softly, and looked again toward Derek and his daughter. Her visits to Egypt had never coincided with his, so this was the first time she had seen them together since the baby's birth. She noted a sort of reverse resemblance between them. Nefi had shiny dark hair that hung in thick Shirley Temple curls around her face, while his was ruthlessly short. She had the same radiant eyes as her natural father, but where his sparkled with joie de vivre, Nefi's seemed more solemn.

"Please, both of you." Auset's voice was raw. "Come and sit down here outside the kitchen." She pointed to a round glass table at the side of the garden that was already set with plates and fruit. "Fahd will bring us some breakfast."

"What a beautiful place." Valerie postponed talking about Yussif. "It's part of your father's business, isn't it?"

Auset blew her nose into a tissue. "Yes, my father's shop is at that end, under the arcade."

Valerie traced the balcony walkway that went around three sides of the courtyard and marked out the upper floor. Though it overlooked the garden full of plants, it also held pots of flowering vines that hung down over the carved balustrades. Behind them she could see the doors and windows to the private rooms.

Derek sat down with Nefi on his lap. "I was planning to stay at the Sheraton," he said to Valerie, "but Auset's father invited me to stay here. I want to spend more time with Nefi, anyhow. Not that I want to replace Yussif, of course."

Valerie saw where his eyes went, toward the photo at the center of the table, and she picked it up. Yussif sat on the ground and leaned against a palm tree in Al Dakhla. On his lap was Nefi at the age of one, already with an explosion of curls. In the three-day beard that he insisted on keeping, Yussif still looked fierce, but his eyes beamed contentment. One of his large hands held his adoptive daughter around the waist; the other held up the brightly clothed Cleopatra doll that Derek had sent as a birthday present from the Munich opera. The first of a series of lovely and impractical gifts from all over the musical world.

Gently laying the picture back down, Valerie thought fondly of

Yussif, that rare kind of man who cheerfully, lovingly raises another man's child. Yet in the gods' scheme of things, he'd been an afterthought when the Child's natural father proved a poor choice as paterfamilias. How had the gods not noticed that Derek was gay? Or that she herself was? Yet the two of them, unrepentantly deviant, carried the bloodline of the chosen priest, Rekemheb.

She looked around again. "It seems like an idyllic place to raise a child."

The houseman set down a wide tray with a metal teapot, numerous glasses, and bowls full of yogurt, tahini, and pita.

Auset thanked him and poured tea for all of them. "It's a safe place for us, for awhile. But my father is religious, and mullahs and imams come and go through the house all the time. If it gets too Islamic, I plan to take a vacation with my other grandparents in Jerusalem."

Jerusalem? Derek's eyebrows went up. "Aren't they religious too? Your mother's family, I mean."

"Yes, they are, but the two religions would sort of balance out, I think. Savti and Babi always made a fuss over me when I was little, and now they have a great-grandchild. They have a shop in the Old City, so I would visit them just to get away from Cairo for a while." She passed around the yogurt, cheered, it seemed, by the talk of travel.

"I thought Egyptians needed visas to get into Israel."

"Not Jews. Remember, there's that right-of-return thing. I've been there lots of times with my mother."

Valerie frowned. "You're as Jewish as I am Christian."

"I'm as Jewish as I need to be. My mother is Jewish, and by Jewish law, both Nefi and I are too. Only my father needs a special visa. Absurd, isn't it?" She added more tea to Valerie's glass. "How long can you stay? I'd love for Nefi to spend time with you."

"I'd love it too. A lot depends on whether I can save Rekemheb."

"Save him? From what?"

"Nekhbet appeared in Brussels suddenly and told me that Rekemheb's ka has disappeared because his mummy is damaged, she thinks. I promised that I'd drive down to his tomb and see if I could save him."

"I never really understood about kas. Just how would you do that?"

"You know that the ka-spirit can migrate to a statue, if it looks like him, but only if you get there in time and do the right ceremonies. We plan to order the statue this afternoon, and when it's done, rush it down to his tomb."

While Valerie spoke, Derek unwrapped the little pink shoes and slid one absentmindedly onto one of Nefi's bare feet. She accepted it, intrigued. "All the pain we went through to save his mummy and it would be for nothing." He buckled on the second shoe.

"That's why it's so urgent that we get to him right away. I estimate two days to get the statue carved and two days to get to the tomb."

Auset took Valerie's wrist. "Wait. You're going to try to save the ka of Rekemheb? Why not Yussif too? Doesn't he have a ka?"

Valerie raised her brow in tentative agreement. "He ought to. But for a ka to live in the underworld, he needs an earthly form."

Auset looked appalled. "You mean I'd have to mummify him first?"

"No. You could make a statue too, I guess, like we're doing for Rekemheb. But I just don't know. When the gods came to Dendara, none of us thought to ask if the rules applied to all of us. And when I asked Nekhbet, she refused to say."

"Well, I guess we better hope Rekemheb makes it, so we can ask him, right?" Then, as if realizing the cumulative weight of the problems, Derek rubbed his forehead. "So how should we do this? Should I go with you, Val? Auset? What do you think? Maybe we could all go together, like before."

He hugged his daughter briefly as she examined the brightly colored objects on her feet.

"What are you thinking, dear?" Auset was adamant. "I couldn't possibly take a small child into the desert. And I won't leave her alone either. She still doesn't understand why *Baba* doesn't come home."

"It's all right, Derek." Valerie touched his hand. "I need you to come with me this afternoon to get the statue made, but you don't have to go to the tomb. I'm the only one who knows the incantations anyhow. You should stay in Cairo with your family."

"Sounds like a plan," he said, obviously relieved. "So when are we visiting this image-maker person?"

"As soon as I've made a quick trip to the hammam for a bath. I'm wearing the same clothes I had on in Brussels, so I apologize if I'm a bit ripe, Auset. I considered going before I came here, but seeing you was more important."

"You can have a bath right here," someone said.

Valerie glanced around to the source of the soothing voice and saw a gray-haired woman in the kitchen doorway wiping her hands on a towel. Hannah Ibrahim opened her arms and Valerie stepped easily into the light maternal embrace. Though they had met only briefly, at Auset's own house, Valerie felt a warmth that had carried over.

"You know you are family here, Valerie, dear. Derek has the guest room, but we can make a place in the library for you to stay with us."

Valerie studied the mother of Auset al Fakhir. Hannah was short and slight of build, but had a force of personality that seemed to lend her substance. She had an age-softened version of her daughter's sensuality, but while Auset confronted the world with wisecracks, Hannah met it with quiet conviction. She had not only stood up to family condemnation for marrying a Moslem, but she had also protected her willful daughter and illegitimate grandchild from hostility on all sides.

"Oh, thank you, Hannah, that's very kind. But I've stayed for so long at Sammed's place, it really feels like home. Besides, he's just evicted a couple of people for me, so it would be impolite not to go back."

"Shuff, *Jaddee!*" Nefi lifted one pink foot toward her grandmother.

Hannah stroked the new shoe with her fingertip. "*Gameel,* habibti," she said, admiring their beauty.

"*Duktura Foret,*" a baritone voice said behind them.

"Oh, Mahmoud al Fakhir, good morning." Valerie knew not to offer her hand to a conservative Muslim, but she inclined her head in what she hoped he understood was sincere warmth.

Auset's father was tall and slightly stooped. In spite of doing regular business with the West and of having sent his daughter to college in New York, he seemed in every other way a traditional Egyptian. A full beard, now shot through with gray, grew down to his collar, and his galabaya and turban were both white. He looked like any of a thousand men prostrating themselves in the Citadel mosque every Friday.

And yet she knew from Auset how very untraditional he was, in spite of himself. At the discovery of his daughter's pregnancy, he had been furious, but after a few weeks of silence he had evidently decided that family was more important than shame, and so he accepted her back. That his daughter and son-in-law had embraced polytheism had not yet been revealed to him.

Al Fakhir sat on the remaining chair and patted his knees. Nefi slid off Derek's lap to climb onto her grandfather's, where she was obviously at home. Reaching over her shoulder he took the knife, cut a piece of melon, and placed it into Nefi's plump hand.

Fahd was suddenly at the table. "*Sayyid. Fee raghel mistaneek barra aiyz yeshufak. Amerikani,*" he said in a rapid, agitated stream.

Auset looked at Derek. "An American? Do you have any idea who it could be?"

Valerie turned toward him as well. "You didn't tell her?"

15

Grandfathers

Harlan Carter entered hesitantly, clearly surprised by the lush, perfumed garden. Valerie suspected that the atmosphere of elegance and prosperity didn't quite fit with the reverend's picture of a squalid people in need of salvation.

The men at the table stood up to receive him. Though he was clearly taken aback, Al Fakhir offered him his hand and gestured toward the remaining chair.

Carter sat down, brushing imaginary dust from his trousers. "Pleased to meet you, Mr. Alfakker, is it? Mrs. Alfakker." Mispronouncing the name, which was not hers in any case, the reverend held out his hand to Hannah.

After an awkward moment, she touched his hand lightly and withdrew it.

"Yes, and oh, there she is, my granddaughter." He reached over to Nefi, who still sat in al Fakhir's lap, and pinched her cheek. "Hello, sweetie. Well, aren't you a beauty. Your daddy's goin' to have to beat the boys away with a stick, isn't he?"

Nefi leaned backward away from him, and al Fakhir raised a protective hand in front of her. "She does not know you."

"Of course she doesn't. Not yet anyhow." He wiggled his fingers at the puzzled child. "Honey, this is your other grandpa, and is he looking forward to spoiling you rotten!"

"Pa, please," Derek said. "She has no idea what you're saying."

"That's all right. She'll understand this." He reached in his pocket and held up a wrapped candy. "See, peppermint. Everybody loves peppermint."

He handed the candy to her, and she opened the crackly cellophane. Without taking her eyes from the stranger, she put the sweet into her mouth with the palm of her hand. She wrinkled her nose for a moment, then took the sticky lump out with her fingers.

Auset scooped it from her hand with a paper napkin. "She's never seen candy. Egyptian children don't eat much of it."

Reverend Carter would not be deterred. "But I bet they love toys as much as American children do." From the other pocket he withdrew a stuffed bear, only slightly larger than his own plump fist. He presented it to the fascinated child, and she smiled broadly as she squeezed its soft plush.

"What are you giving her? Derek asked. "A toy bear with armor?

"This is the Armor-of-God stuffed bear. Look, he's wearing the shield of Faith, the Breastplate of Righteousness, the Sword of the Spirit, and the Helmet of Salvation. It teaches kids that God is their salvation."

Nefi squeezed the soft plush bear, clearly pleased.

Al Fakhir, who still held her in his lap, forced a polite smile and spoke to Nefi in Arabic.

"*Shukran,*" she said dutifully.

"She says 'thank you.'"

"Doesn't she speak English?"

"Not much, Pa. I see her only twice a year. And I try to speak to her in Arabic."

"Well, she can learn, of course. She's a smart girl, I can see that." Reverend Carter took hold of one of the little hands, "I am your grandpa. Say 'grandpa...grand...pa.'"

Nefi yanked her hand away and Auset intervened. "Perhaps we could have the English lesson some other time, Reverend."

Carter stood up. "Of course. There's plenty of time for that. I won't disturb your little family any longer." He addressed Derek. "Would you come by the hotel today? I have something important to discuss with you."

"Sure, Pa. But only for a few minutes. Valerie and I have urgent business this afternoon."

"Just stop by before you go. It's very important." He nodded toward al Fakhir, who set Nefi down in order to rise courteously but didn't speak.

Fahd came to escort the stranger out.

"Don't forget." Reverend Carter squeezed Derek's arm as he turned to leave. He followed the housemaster out, his blue polyester suit seeming somehow alien in the Arab garden.

Valerie glanced over at the rival grandfather. Al Fakhir had watched the clergyman depart and still stared at the empty path. She detected more than simple dislike in his expression. Something very old, some archaic battle that once was fought with swords, seemed to have awakened in him. How could it not have? The terrorist's hand had reached into his family, and now some know-nothing foreigner had invaded his house as well.

16

Hammam

Valerie strode along the narrower alleys of the souq. Over her head, elaborate screens of Mameluke bay windows overhung the street. Behind them, she was certain, idle women gazed down onto the activity below. A wide red carpet hung from below one of them, waiting to be dusted.

The Khan was timeless. It seemed to always have the same heat, colors, sounds, and smells, and when she returned here after an absence, it was as if she had never been away. In the spice souq, the shops were doing brisk business, and as she passed them, she suddenly smelled cardamom, clove, and incense.

She passed the wood-carvers working on their elaborate screens under the shade of an awning. Their decorations, like their script, curled in languid arabesques. But languid was one thing she was not today.

It was the hot part of the day and she was already sweating. She quickened her step. El Fishawy cafe was full of tourists as she passed through it and found the nameless alley that led toward the Hammam Sallahhudin.

She loved the hammam, and not only for the delicious pleasure of a vigorous scrubbing in the company of women. Like the mosque, the bakery, and the souq itself, it had always been one of the basic elements of Arab life. The Muslims used the hammam to purify themselves before prayer, yet, throughout history it was also a place for sensuality and openness. As the mosque called them all to God, so the hammam called them back to the needs of the flesh. She wondered how many deals had been struck, how many marriages arranged, how many illicit affairs begun in its steamy semi-darkness.

"*Shukran.*" She handed over her Egyptian pounds and received a folded cotton bath cloth, a plastic tube of liquid soap, rubber flip-flops, a brass bucket, and a locker key. It was a relief, in the moist warm air of the hamman dressing chamber, to finally take off her boots. She placed her folded clothing in the wooden locker and hooked the flimsy lock over the latch. As she entered the domed hot room wrapped in her bath cloth she felt reprieved, if only for an hour. She exhaled the dust of the street and inhaled the smell of soap and rosewater, of henna, and behind it, the faint whiff of chlorine on the marble floor.

The circular bath hall was dim and mysterious, almost temple-like. Its only light penetrated from high above through glass "eyes" scattered over the dome. The midday sunlight shone down in a spray of narrow beams onto the marble platform below, where several bathers lay. From the dark periphery, where columned arcades covered niches, Valerie could hear the gush of water and the banging of metal buckets against the brass spigots. As her eyes adapted, she discerned the figures of women in small groups, their voices bright as they washed each other's hair or let themselves be scrubbed by the hamman's own scrubber.

Businesslike, she washed herself thoroughly, declining the assistance of the burly female attendant, and savored the slight lasciviousness of bathing in a half-lit public place. Then she wrapped her towel around her hips and lay down on the platform a respectful distance from the others.

"Ahhhh." Something between sound and thought escaped her. She moved her head and felt white light pour onto her from the dome. It occurred to her that the other women on the dais lay under such light beams as well, each one in her own revelation. A good metaphor for religion, she thought. Then she dozed, recalling the painted scenes of pharaoh touched by the fingers of sunlight. Her sleep-addled scientist's brain added, "But it's only photons from burning hydrogen."

Some small noise, the tap of a slippered foot on the dais or an exhalation, penetrated her sleep. Her eyes fluttered open and were blinded by white light until she jerked her head to the side. Her glance fell on a towel-covered hip, then traveled up along a smooth bare arm and shoulder to a face that was studying her. The light that poured down from the dome illuminated the top of the stranger's head and cast a shadow across her eyes. Valerie smelled the woman's skin, like steaming food, then recognized her.

She sat up. "Is this some kind of joke?"

The woman shifted her weight and turned toward her, leaning on her elbow. "I'm sorry. I wondered what I could say that wouldn't make it sound like I'd crept up on you. I couldn't think of anything, so I thought it was best to leave you asleep."

Annoyed at being watched while she slept, Valerie snapped, "What are you doing here?"

"Bathing, like everyone else. And I was just as surprised as you."

Valerie became aware of the other woman's half-nude body, the well-formed breasts a shade lighter than Jameela's but still unmistakably Arab. They were full, but firm enough to swell upward, and they left an expanse of midriff exposed beneath them. Valerie averted her eyes, but not before she noticed the thin line of intimate dark hair that descended from the navel into the towel.

"You mean it's pure coincidence that you showed up at the same time I did in an obscure hammam?"

Najya Khoury shrugged slightly with one shoulder. "It's not obscure at all. Every journalist who comes to Cairo knows this place."

"But what are you doing in the souq anyhow? I know who you are. A big-name Worldnews journalist wouldn't stay in a place like Sammed's."

Najya laughed softly. "I might ask you the same thing, Dr. Foret. You see, I know you too. Did you think any journalist in the Middle East wouldn't recognize this century's Howard Carter?" She shifted her weight again and her breasts drew attention once more. "Look, this morning was unfortunate. Can we start over now? I'm Najya Khoury, journalist." She held out her hand. "And in case you're worried, no, you weren't snoring. You looked very peaceful and I really tried not to wake you."

Valerie sat up in order to be able to shake hands, conscious now of her own breasts. "In that case, Valerie Foret, archaeologist. Sorry I threw you out of your room."

"No harm done. It was Harry's idea to go there anyhow. We're staying at the Blue Nile hotel now, only a few streets away from Sammed's."

"Not much of a step up. So what *are* you doing here?"

"I came here from our Israeli office to do a story on fundamentalism and martyrdom. Then the train explosion happened. I'm just staying on a few days to talk to some more people. I can get better interviews here in the souq than in modern Cairo."

"Fundamentalism. So you think it was the Brotherhood that blew up the coach?"

"I can't imagine who else would do it. But if they were trying to frighten the West, they got very little for their efforts. Only one coach exploded. Just a couple of people killed, a few more injured. It'll scare the tourists away for a few months, but they'll come back."

"One of my good friends, a family member in a way, was killed. I only learned about it from your broadcast. Can you give me any more details?"

"Oh, I'm so sorry. For us it's a flashy news story. We forget sometimes that for the victims and their families, such an event is shattering. And I'm sorry to say I don't know any more than what was broadcast the last few days. The evening train from Luxor. Only damage was to the first-class coach, the one the tourists take. Everyone's saying fundamentalist terrorism, and that's what I'm here to write about."

Valerie shook her head. "Don't take this personally, but I'm not sure an Israeli journalist is the right person to address the complexities of Arab fundamentalism."

"I *do* take it personally. And I'm *exactly* the right person to address it. I'm a Palestinian Israeli, born in Jerusalem. I have a degree in international law as well as journalism. I'm perfectly aware of the difference between the intifada and purely religious violence. Conflict and Jerusalem are in my blood, so to speak."

Valerie studied the earnest face, which had put her off at first. But now it seemed more intelligent than hard. It was the face of a woman who didn't suffer fools gladly. In their brief confrontation at Sammed's she had looked heavily mascaraed, as if her eyes were rimmed with kohl. But Valerie saw now it was her lashes, lush and black, that made her look Egyptian. Valerie imagined Hatchepsut, the female pharaoh.

The compressed muscle around the mouth, which had at first seemed to indicate annoyance, now suggested a certain verbal restraint, as if the well-cushioned lips held something back. It was, in fact, a rather nice mouth. "So to speak…?" Valerie echoed.

Najya gathered up her hair from where it lay between her shoulder blades, twisted it into a single coil, and curled it around itself. Her raised arms showed a softly curved musculature, though less defined than Valerie's own. Najya let the coil of hair fall at the back of her neck and drew the strands of loose hair over her ears. "I've lived in Jerusalem most of my life, and I know every street in every sector. I even led tours when I was a student at Al Quds University. I also have a…well, you could call it a 'genetic' connection with the Old City. My father tells me our family goes back to Jerusalem before the crusades."

"Very impressive." Valerie dropped her eyes before her interest became obvious. "But if you want to write about conflict and fundamentalism, Israel has its own version of it. Why don't you start with the militant Jewish settlers?"

Najya's arms dropped again, the hint of biceps disappearing under bronze-colored skin "Oh, I have. I have reams of interviews with them, with some of the most militant. You'd be surprised how similar their views are to those of the Islamists."

"I wouldn't be surprised at all. I know all about dogma. I spent years in a Catholic orphanage that had a single theme—revelation—and a single lesson—obedience. I don't have a very high opinion of religion."

Najya looked directly at her now, though when she lowered her head, the harsh light beam that streamed from overhead cast her eyes in shadow and obscured their color. "I can see how that could sour you. But, aside from religion being a part of a person's identity, I think religious dogma arises more from a yearning for order and sense. A noble longing, in fact."

Valerie was distracted by the light play. "Religion and superstition noble? I'm sorry, I don't follow."

"I think humans crave morality, as well as order. I'm saying that religion does not make us moral. Quite the opposite. Our innate morality makes religion. In fact, I believe in people, not God. That's why I studied international law before I went into journalism."

"Morality makes religion." Valerie smiled from the side of her mouth. "Pretty clever. Did you come up with all that just now?"

"You mean lying here naked? Unfortunately, no. I didn't come up with it at all. I got it from Salman Rushdie."

"I'm so glad. I was beginning to feel a little stupid not being able to formulate a brilliant worldview while lying dazed in a hammam. But I do have a good formulation for you, before I leave, which I have to do right now. I'm already late." Valerie stood up. "If people can dream up a law-giving spirit in the sky, they can also dream 'down' a spirit-filled nature around them."

"You mean animism? I'd have thought that's over and done with. What's the point of projecting your ideals into trees and animals?"

Valerie re-tucked her towel around her and stepped into her flip-flops.

"'The story that you tell is the story that tells you.'"

"That sounds mysterious. Who said that? Definitely not Salman Rushdie."

"No. It's from Jehuti, Egyptian God of Scribes. But I guess you had to be there."

As Valerie walked away, she felt the glance of the other woman on her back and wondered if it was lascivious. For the briefest moment she imagined caressing those beautiful dark breasts. Then she remembered a man's pants folded over the back of the chair in her room.

Damn, she hated it when straight women flirted with her.

17

Caravanserai

The last stretch of desert to the shelter of the caravanserai seemed endless. But finally the line of their heavily laden camels trudged alongside it. Faaria could count the blind archways that made up the wall: ten of them, each one a camel's length in width. The small windows at the top of each archway revealed two stories, one below, presumably for beasts and fodder, and one above for people.

The drovers brought the caravan around to the main portal, which rose to a peaked arch. Mud-brick walls supported wide wooden doors that could be shut against marauders. The refuse and desert sand that had collected along their lower edges showed that had not been necessary for some time. As the camels filed one by one into the shade of the entrance tunnel, Faaria felt immediate relief

The central courtyard, as she expected, was open to the sky, but around the four walls many of the niches and archways supported cloth awnings. The parched caravan passed to the far end of the oblong court where a cistern lay. Smelling the water, the camels strained against their reins.

The men dismounted and quenched their thirst, then carried bowls of the cool water to the two women.

Amhara dribbled it between the baby's lips, then wiped her face with it. The child began to cry, and Amhara smiled relief at her full-throated wail.

Finally unleashed, the camels jostled one another to drink, scarcely fitting around the periphery with their wide loads. When the camels had drunk enough, the drovers hauled them back and urged them toward one side of the court to be unloaded for the night.

At one end of the cistern, Amhara perched her baby on the stone wall and continued to splash cool water over the little head and back.

The child seemed revitalized. Her whimpering became chortles of pleasure, then breathless excitement as a yellow bird suddenly appeared and lit close to her on the wall.

"Look Reni, it's a bird," Amhara cooed. "A yellow bird."

Reni pointed with her entire baby arm toward the fluttering creature and said, "burd."

"Did you hear that?" Amhara called to Faaria, who had returned with the empty goatskins. "Reni said her first word!"

"What an odd word—" The noise at the gate drew Faaria's attention. A second caravan was arriving behind them and moving to the north end of the caravanserai to unload their goods at one of the bays. She knew the men would do a little trading that evening and exchange news.

Faaria hurried to fill the goatskins before the new drovers brought their camels to the cistern. She glanced idly back at the yellow bird, which still perched on the wall with its tail toward her. Strange, for a bird like that to be in the desert, she thought. Then, as the creature hopped around to face her, she nearly dropped her goatskins into the pool. Where it should have had a beak it had a nose and, behind it, a tiny human face. A thin black feather—no, it was a minute black twist of hair—hung down one side of its head.

"Hurry up there, woman," someone barked behind her. "Men from the Negev are here, and we can't wait all day!"

The strange bird took flight, and Faaria gathered her goatskins in her arms.

"Come on, before the others take the good rooms." Amhara was already following a servant to a narrow staircase on the inner wall. At the top of the stairs, on the second story, were the sleeping rooms, empty but for a pile of straw and a coarse woven curtain at the front.

Once inside, Faaria noticed the tiny window high on the outside wall. It would let in little heat and just enough light to tell them when it was dawn. She dropped the armload of goatskins on the walkway just outside the room, then went inside and found a spot on the straw that suited her. This was where she would lay out her sleeping carpet.

Amhara perused the room once and nodded with satisfaction. "Rest later, Faaria. Didn't you smell it? They're cooking in the courtyard. Lentils and fresh bread."

"*Alhamdullilah*!" Faaria sat up again and stretched aching muscles. "Supper. And then a bath."

❖

An hour later, Faaria and Amhara left the central courtyard for the hamman built over a secondary cistern. At the gate, a donkey cart full of camel chips passed them, the battered wooden wheels rumbling over the rocks. It drew up at the rear of the bath building, and the driver, a mere boy, shoveled the camel dung onto a pile against the wall. Another boy shoveled the chips with a wooden rake toward the fire that smoldered under the stone floor of the building.

They walked to the front, and at the entrance they saw that the single bathhouse had been divided in half along its length. The men's and women's entrances were at the same end, but discreetly separated by the central wall.

In the antechamber of the women's bath several abayas and undergarments already hung on the hooks, and Faaria could hear the laughter of the other women and their children coming from inside.

Amhara undressed Reni, who stood bow-legged and giggling with her hands on her toddler's belly. Then she drew off her own abaya and underclothes.

Faaria averted her eyes, staring at the wall as she herself disrobed, realizing that in spite of all the nights they had slept side by side, she had never seen Amhara naked. Still glancing off to the side, she said, "It will be a relief to wash the Sinai out of my hair" a bit too quickly and marched ahead through the doorway.

The second room, as always, was the cool room. The circular cistern was divided down the middle by the wall that separated the men from the women. Leaning over the wall, Faaria could hear the voices of the men on the other side.

They hauled up buckets of water and took them into the hot room. Three women from the Negev caravan were already lying on the hot stone at the center of the room, and two others scrubbed children in the tubs on the side wall. They greeted the newcomers as they entered and returned to their own conversation.

Amhara drew out a flask of washing oil after they sat down in a corner. She scrubbed the squirming Reni first, starting with her hair and ending with her toes. When the ordeal was over, the baby slapped her flat hands in the bucket and called out "burd" with each little fountain.

"Come on, it's your turn." Amhara grasped Faaria's wrist and drew her in front of her. Humming some fragment of a tune, she poured the fragrant oil over Faaria's hair and rubbed it into a froth. "I love the color of your hair. It sets you apart. But why do you keep it so short?"

Faaria tilted her head back. "I cut it in mourning when my parents died. But then I left it short, to keep Sharif from marrying me to the nearest merchant to get me off his hands."

"Your brother doesn't seem to try very hard to get you married to anyone. He isn't even married himself." Amhara poured handfuls of clear water over the shoulder-length strands, then lathered them again.

"Oh, no. He is dedicated to Husaam. Haven't you noticed? They make a perfect couple. I don't think either one of them wants a wife now."

"Shhhh!" Amhara giggled as the other women got up from the platform, still chattering among themselves, and left the hammam. Only the two women at the tubs still scrubbed children.

Faaria sputtered as Amhara poured the remaining water from the first bucket over her head. Then they switched places and Faaria moved behind. She poured handfuls of water on the long hair, then drizzled the washing oil down the length of it. She gathered the thick hair in handfuls and squeezed the lather through it from the scalp down the length of Amhara's back. Finally she rinsed with handfuls of water until the froth was gone.

Sitting in front of both of them, Reni let herself be splashed, then crawled onto her mother's lap, sucking her thumb.

Amhara kissed the top of her head. "Why don't you want to marry?" she asked over her shoulder. "Don't you want to have children?"

Faaria combed water from the long hair with her fingers. "Yes, of course I would. But I wouldn't like that—what men do to make you pregnant. They are too rough."

"Not all men are rough. Samek was tender."

"Was he?" Faaria was torn between desire to hear Amhara talk about love and resentment that she had given herself to a near stranger.

"Yes," Amhara confided. "He came to me only once, while the men were preparing the winter caravan. He was supposed to be one of the drovers. I knew it was wrong, but something came over me. He was different from the other men."

"He must have been. I mean, you wouldn't have otherwise…" She resumed combing.

"No, I wouldn't have. He came from the South. From a people he said worshipped the old gods."

"Did you love him?" Faaria asked, sullen.

"I had no time for that kind of love, but I would have loved his whole people, the idea of them. He said they made gifts to the water and to the animals. I wanted to be like him and know the names of his gods."

"What happened to him?"

"He was caught the moment he left my room. They tied him up, but he escaped and ran away. A month later I knew I carried his child."

Faaria was silent for a moment. "I would be tender," she said finally, and trickled water once again through the hair. "And I would know what to do to please a woman. If I were a man, I mean."

Amhara glanced at the two women from the other caravan, who seemed engrossed in their own conversation, then said softly, looking nowhere in particular, "Really? What would you do? If you were a man, I mean."

Faaria dropped her voice. "I would take my time and touch her in all the soft places." She added a bit more oil to the hair so as to have something to do with her hands. The back of her fingers touched the slender neck as she worked up the lather again. "She would know what comes at the end and would want me to hurry, but I would not."

"Do you know what is at the end? You aren't supposed to know that, you harlot," Amhara whispered back.

"Oh, yes. I do know, and I would press my lips against her throat and caress her breasts to make her long for it."

"I am sure she would like that." Amhara sat motionless, with her back toward Faaria as she played with her hair.

"Do you think so?" Faaria stilled her hands. Her palms warmed from the heat of Amhara's neck while the backs of her hands were cool against the wet hair—a confusing sensation that seemed the physical form of what was happening in her mind. "Do you think she would want to kiss me back, deeply, like a lover?" She leaned forward as closely as she dared.

Amhara didn't move. Only her shoulders rose faintly as she inhaled. "Kiss you? Yes, I am sure she would. But the girls kiss all the time in the harem. You must know the things to do to reach the end."

"Oh, I know them. I would put my hand on that lovely place every woman who is not mutilated knows. I would make her sweet juices flow over my fingers." Faaria closed her eyes and allowed her lips to brush softly against the damp hair. "I would go where men want to go, but I would do it so gently that she would moan with happiness."

"Because of what's at the end." Amhara's voice had grown tight.

"Yes," Faaria breathed. "That moment when the air becomes honey and your head swims with happiness."

Amhara reached back and stilled the hand that stroked her hair. "I think my hair is clean enough."

"We can go back to our own room then, and we'll be alone."

Amhara didn't answer but stood up, her sleeping baby in her arms.

Faaria gathered up the buckets. They dressed without speaking in the anteroom and walked, not looking at one another, out of the hammam.

The caravanserai had settled into its evening quiet. The unsaddled camels clustered in two groups near the portal, chewing contentedly on fodder. At the far end, the cooking fire continued to burn, fed from an inexhaustible supply of camel chips. The men of the two caravans crouched together in a circle around it, wrapped in their burnooses and exchanging news or rambling tales. She could smell the coffee they had just boiled, but had no interest in it. Tonight she would be with Amhara.

Faaria's heart was pounding as they approached the curtain over their doorway that cut them off from the sight of men. In a few moments they would be in a private place, alone for the night, and she would make Amhara moan with happiness. She drew back the curtain.

Five women sat or lay on carpets. Two held infants at their breasts, while the others scolded small children who, for their part, whined or tussled among themselves. A boy of about three urinated into a clay pot in the corner.

Faaria stood at the entrance, biting her lip, still gripping the curtain. Forty days of growing infatuation had seemed to climax in the intimacy of the hammam. And then, at the very doorway of the room in which they would lie, it was snatched away. Her mouth, which half a day before was dry as sand, filled now with the taste of bile.

18

Family Values

Derek was standing in the lobby as Valerie arrived at the Cairo Sheraton. He embraced her again, as if he had not just seen her an hour before.

"Umm, you smell nice. You must let me have some of your shampoo."

"Silly queen. Get your own shampoo." She had forgotten how much fun he was to be with, how he reminded her of every little thing that was good, even the smell of freshly washed hair.

"I've just spent a nice hour at the hammam, and you should try it too. It'll take your mind off the heat."

"Mmmm. I'm not sure I'd know how to behave in one of those places. I'd have trouble knowing where to look." He blinked with beautiful long eyelashes.

She linked her arm in his. "Ready to go to the souq, girlfriend? You can tell me about your big important meeting with the reverend while we're in the taxi."

"Uh, I haven't really had the big important meeting yet," he said sheepishly. "I thought if you were here with me and we said we were in a hurry, he'd get to the point faster. Otherwise I know I'll get a sermon."

She looked at her watch. "Oh, Derek! We *are* in a hurry. Tomorrow is the Muslim Sabbath so the shops will close early. We're really cutting this close."

"I know that. Rekemheb is my ancestor too. Look, I promise we'll be out of here in five minutes." He led her to the elevator.

Valerie sighed. "We came here for serious things, and dealing with Reverend Carter wasn't one of them."

"I know, Val. But you shouldn't be so hard on him. He really believes he's offering the Egyptians salvation."

"They'll recognize that offer. They had it once from the crusaders."

They stepped into the elevator together. "I suppose so, but he's basically a good man. He just has this Christ-and-Judgment-Day thing."

"That can't have been a very nice atmosphere to grow up in."

"He was a good enough father when I was young. At least until I told him I was gay. He slapped me and said we'd never speak of it again. And we never did. But I still had a home. And think about it, Valerie. You and I both lost our fathers, but you got put in an institution while I had the benefit of a decent stepfather."

"If he's such a decent, fun-loving guy, why does he travel with bodyguards?"

"I guess he figures he's going to meet some hostility."

"He's right about that. And when he does, his two goons, who don't speak a word of Arabic, will be useless."

The elevator pinged and the doors opened on the fourteenth floor. They stepped out together. "Well, I guess it'll be my job to see that it doesn't come to that."

"But it *will* come to that," she insisted. "Don't you remember two years ago in Al Amarna, how furious those people were that we entered their shrine? It's far worse now. Egypt—the whole Middle East—doesn't welcome crusaders." She walked beside him along the red-carpeted corridor.

"Al Amarna," he said nostalgically. "Seems a lifetime ago, doesn't it? Lordy, Lordy," he added softly, shaking his head. "If I'd known what we were in for…that we were going to both die…and *then* be resurrected—"

"Yes, but not in that big-spectacle way that Reverend Carter preaches about." Valerie checked her watch again as he knocked on the door. "We really only have five minutes, Derek."

The door opened to a view of the entire room with Reverend Carter standing at the center, in front of the television set. News was being broadcast—something about melting glaciers—and he flicked it off. Annoyance registered for an instant on his face when he saw Valerie, then he waved them both in.

"Uh, Pa. Can we take care of this quickly? We're in sort of a hurry here. We have to get to the souq before it closes."

"This is more important than shopping, son. This is family business."

"Ours is family business too, Reverend," Valerie countered as she entered. "For a family member in the South. And I'm afraid we're really pressed for time."

Carter didn't reply, though she could feel the air in the room crackle with his hostility.

"All right, Pa. What is it?"

"Please. Take a seat." Carter motioned toward the chair in front of the hotel television set.

"No, Pa. We can't sit down. Please just tell me what you want to discuss."

"What I want to discuss, my son, is salvation, so you had better sit down."

"What? Oh, please. Not that again." Derek took a step toward the door. At that moment, the two bodyguards entered from outside. One confronted Derek and the other one took up position by Valerie's side.

"What the hell's going on?" Valerie looked around.

"I will thank you to keep a civil tongue in your head, Ms. Foret."

Carter turned to Derek. "You know your momma and I love you, and you must understand that this comes from my heart." He set a second chair down next to the first.

"This? This what?" Derek held out both hands.

The burly guards took Derek and Valerie both by their shoulders and pressed them down into the two chairs.

"This intervention." Carter sat in the bed next to Derek's chair and laid a hand on his forearm. "You have no idea how much it pains me to have to do it this way, but one day you will thank me. Perhaps very soon, when we are all standing before God."

Derek leaned away from him. "Pa, if an intervention didn't work when I was sixteen, it's not going to work now. I'm a grown man and I like who I am. Now we've got urgent things to do, and you've got to let us go and do them."

Carter still held onto his arm. "I know who you are. You're that little boy who used to sing like an angel in our church. Your momma and I were so proud of you. You were filled with the Holy Spirit until you fell into bad company." He shook his head, seeming to recall the ruinous moment.

"You've got to fight it, boy, and you can! We're your family and want to help you push away those unnatural influences." He didn't need to glance at Valerie for the accusation to hang in the air.

Derek jerked his arm from the grasp. "It's not unnatural. You always said God is love."

"Of course He is. And God loves the sinner always. It is just the sin that He hates." Carter opened the briefcase at the side of the bed and drew out a battered Bible. "Let me read you the passage where it says so." He opened a bookmarked section.

Derek shook his head. "Pa, you're way out of your element here, and you have no idea how ridiculous you sound."

Carter was near tears. "Don't talk that way. I'm a pastor, the shepherd of a flock. God has called on me to save as many as I can before the Reckoning. It's coming soon, Derek. The wars, the hatred, all the signs prove it. I want my family to stand beside me when that awesome day arrives."

Abruptly Valerie stood up and confronted him. "It is illegal to hold people against their will in Egypt, just as it is in Georgia. If you don't let us go, I *will* call the police." She reached past him to the hotel phone. The five minutes had become twenty, and now they'd never make it to the souq. She was furious.

Carter seized the handset from her and placed it back on the cradle. "Have it your own way. You who are unrepentant can go with your sins upon you. It is my family I care about."

He signaled to the men to unlock the door and turned back to Derek, then began to talk faster. "Please listen to me, son. Don't you see? God made that baby to show you who you are. That woman needs you to marry her, and her baby needs a daddy. You've got a chance to take them back home to America and start over as a Christian man with a Christian family."

Derek brushed aside the Bible and got up. He opened the door for Valerie, then glanced back to Harlan Carter. "You're right, Pa. This baby showed me who I am, but who I really am is way off your radar. There's just so much you don't know."

"I know about the Resurrection!" With his Bible across his chest the reverend spoke in a tone he was clearly accustomed to using before a congregation.

"There are all kinds of resurrections, Pa." Derek shook his head as he followed Valerie out. "And you may have just ruined one of them."

19

Books

A lamp still burned in the alcove where Sharif guarded the most precious part of the caravan's goods. Faaria slid back the carpet that covered the doorway and watched her brother. It comforted her to see him solitary, as she was. They were two of a kind.

He sat curled over one of the manuscripts that was open on his knees. Hearing her, he lifted his head slowly, as if loath to be drawn away from his private world. "Why aren't you sleeping, little sister? It's late."

"Why aren't *you*? You worked harder than I did today."

"I will soon enough." He glanced toward his pallet laid out in the corner.

"What are you brooding over like a big hen?"

Sharif waved her to his side with a slender hand. "Something wonderful, that passes from land to land and generation to generation."

She sat down next to him and leaned against his shoulder . "Stop making riddles, Sharif, and show me what it is."

"What it is…is science. Look." He moved the lantern over to her side of the open volume.

"Books? I have seen books before. Cairo is full of them. I myself have held a Quran in my hands."

"These are different. Qurans carry revelations, commandments, the way men want the world to be. But science is observation of what the world is. Let me show you." He turned back to the first page. In large calligraphic letters was the title *Canon of Medical Sciences*. "This was written by a man of great learning, Abu Ali Ibn Sina. In the North, the Franks call him Avicenna."

He laid the medical volume aside and pulled one of the tassled camel bags closer. "And you must see these too." He withdrew two large manuscripts bound in dark leather and tied together, undid the cord, and opened the first volume. "These are called *The Book of Strange Arts*. The first part tells of celestial and the second of terrestrial matters. See, this one has a world map." He traced his finger delicately around the edge. "Did you know the world had so much water all around it?"

Faaria stared at the meaningless shapes, trying to fathom how water could surround the world rather than be in it.

Sharif had become animated. "But before science, you must have logic. He reached again into the camel bag. "Here is Al Farabi's *Agreement between the Two Philosophers, Plato and Aristotle.* Those were Greek men of science, who also turned their eyes away from heaven toward the world."

He opened another volume of vellum, covered with script and shapes and numbers. "And once you grasp logic, you can study this. This is a translation of another Greek, Euclid. The title is simple, *Elements.* But do not let it fool you. It shows that the shapes of things—circles, squares, triangles—are not random. They follow principles and work together through the art of numbers."

His eyes seemed to shine, even in the dim, flickering light of the oil lamp. "Science," he repeated almost in a whisper. "It shows that things are not present simply at the whim of God. There is an order to them, of and by themselves, and…" He paused dramatically and held up an index finger. "One can know that order. Science *wants* to know. It is a hunger that increases as it consumes."

Faaria considered the alien concept—a study of the rules of things in themselves. It seemed almost rebellious, and she liked that.

"Amhara says," she blurted suddenly, "that there could be gods in all the things: the wind and waters, in the beasts and birds too. The father of her baby told her that. Is it allowed to even think about such things?"

Sharif chuckled. "Many people think about such things—and write about them too. And not just mystics or madmen. There is even a great mathematician who says them." He drew a slender volume from inside the camel bag, scarcely twenty pages of parchment, and leafed through it gently. "These are in Persian and Arabic." He held the oil lamp over the open page, then began to read out loud.

> *Men say I hold a loose and dubious creed*
> *And set my soul precariously on good deed*
> *But let this virtue my atonement be*
> *The One for many I never did misread.*

"Are you sure he's talking about religion?" Faaria was skeptical.

Sharif shrugged. "From what I know of this man, he *only* writes about religion, even when he writes of love. Umar al Khayyam he calls himself, the son of a tentmaker. Men hold him both in awe and in suspicion, for obvious reasons." He closed the manuscript and laid it between the two books of medicine.

"What's going on here?" Hussaam al Noori stepped into the alcove.

The merchant looked haggard, though one would have had to know him well to notice his fatigue. He was a youthful fifty, with a full head of graying hair, and his round face always gave him the appearance of prosperity. His beard, which had been regularly trimmed by his daughter and now by Sharif, showed almost no gray, though he had an old man's habit of stroking it when in thought.

"Is something amiss?" Husaam leaned forward and sat on one of the bales. It sagged with a crackling of flax fibers under his weight.

"Not at all, sayyid. I thought to examine the vellum for vermin. Faaria was simply curious, and I was pleased to show the books to her." Sharif slid the pile of manuscripts carefully back into the camel bag. "You will see, sayyid, these works are of great worth, both in coin and to the spirit of men."

"Value to the spirit of men, eh?" Husaam touched Sharif on the shoulder and let his hand rest there while he spoke. Like a father, Faaria thought, though she could not remember her own.

"I'm glad to know it," Husaam said. "But I have a business to run, so please calculate their value in coin so we can sell them. In the meantime you must disguise them. Wrap them in straw. The trade route is blocked, and we'll have to take a detour, which itself is a great risk."

Sharif slipped all the volumes back into their woolen bags. "We aren't going to Damascus?"

"No. The caravan that arrived just after us and took half our rooms came from the Negev. But they crossed paths with travelers from the north. These people reported that the Frankish armies have taken Antioch and are moving south, seizing every town along the way."

"But they fight the Seljuk Turks, not us. Isn't it common wisdom that the enemy of my enemy is my friend?"

"The Seljuks are not my enemy. Not my friends either. I have contracts with them for goods. So these Franks can only keep me from my business."

"Where can we go then? Where is it safe?"

"Nowhere is safe. The Franks claim everything in their path, but some cities have been able to placate them and buy them off." He squeezed Sharif's shoulder with his large hand. "I have a friend, an old and powerful friend in a great city. He has high walls and, if need be, a large and skilled army. If anyone can stand up to the foreigners, he can. I have decided to go to him and beg the use of a warehouse and stables, rather than turn around with twenty fully laden camels and flee back through the Sinai."

"Who is this great man, sayyid?"

"Idris ad Dawla, emir of the city. We are going to Jerusalem."

20

El Fishawy

A llaaaah uakbar" sounded over the roofs of the Cairo souq and roused Valerie from her half sleep. It repeated three more times as she washed her face at the sink. Refreshed, if only momentarily, she went out.

"Ashhadu an la ilaha illa'llah," the muezzin sang, bearing witness that there was no deity but God.

She descended the outside steps, not quite sure where she was going, just needing to move and shake off the looming dread.

"Ashhadu anna Muhammadan Rasululu'llah," the voice persisted, declaring that Mohammed was God's Messenger.

The musical call to prayer—like the muezzin and the minaret itself, a delightful medieval anachronism—didn't evoke the usual nostalgia today, but only annoyance. Today the shopkeepers were all at the mosque instead of minding the store, and their piety kept her from her urgent business just as Reverend Carter's had.

Derek, to his credit, was spending quality time with his daughter. Teaching her how to tap dance in her new shoes, probably. Valerie, on the other hand, was spinning her wheels in the sand, and she hated it.

At least El Fishawy was doing business. The open air coffee house—which was no house at all, but a row of chairs and wobbly round tables along both sides of a small closed alley—was in fact full of customers. Obviously, not everyone went to Friday prayers. She spotted a single table in the corner near the entrance and sat down.

Not until after the waiter had taken her order and moved away did she notice the two of them, and she felt a mix of pleasure and embarrassment. How many coincidences could there be?

At a long table at the opposite end of the coffee house, Najya Khoury leaned forward listening intently to two men in headscarves. She held a small metal box in her hand in front of her, no bigger than a pack of cigarettes. Presumably a tape recorder. A few meters behind her, her photographer was taking snapshots. What was his name?

Harry. Right. When one of the men objected, he stopped and sat down beside Najya.

Valerie's waiter returned with the usual chipped enamel teapot and tea glass, and as he set it down, the hookah man—the same old man who had served her two years before—limped to her table with the water pipe. His boy dropped a large hot coal from his cauldron onto the plug of sheesha at the top.

She sipped the mint tea first, gripping the hot glass with her fingertips at the top and bottom, then took a long pull on the hookah. The water gurgled pleasantly in the pipe, and she held the sweet smoke in her mouth, letting it mix with the mint. She could understand why for centuries men had filled their idle hours doing just that—the soothing effect of sound and taste and inactivity made the world seem a friendlier place.

She watched the interview at the far end of the street. Sheer coincidence had brought her just at that hour, of course. But the pleasure she felt watching a beautiful woman who didn't know she was being watched made her feel a little guilty.

How skillful the journalist was, deferential and yet assertive. As she listened to the men, the position of her head and the squint of her eyes subtly suggested either understanding or skepticism. She shifted position away from them when they were vehement, leaned forward again when they seemed to want to confide, and always appeared interested. Valerie thought it must be a pleasure to be interviewed by Najya Khoury.

Harry, for his part, fiddled with his camera lens, then his camera case, then a coffee cup. He shifted in his seat, said something to Najya, and got up to leave. As he passed Valerie's table near the entrance, he looked straight ahead and, to her relief, seemed not to notice her.

Valerie directed her attention back to Najya and felt her face warm suddenly when she realized the journalist had caught sight of her. Najya continued the interview, seemingly unperturbed, and Valerie wondered how she was going to explain her sudden appearance in the same place at the same time. Then she realized that it would make no difference.

She leaned sideways and took another long draw on the hookah, letting her eyes half close, and continued to watch. In a few minutes, the interview was over. Najya stood up, took leave of the two men, dropped her tape recorder into her bag, and swung it on her shoulder.

As graceful as a dancer, she pivoted and glided toward Valerie.

It was a long walk down the center of the alley that was El Fishawy, ten tables at least, and every step Najya took between them seemed to be in slow motion. Valerie watched the line of Najya's body shift languidly onto each leg as she ambled and thought she saw the long hair lift slightly with each step.

Najya held her glance, as if pulled along by it, the dark eyes focused but expressionless. They seemed to begin a conversation without words, without even thoughts, for everything was still a question. Yet they already had a sort of understanding, the way a wave understands the shore it swells toward. And so she came, step by lovely step, until she was at Valerie's table. The expression that formed on her face was a piquant mix of surprise, pleasure, curiosity, and a hint of revenge.

"Don't tell me. Just another odd coincidence."

Valerie still held the mouthpiece to the hookah and allowed herself another puff. "Not at all," she parried. "I've been stalking you for days."

Najya smiled and Valerie realized what she had found so attractive before. She tended to smile from one side of her mouth, letting it curve upward and open slightly, which allowed a glimpse of teeth. An arabesque of a smile.

"All right. We're even. But now I'm allowed to ask what brings *you* here."

"Nothing really." Valerie shrugged. "I have business with a certain merchant, but his shop's not open today, so I'm killing time, or at least beating it up a little. You, I see, are working."

"Yes. Getting as much information as possible before I have to leave in a few days. And you? Are you in Cairo to look after your exhibit or for personal reasons?"

"Mostly personal reasons. The exhibit takes care of itself these days. I'm here mainly to help out a…uh…relative in the South, but he needs something I can only get from the souq."

"A relative? You have family in Egypt?" Najya remained standing, rolling a ballpoint pen slowly between her fingers.

The gesture reminded Valerie of herself, playing with chalk while she lectured.

"This one is a distant relative. A…priest, in fact." *Why are you telling her this? You can't possibly explain.* "But no longer active.

Retired. Sort of."

"A Catholic priest? In southern Egypt? Sounds intriguing."

You have no idea. "No, not Catholic. A little closer to home than that. But it's a story that will have to wait for another day."

Najya finally slid her ballpoint pen into a pocket, but she still didn't sit down. "Yes, I suppose it will. It seems that one or another of us is always in a hurry. I wish we'd talked more yesterday."

"I do too. Especially since the rush was all for nothing anyhow. I met other obstacles."

"Yes, you did rush off, didn't you? And with a provocative last remark. Do you remember? You said 'the story that you tell is the story that tells you.' Maybe you can let me know now what that was supposed to mean."

Valerie paused, ordering her thoughts. "It's the *Rashomon* effect," if you know the great film by Kurasawa. The idea that absolute truth is impossible because each person has their own story, so to speak. And whatever story you inherit colors your perception of all reality, including, in the eyes of some, your experience of death."

"'Including the experience of death.' Now there's a remark that begs discussion." Najya drummed her fingers on the back of a chair. "Look, Harry's waiting for me to show up and start the next interview, and we've got them all day tomorrow. But maybe we, you and I, can get together the day after. It seems like there's a really great conversation just waiting for us to have."

Valerie smiled. "I think so too. Unfortunately, I've got urgent family business that will involve a trip to El Kharga to my relative. But I'd love to get together when I get back."

"Ah, the mysterious priest of the mysterious religion."

"It's not such a mystery. If all goes well with him, I'll give you a call and we can talk about him. It's a story you won't have heard before."

"Don't forget, I'm a journalist. I've spent much of my adult life reporting other people's stories. I'm hard to surprise."

Najya glanced past her, and Valerie turned her head to see what had caught her eye. But it was just Harry standing in the shadows outside the coffee house.

"Yes, please call me. See if you can shock me," Najya said and went to join him.

Valerie watched the two of them disappear. "No problem."

21

Graven Images

Valerie checked the scrap of paper in her hand. "This is the corner, the crossing of Sharia' Suyufia and Shari' el Muzafar." She squinted, struggling to read the heavily calligraphied Arabic letters. "That must be it right there. The shop called Mahal Tamaatheel Manhoota."

Derek squinted as well, in solidarity. "What does that mean?"

"Shop of Graven Images."

"Well, duh." He indicated the rows of plaster and ceramic figurines displayed on the steps at both sides of the entrance.

It was the usual: Anubis in large and small, Horus in three sizes and two colors, Isis and infant, clunky and mass produced. "It's the same stuff they sell all over Cairo," she agreed, a little disappointed.

They stepped from the bright light of the market street into the dimly lit shop. A man stood behind a narrow counter—small, turbaned, and clean shaven. The sleeves of his galabaya were rolled up to the elbows, exposing well-muscled forearms and knotted hands. The hands of a craftsman in some hard material.

"*Sabah el kheer,*" Valerie said.

"*Sabah el noor,*" he replied, but made no attempt to sell. He seemed to wait, rather, for them to explain themselves.

"I…uh, see you sell statues," Valerie began awkwardly. She realized suddenly that she hadn't planned what to say. The ordering of a statue with a personal identity, the identity of a dead man, was not a transaction you could initiate without explanation.

The merchant nodded, his hands flat on the counter in front of him.

"Do you also make them?" Derek asked.

"Yes, I do," he answered cautiously in English.

"Oh, then could you make one of me?" Derek laid his open hand on his chest, in case there was some doubt as to who "me" referred to.

The man's eyes shone with sudden interest. "Yes, yes, of course. A very good one." He studied Derek's face as if smitten.

"In what material?" He took up a small sketch pad and walked a half circle around Derek, scrutinizing, then sketching each feature. He nodded faintly to himself as if in some inner dialogue. "And how large?"

"Whatever you can make fast. And about this high." Valerie held one palm about forty centimeters above the other. "Small enough to fit into a knapsack."

"That would be wood. Painted, of course," the shopkeeper said.

Valerie thought for a moment. "Yes, but a shade lighter than him, and slightly more slender. The face should be the same, but with a braid of hair on one side of his head."

"Ah, like a priest, you mean." The craftsman made another circle around Derek's head, sketching him in profile and three-quarter, then from front and back.

"Yes, exactly. Like an ancient priest. Oh, and one other thing. Please add a small scar." She turned Derek by the arm and pointed to a spot under his right shoulder blade. "Right here."

Derek looked doubtfully at the sketch. "I can leave you a picture, you know. Not to take anything away from your drawing."

"If you like," the Egyptian said, laying the pad aside. "A picture will be fine."

Valerie couldn't tell whether he was offended.

Derek fished a small leather calendar book from his shoulder bag. From its middle he drew a glossy flyer folded in quarters and opened it. Dashing black man, in tuxedo and white tie. The caption was straightforward. Derek Ragin. Countertenor.

"You carry publicity photos with you?" Valerie asked, surprised.

"Of course. Opera singers aren't like archaeologists. We have to advertise."

Taciturn, the Egyptian laid the photo on the counter. "In two days. You can pick it up and we will discuss price."

Valerie hesitated, instinctively reluctant to agree to a transaction without a stated price. Then she realized that under the circumstances, they were prepared to pay almost anything anyhow.

Derek hesitated too, scratching something just below his ear. "Um…maybe I'm vain. I dunno. But could you show us some of your work? I'm just curious. Do you have any figures like this that you've already made? Of real people, I mean."

The Egyptian looked at him for a long moment, as if having to make a decision. Finally he nodded. "In the back."

He led them toward a corner of the already tiny shop to a hanging carpet that had seen much better days. Dust wafted off its fringes as he moved it aside to expose a narrow door. Taking a key from the pocket of his galabaya, he unlocked the padlock that hung through an iron loop over the door handle, then laid back the rusted hasp and tugged on the door. It hung badly with age and so scraped along the floor as he opened it.

"Just a moment. No light in there." He moved away briefly and returned with a battery-powered lantern, then led them into an airless room.

Shelves were hung on three sides, and on every one, from floor to ceiling, hundreds of faces stared back at them. Statues, dolls, figurines, from a few centimeters to a meter in height. They were made of wood, painted and plain, plaster, ceramic, and polished stone. Some had cloth costumes and woolen hair, like dolls. Others were statuettes, their hair and garments cut into the wood or carved on the stone.

"Did you make all of these?" Valerie asked incredulously.

"Only a few," the Egyptian said. "It is my calling to look after them."

"May I?" Valerie took the lantern from his hand and held it up closer to the figures, trying to make sense of them. Finally, she realized that they were organized historically.

The most numerous ones on the highest shelves were pharaonic and mostly basalt: noblemen, military figures, priests, high-ranking women. On the shelf below stood similar statues, both in stone and in terra cotta, but more elaborately carved or costumed. Greco-Roman costumes identified them as Ptolemaic. Below these, there were fewer, and their costumes varied greatly: rich Byzantine gowns, Saracen silks, and wide Bedouin haiks. In the corner were some dozen more, of various races. Black ones appeared to be Nubian, the white ones European peasants. Curiously, many of them had broken noses, and some even had their entire faces smashed away.

"Who are all of these people? I mean, who were they made *for*?" Valerie asked.

"The lost ones," the Egyptian said enigmatically.

At her shoulder, Derek faced the shelves on the opposite side of the tiny closet. "What are those?" He pointed to an open ebony chest on the shelf above them where some of the figurines were set aside, though only the heads were visible. Without waiting for an answer, he reached overhead and took two of the figures from the open box.

He held one in each hand. "They're so beautiful—so realistic. This one here with the pointy helmet looks like a Saracen, or whatever they call them. And this other one, with the big red cross over his armor, even has blond hair. It's a crusader, isn't it?" he asked the shopkeeper over his shoulder.

"Please leave them in their place." The man took them gently out of Derek's hands, set them back in their chest, and flicked off the lantern. "I think that will be all," he said, ushering them out. He closed the door behind them and threaded the padlock through the staple, pressing it from both sides until it clicked into place.

He was suddenly businesslike, impatient. "You must go now so I can make your likeness," he said and urged them through the front door of the shop. "Come back in two days."

The door closed behind them and they stared at each other. Derek pursed his lips, then threaded her arm in his. "Did that closet give you the creeps the way it did me?"

"A little bit. Those figures obviously weren't made for tourists."

"The two that I held were like chess pieces, except with real faces. Like they were alive once. And the whole room was like a...I don't know...like a haunted house. Didn't you feel it?"

She thought for a minute. "No, to me it felt like a graveyard."

"I'll tell you what the creepiest thing of all was. That crusader."

"Why?"

"Except for the blond hair, he looked a lot like you."

22

Miles Christi—1097

S ir Ludolf of Tournai kneed his horse closer to the promontory and dismounted, dazzled by the sight.

Constantinople spread over the hills before him, and on the plain below, twenty thousand men were gathered. At the eastern edge of the encampment he could see the standards of Flanders with their green crosses. Beneath them he thought he could make out his own tent where his grooms cleaned his armor and prepared his supper.

The spring wind blew through his honey blond hair and cooled his sweat. So this was it, then. His quiet euphoria and the pounding in his chest were what the bishops had meant by the "rejoicing in the Lord."

How much his life had changed and was about to change since Antwerp.

He had far too long been the useless youngest son. His long face and too-full lips made him look effeminate, he knew, and his wide hips and long torso made him the butt of the men's jokes. When his family had finally brokered a match for him with some tiny docile creature, he had known contentment of a sort, particularly when she informed him a child was on the way. But evil had touched his land and household, and his wife had died along with the babe she was trying to bear. For months he had wallowed in bitterness, resenting every offspring gotten by his brothers. But then he heard Pope Urban at Clermont, and had the Dream, and pledged his sword to God.

Suddenly he had a purpose, a noble one, that set him above the others. For a year he had been on the march, along with a troop of twenty vassals and their grooms and servants.

The preparations had at first seemed endless, organizing horse and household. But finally he joined Godfrey of Bouillon and Raymond of Toulouse, as they gathered infantry, then marched across the mountains to Genoa and down the western side of Italy.

Rome had been a disappointment. His Holiness had issued the call for the entire endeavor, but the Holy See from which he drew his authority held little glory. The ancient Basilica of St. Peter where Ludolf had gone to pray was in disrepair. And it disgusted him that sheep were grazing in the Forum and in many of the city's quarters.

No matter. He was sworn to a holier pilgrimage. The trip across the Adriatic had been the real test of his faith. One of their ships had foundered in the storm, dashed against rocks. But he himself felt no fear. His faith and the certainty that God had chosen him for a nobler contest had sustained him.

He startled at the sound of hoof on gravel and turned to see his cousin dismount. The ruddy knight tethered his horse and strode toward him.

"What a sight, eh, Ludolf?" The other knight took off his helmet and held it in the crook of his arm, its plumes still fluttering in the breeze that blew over the promontory. "Here we are, standing before the richest city in Christendom!"

"Do not be so easily dazzled, Gilbert. Splendor means nothing without the True Faith," Ludolf said somberly.

"Ever pious, eh, Ludolf?" Gilbert lifted his head and let the breeze dry his neck. "Myself, I will leave the bishops to judge if these Byzantines are of the Faith. I was in the Basilica of St. Sophia yesterday, though, and it certainly looked Christian to me."

Ludolf did not reply.

Gilbert seemed not to notice. "Oh, yes. It's vast, with a great dome way overhead. The walls seem to glow with frescoes and mosaics. There are even mosaics on the floor. And the relics! God's wounds, Ludolf, you wouldn't believe the relics. Christ's Crown of Thorns, pieces of the Holy Cross, the Virgin's robe—and even the head of John the Baptist."

"The Crown of Thorns? Really?" Ludolf was skeptical. "Are you sure it's authentic?"

"It has to be. They wouldn't have it in the church otherwise."

Ludolf let the remark hang in the air.

Gilbert looked unperturbed. "Rome's got no palaces like this Byzantine has, that's for sure. Over there." He nodded toward the northwest corner of the city. "He's got more gold than I've ever laid eyes on. Marble too, colored marble all over the floors and walls. He is a great emperor."

"Not so great that he doesn't need help from the West." Ludolf scratched something from his tabard. "Are you going to swear loyalty to him, as he demands?"

"Why not? Alexius has been very generous. He's given us armor, horses, silks—and rather a lot of money for provisions. Besides, Godfrey of Bouillon has taken the oath, and no one's greater than he is."

"The one who died on the Cross is greater than the Duke of Bouillon. I have already taken an oath to the Cross. That is enough."

"Don't be so righteous, old man. Every free man in the camp has taken the oath to the Cross." He glanced toward the field of tents on the plain below them.

Ludolf shook his head. "Some have sworn lightly, with less faith than urge for battle and gain. But I took a second and private oath—with my blood."

He ran his hand down the front of his tabard, so Gilbert could see that the entire crimson cross that reached from his throat to his hem and from shoulder to shoulder was outlined with reddish-brown blood.

Gilbert averted his eyes. "Well, no one will ever accuse you of laxity."

Ludolf half closed his eyes again. "No, they never will. On my knees before the cross and with blood running from my hands, I swore on my soul to be a soldier for the True Faith."

He drew his sword from his side and held it by the blade up to heaven. "I have sworn this in Rome, and I swear it again here before this city of sickly Christians. I am for God, and all my lineage shall be for God, through all generations—or my curse is on them!" He lowered his sword and whispered the declaration of God's will that was emblazoned on their banners. "*Deus lo volt.*"

23

Rekemheb

It was late morning as Valerie drove her rented jeep south from Luxor, and from the east the sun shone hard on one side of her face.

She met only sparse traffic on the highway, little to distract her from her brooding. Here she was again, driving over the desert for Rekemheb. Now at least she understood why. The ka was family, the founder of the family, in fact. And what a strange lineage they were. How could she ever explain them to a stranger? To Najya Khoury, for example.

Najya Khoury. Through the long night of driving, Valerie had thought a lot about the handsome Palestinian journalist. An intriguing, complicated woman, unlike anyone she'd met in a long time. Maybe ever.

Curious that Najya could be so unsentimental and at the same time "believe in people," as she said. Still, she was worth having another conversation with, dressed or undressed. Valerie smiled to herself thinking of which alternative she preferred.

Then she remembered the trousers thrown over the foot of her bed at Sammad's place. And Harry. He had been undressed—with Najya—in the upstairs room. The image of their coupling on her bed flashed through Valerie's mind, and she felt herself grimace. She hated the ease with which men got women into bed.

She wondered if Najya ever had a lesbian thought.

Banzeen, the sign said, over an arrow pointing off the road. She checked the fuel gauge—time to tank up. In less than a kilometer she reached the station, although the line of busses showed her where it was long before she reached it. She pulled in and waited.

Nervous and bored at the same time, she first drummed her fingers on the steering wheel, then reached for the statue of Rekemheb. For some reason, the shopkeeper had handed it to her wrapped in linen rather than laid in a box. She had checked it briefly in the shop, decided it was suitable, then paid the charge. She was surprised that the price was reasonable and so added a small *baksheesh* to show her satisfaction. He didn't seem to notice.

She undid the cord and studied the statue more closely. It seemed even better made than she had first judged. The face was strikingly accurate, and the sculptor had captured the lightness around Derek's eyes so that the statue had the same facial radiance that he had. But of course it was not Derek; it was Rekemheb, complete with priestly sidelock and painted a shade lighter brown than the more African Derek.

The shoulders also were excessively wide, and the relative flatness of the chest was unmistakably Egyptian, reminiscent of the lean, spare statues of the temples. One hand hung down at his side in the archaic style and held a sistrum. The other one, laid across his chest, held a tiny object. She hadn't paid attention to it before, but she saw now it was an amulet. The image on it was miniscule, but holding it close, she could make it out. It was the Balance in the underworld. A single red dot on one side signified the heart, a single vertical white hyphen on the other was the feather.

She turned it over and studied the back. The well-formed hips and legs were covered by the long pleated white kilt of the priest, and above it, slightly to the right, was the mark where the deadly spear had pierced his back.

The whole object was extraordinary. In the sweetness and precision of its face, it was a doll in the formal rigidity of its body, a pharaonic statue.

Suddenly the gas line opened up and she set the doll aside to pull into the station.

❖

Valerie forced the jeep across the hard-packed sand between the oasis and the great rock wall. There it was finally, the escarpment where the lines of shadow on the cliff formed the Eye of Horus. She drove as closely as possible to the cliff wall, to take advantage of the narrow band of shade. Gathering up canteen, flashlight, and backpack, she climbed out and hiked up to the cave entrance.

It took all her strength to dislodge the stone, and when she finally managed it, she was exhausted and dehydrated. Panting, she stepped into the familiar tunnel and took a long drink of water from her canteen before she started down. As she walked, the light of her flashlight beam ovaled and sprang back to a circle along the walls and floor, revealing nothing new.

Memories returned in a rush, of the four of them, pleased with themselves, carrying the mummy of Rekemheb to his new tomb; of the sudden reappearance of Vanderschmitt and his shooting of the Bedouin woman; of her own reawakening there with Derek after their release from the underworld. All that coming and going, she thought. The place was not so much a tomb as a sort of spiritual bus stop.

When she came, finally, to the sarcophagus, she called Rekemheb's name. She wasn't sure of the ritual; it would be good to have his guidance. Silence. Nothing but the sound of her own breathing. Bleakly, she laid down her knapsack and put her shoulder to the sarcophagus lid, inching it far enough along to reveal the head and chest of the mummy.

"Oh, no," she whispered. She knew in an instant she couldn't rescue him.

Someone had opened the sarcophagus and dropped a stone onto the mummy's chest, shattering its ribs and spine. She felt nauseous with fear as she grasped what the dropped stone meant. Whoever, whatever had been there hadn't smashed the mummy cleanly, but had mortally wounded it, letting it ebb slowly, consciously, toward the moment when its ka could no longer be sustained. It was not only spiritual murder it was torture unto final endless death.

She called his name again, clutching at straws, but it was no use. He was gone. The ritual was pointless. She took another drink from her canteen and wiped her neck with her bandana, indecisive. She had come so far for him, they all had. She exhaled in a sort of weak decision. Like the rescuer who leaves the oxygen mask on the victim past the point of hope, she would perform the ceremony to pay him a last respect.

She drew the wooden statue from her pack and placed it on the stone lid in the light of her flashlight. The painted face looked at her serenely. With trembling hands she laid out the adz and the tiny alabaster dish of myrrh. She drew her battered Zippo lighter from her pocket and held the flame to the myrrh until it caught. When the fragrant smoke was strong enough to cover the dank smell of the sarcophagus, she began the familiar invocation in Egyptian.

"*Chesu, Neteru!* Hail to you, Great Gods, and to you, Lords of Justice. You live on truth and gulp down truth. I know you and I know your names. Behold, I am without falsehood and there is no one who testifies against me."

She reached down into the sarcophagus with the bronze adz and pressed its curved tip against the mummy's mouth. "Jehuti comes filled with magic," she intoned. "He has cast away the bonds of Seth which held my words. My mouth is split open with the instrument that touched the mouth of the gods. I am Osiris, who dwells with souls, and I shall speak."

The dry lips crumbled at the touch and she quickly withdrew the instrument, placing it against the carved mouth of the statue. "I am Osiris who dwells with souls. I shall take breath."

She reached down again, this time touching the mummy's sunken eyes and desiccated nose and ears. She withdrew the tool and laid it on the head of the statue. Mechanically, she touched the adz to the four limbs and to the respective parts of the statue and spoke the final incantation. "My eyes are opened by the god and my ears to hear, my legs to walk, and my arms to fell my enemy. My flesh shall not be halted at the portals of the West, and I may go in and out in peace."

Nothing happened. She hadn't expected anything to.

"Jehuti! Nekhbet! Where are you?" she called into the darkness. "Your priest is gone now, just like the caretaker of the Child! How can you make a prophecy and not defend it? How can you not even show up?"

Her own voice echoed foolishly in the stone tunnel. She leaned her arms on the sarcophagus for a few moments, giving the gods time to answer. They had to answer. Nothing. The silence mocked her. She grasped the stone lid to slide it closed.

Then, on impulse, she stopped and shone her light down into the coffin again. If the mummy was going to disintegrate, there was something she wanted. She reached down to the fleshless jaw of the corpse, seized hold of a large tooth at the back of the jaw, and drew it easily from the porous bone. A quick perusal under the flashlight revealed it was intact, and she dropped it into her pocket.

"So much for 'forever,'" she muttered and shoved the stone lid back into place. At the last nudge of the tablet, the ceremonial objects tumbled to the ground and lay in the silt. When she retrieved them, they felt like stupid toys. What had she been thinking? She tossed them carelessly into her knapsack. The statue of Rekemheb, which she still held in her hand, looked toy-like as well. A painted doll. Sick with the sense of betrayal, she rolled it in its linen wrapping and started up the tunnel to the entrance.

It was the hottest part of the day. The jeep shimmered in the sunlight. If she tried to drive in it, she would slowly cook. Worse, the pulsing line of orange-gray on the horizon told her that a sandstorm was approaching. She would have to wait it out.

She withdrew halfway down the tunnel where the dust would be tolerable, leaned back against the stone wall, and drew her knees up, wrapping her arms around them. Mumbling *"Merde...merde...merde,"* she let herself fall into a brief, tormented sleep.

❖

Though it was evening, the desert wind still blew hot against her as she drove, brooding again. There are no coincidences, Derek had said. For us, everything is connected. Yussif and Rekemheb struck down in the same week. No, it wasn't a coincidence. Someone, something was persecuting them.

How could it be, though? Who even knew where the mummy lay? Only Vanderschmitt had followed them, driven, in some way she couldn't understand, by the urges of the Aton. But he was dead, his vulture-stripped remains interred somewhere in Belgium. And though he was—she shuddered at the thought—her father, she had no interest in knowing where.

She cringed inwardly whenever she thought of Volker Vanderschmitt and was alternately repulsed and angry at having to acknowledge his paternity. Horrifying enough to discover that her father was a murderer. All the more monstrous to learn that her own murderer was her father. Yet she carried his genes, which caused the greatest revulsion of all; it was enough to make her crazy. She slammed the door in her mind on the thought of him and ruminated on the subject from another direction.

What was different now from every other day in the last two years when nothing had threatened them? What had happened at exactly the time of Yussif's death?

She almost braked when it came to her, when the full weight of the danger descended on her like a stone.

The Book.

Her manuscript had been accepted for publication only a week before the train explosion. The moment had come when the story of the gods would be told to the world. What's more, once the machinery of publication had begun, it would not be stopped. The electronic existence of the manuscript in half a dozen places ensured its safety. Even from "acts of God."

"Is that what you're worried about?" she shouted into the empty air. "You think my little adventure tale is going to lead to a wave of apostasy?" She laughed bitterly. "You snuffed out two beautiful spirits because you're afraid of *me*?"

The engine roared as she pushed the jeep as hard as it could go over the rocky ground. It was already evening. She had water and trail food and could drive all night. She had to get back and warn the others.

24

Obedience

From his vantage point, he watched the two men, the black one and the white one, emerge from the hotel. As soon as they stepped into a taxi, he called another one over to the curb and followed them. They got out in front of some small church, and once they were inside, he stepped out of his taxi onto the street.

He was prepared to wait indefinitely, but they emerged again in less than an hour. They hailed another taxi, and when they were out of sight, he entered the church himself.

He walked along the side aisles until he found a good spot. Yes, he could stand here, in a straight line to the pulpit, and be concealed. If the opportunity presented itself, he could move in close for a sure thing—but he could probably do it even from cover.

Satisfied, he returned to the center aisle at the front of the church and stood before the altar. It was a simple affair, a block of hardwood with a white altar cloth and a plain meter-high bronze cross at the center.

The purity and straightforwardness of it appealed to him. It wasn't the church in which he was raised, but in the semi-darkness, he definitely felt the Presence. It began as a pressure behind his eyes and a rushing in his ears. On an impulse, he knelt down and let the spirit settle over him. Then, as so often in his boyhood, he raised his hands and clasped them under his chin.

"Forgive me, Lord," he began, as he always had, enumerating his failures before making any requests. "I'm sorry, Lord, for what I did to that little girl, but I was only a child myself. And I'm sorry for any evil thoughts I might have had for my parents. I'm sorry for the animals I hurt, but you know that was my foolish anger."

His head began to ache. The pain started behind his eyes, then spread over the top of his skull. He moved his confession up in time. "I beg forgiveness for my carelessness with my wife and children, and I accept their leaving me as my punishment. But you can see, Lord, I've given myself to a higher calling." The throbbing was severe now, but he took it as a sign of the importance of the moment. God spoke to him through pain, and always he measured his suffering against the agony of Christ; each shuddering wave that washed against his skull brought Him closer. Though he had begun his prayer sitting upright, like an altarboy, he had slowly curled over until he formed a tight ball of contrition.

Then the light appeared. The jagged psychedelic rings of lights in harsh colors flashed and sparkled around the emptiness in the middle. He was blind now, but for a thin ring of vision on the periphery. He crawled toward the emptiness, the opening toward the infinite, and groped along the edge of the altar cloth until he felt the metal base of the cross.

"Forgive me, Lord, for my weakness, for my doubts in You or in this mission. I have seen Your signs, and I know what I must do. I offer my life, my strength to You. For I was a shadow and now I am a man. Guide my hand as I wipe out the abomination and make the world clean again for You."

The flashing neon rings stopped finally, and the pain subsided to a dull ache. He stood up from the altar, plucked his clammy shirt away from his skin, and exhaled slowly. His vision restored, he looked around the sanctuary once more and saw how the afternoon light had changed.

He had to take a shower, change his clothes again. The day's work wasn't finished. He ran his hand over his head, feeling that the headache was now gone, and his fingers lingered for a moment at the edge of his brow where he imagined once the crown of thorns had rested.

25

Assassin

*M*erde! *Merde! Merde!* Why hadn't she thought to get
Auset's parents' telephone number? And why wasn't Derek
answering his cell phone? She'd called three times from towns on the
way north but never got through. What the hell good was it to have one
of those gadgets if you didn't turn it on?

Zamalak, the road sign said. Finally. She careened around a corner
to the house of Mahmoud al Fakhir and parked the rented jeep half on
the sidewalk. She rang. And rang again, shifting her weight from one
foot to the other.

The housemaster opened. "*Ah, Duktura. Ahlan wa sahlan.*" He
stepped back to admit her; his always-solemn face told nothing.

"She took a breath. "Is everyone all right?"

"*Alhamdullilah,*" he reassured her and led her down the corridor
to the garden. Auset sat again at the tea table next to the kitchen.

Valerie looked around, alarmed. "Where's Nefi?"

Auset stared at her with a puzzled expression. "Nefi's fine. She's
with my mother, upstairs. Are you all right? You look harried."

"I came as fast as I could. Someone was in the tomb and opened
the sarcophagus. Rekemheb's mummy was smashed. There was no ka,
of course. I did the ceremony, but it was all useless. He's gone."

"Oh, no." Auset dropped her eyes wearily. "I'm sorry. What does
that mean for us, then? Do you suppose—?"

"That's what I rushed back to tell you. It can't be a coincidence
that Rekemheb's mummy was smashed and Yussif was killed in the
same week. I'm sure now that someone—or something—is out to harm
us all." She glanced up toward the second story where the private rooms
were. "Where's Derek?"

"He's with his stepfather at the Evangelical Church. There were
hecklers at the sermon yesterday in Alexandria so Derek went along
today. To 'keep things calm,' he said."

"The Evangelical Church. That's in Al Qal'a, street, isn't it?"
Valerie was on her feet.

"Yes, why? I don't think you need to worry. They've got guards, after all."

"Yussif's train had guards too." Valerie hurried toward the door.

❖

She heard the reverend's voice in the atrium even before she opened the double doors to the sanctuary and saw him.

Carter stood at the center, on the top step before the altar, and held up a Bible. A finger was tucked between the pages, as if he had just been reading from it. He spoke, full throated, like a man used to preaching in large spaces. "Thessalonians tells us that the Lord will descend from heaven with a thunderous cry…and the dead in Christ shall rise up." An interpreter stood just behind him with a microphone and repeated each sentence in Arabic. Reverend Carter seemed to be used to a staccato delivery. He spoke in short phrases and paused after each one, letting his argument build.

The air was electric. Voices from the front rows said "Amen," but another, from the rear, called out "*Kazaab!*" Carter clearly did not understand that he was called a liar, and he held his Bible up higher. "And in Revelation, 'I saw heaven open up…and there was a rider called Faithful who judges and makes war. His eyes are like blazing fire.'" He widened his eyes and said "blazing fire" a notch louder, as if to impress upon them the mortal peril they were in.

One or two voices called out again, "*Kazaab!*"

Then he dropped his voice, and the audience fell silent. "He is dressed in a robe that is stained with blood…and his name is the Word of God."

Valerie noticed the two goons standing at a slight distance on both sides of him. They held their hands loosely clasped together in front of them, but it was impossible not to know that they were bodyguards. Their presence made it seem like he was delivering an ultimatum instead of a sermon.

Derek was harder to find, but then she spotted the back of his head. He sat in the front pew leaning forward. How he must have hated being there. She wondered if the good reverend had preached about the sin of homosexuality.

Keeping Derek in sight, she edged along the side aisle of the church, glancing around quickly for anything that seemed abnormal. But there was no *normal*. The whole event, a Christian evangelical preacher's attempt at a tent revival in the middle of Cairo, was already bizarre. And every face in the congregation seemed angry. She had almost reached the front row and wondered how to get Derek's attention without disruption.

Derek sat up suddenly, and she realized the tone of the sermon had changed. She had missed a few important words.

"...for you are my brothers in Christ, if only you let yourselves be. But I tell you, the land bordered by the Nile on one side, and the Euphrates on the other..." He reached out an arm as if to show the direction. "By the Mediterranean Sea and by the wilderness of Jordan." The translator repeated each phrase in Arabic right after him. "All this is the land given by God to Israel..." The rumbling in the crowd started. "And will once again be Israel! My brothers—"

As if they had been waiting for those very words, a dozen dissenters rose en masse. Another handful joined them shouting, "Liar. Crusader, go home!" They repeated the words again and again, shaking their fists over their heads; some of them left the pews and advanced toward the steps where Carter stood. From behind the protesters, others, apparent evangelicals, shouted their own slogans and advanced as well, so that the audience as a whole seemed to swell in two waves toward the front.

The two bodyguards moved in to stand by Carter. Derek stood up and pivoted around, holding out his arms on both sides as if to catch something, though nothing was thrown. Then the belligerent crowd closed in around the four foreigners and Valerie lost sight of them.

A gunshot sounded, and the entire pack exploded outward from the center. Valerie ran along the front pew, buffeted by terrified men trying to flee.

Reverend Carter had moved to the side and leaned panting up against the pulpit that he had not used. His two guards were nowhere in sight. Maybe they were chasing the gunman; she didn't know. All she could see was the appalling sight in front of her.

Derek lay on his back on the steps, and she rushed to take him into her arms. She ripped open his shirt to see a thin stream of blood pumping from the center of his chest and covered it with her hand, unnecessarily, for soon the bloodstream stopped as the heart ceased to pump.

Kneeling over the limp body, she looked up at the trembling clergyman. "You bastard," she wailed in helpless fury. "You smug, ignorant bastard!"

26

Antioch, June 1098

There it lay, on a silver platform on the altar. Four candles illuminated it in the somber darkness of the church. A crumbling, rusted spearhead with a handbreadth of rotted wood remaining for its shaft, lay in all its holy power upon a silken pillow. Ludolf dropped to his knees before it, his hands shaking, wondering if he dared touch it, the Holy Lance that had pierced the side of the Son of God.

He placed a hand on his own side, imagining for a moment what it must have felt like to be pierced. His own battle wounds had thus far only been bruises and a blow to the head. He shivered at the thought of the exquisite pain of the new lance blade slicing through naked flesh.

He covered his face and prayed. "Thank you, Lord, for this miracle and sign that has reawakened us to victory. Grant that we prove worthy of it and of His sacrifice."

Truly it had been a miracle that had saved them, snatched them from the very jaws of defeat. The weeks and months had been a sore test indeed. Famine had tortured them all, man and knight, so that a horse's head without the tongue was sold for three solidi, the guts of a goat for five. And then—his heart swelled to think of it—the Holy Lance had been found under the floor of the church. Despite their ravening hunger and exhaustion, the wounds on their feet from the days of penitence, they had borne it before them as they advanced against the Turks, and it had brought them victory.

"I knew you'd be here, Ludolf. The first place you would come when you woke up from your injury."

He looked back over his shoulder toward the familiar voice. Even in the dim light, he recognized his cousin's bulky outline. "You know me well, Gilbert."

Ludolf took hold of the proffered arm and drew himself up. He blessed himself elaborately and allowed himself to be led away from the altar. "Antioch is Christian again, Gilbert."

"Yes, though it reeks of slaughter."

"That is the smell of sacrifice. Salvation is costly."

They reached the portal together and stepped one by one around the great wooden door of the church. By the morning light, Ludolf could see what darkness had concealed when he arrived. Bodies were piled in the corners of the square, where they had obviously been dragged after the slaughter. Emaciated dogs gnawed on them here and there until someone shooed them away.

I do not think God asks for *that* kind of sacrifice." Gilbert nodded toward the three cadavers that still hung from their heels on a scaffold at the south end of the square. Their torsos were slit open from crotch to chest, and half-dried viscera hung out over their faces. "It was said they had swallowed their gold to hide it from us." He shrugged. "The soldiers never found any, though."

"You see it backward, my friend. The death of heathens is not *their* sacrifice. Rather it is *our* suffering and sacrifice to shed their blood against our gentler natures. We are the martyrs here, and God has rewarded us for our piety."

A rumbling from a side street drew their attention. Two women, old and bent with exhaustion, were drawing a handcart into the square.

Ludolf stepped forward to confront them, laying his hand on the hilt of his sword. But as they neared, he saw the wooden crosses hanging from their necks. "What's this?" he demanded. "Christians in Antioch? Or is this some mockery?"

The two women let the cart handle fall and groveled before him.

"What are they saying, Gilbert? You speak their Greek. Tell me."

"They say they are daughters of Italian pilgrims who settled here a long time ago and never left. They come from their quarter, a Christian quarter, which is burning now. They ask if they can pass and leave the city to bury their children."

Ludolf walked to the rear of the cart and lifted the cloth that covered it. Five cadavers lay there, two young men and two women, variously slashed and battered, and the torn skirt on one of them suggested rape. A small child lay horizontally across the others. Ludolf dropped the cloth.

"If they do not follow Rome, they are not Christians," he sniffed. "Let them go. God will reckon with them later."

The two women leaned their weight onto the crossbar and forced the cart into motion again.

Ludolf turned away from the sight of them. "Salvation is costly."

27

Mourning

The fountain in the center of Mahmoud al Fakhir's garden gurgled peacefully, indifferent to the pall of sorrow over Valerie and Auset, who watched it numbly. Auset sat with crossed legs, tapping the fingers of her open hand on her knee to some senseless inner rhythm.

Valerie propped one elbow on the back of the garden bench and rested her cheek on her knuckles.

They watched the two-year-old Nefi, who didn't know what death was, feed crumbs of pita bread to half a dozen swallows.

Auset shifted in her seat and sighed. "They've abandoned us, haven't they? The gods, I mean."

Valerie brooded for a moment. "I don't understand. Nekhbet sent us here. Derek's job was to look after you, and I was supposed to rescue Rekemheb. But both efforts have ended in disaster. And we still don't even know if Derek and Yussif are in the underworld."

"Underworld!" Auset spat out the word. "Don't tell me about the underworld. Yussif has been dead for two weeks now and Derek for four days. If there was any chance they would come back as kas, we would have seen them by now. Besides, the gods never told us—were we supposed to have them embalmed like the pharaohs? Impossible, with my father stepping in and arranging a quick Muslim burial, and the good reverend shipping his stepson to Georgia for a Christian one."

"You're right." Valerie spoke in a monotone. "They never told us the rules. And there's been no sign. Nothing."

More birds had come to join the swallows. Hoopoes and iridescent green-winged sunbirds lit on the rim of the fountain or the flat stones below it. They assembled with unbirdlike calm, except for an occasional twitch when a droplet of fountain spray struck them.

"Will you go home now?" Auset asked. "Please don't. Not right away."

Valerie shook her head. "I've nothing to go home for. I would have gone to Derek's funeral in the US on Friday, but Reverend Carter made it clear I'm not welcome there."

"Despicable, isn't it, that he can come here and claim Derek that way. Simply take him away from us. A man who disapproved of his very identity. Well, he won't get his hands on everything." Auset took hold of a black canvas travel bag beside the bench and dragged it around in front of her.

"Oh, God, I forgot about his personal things. I suppose Carter will want those before he leaves."

"I'm sure he will, but in the meantime, I removed what I know Derek would want you to have." She drew out a small leather case with a belt hook at the back.

"First of all, his cell phone. It's one of those you can put a card in for each country. There's a battery charger too."

Valerie sat down, appalled at handling an object that still seemed to have Derek's touch. Yet it was a sort of relief to have something purposeful to do that he would have wanted. She caressed the metal casing. "He always told me I should have one of these. But it seemed like such an expensive toy."

"The phone is nothing. Look what that foolish man carried around with him. Just imagine the trouble he would have gotten into if they'd inspected his bags at the airport." Auset handed over something flat and heavy, wrapped in a silk handkerchief.

Valerie's eyes pooled again as she unwrapped it. "The amulet," she whispered and tilted it in the light, studying the filigree gold plaque with the image of the Great Balance, attended by the gods of the underworld. "I think he must have brought this to give to Nefi. She's the next one in Rekemheb's line."

"If you say so. I'll put it in a safe place until it's the right time to explain everything to her." Auset slid it into the side pocket of her skirt and continued the inventory. "He had a lot of money in his wallet and I left it all there. I don't want it and don't want to be accused of stealing. But I did take these." She handed over two photographs.

Valerie studied them with a wan smile. "Nefi, looking with great solemnity up into the camera. So adorable. And this must be one of your wedding pictures. Bride and groom. And Derek standing right next to them, as if it were the most natural thing in the world to have two fathers in the family."

"It's a good likeness of both of them, isn't it?"

"A likeness," Valerie repeated. "On that subject, I guess you should take this. It doesn't seem to have worked." She drew the linen-wrapped bundle from her knapsack and held it out. "If nothing else, Nefi can play with it as a doll."

Auset took the statue without unwrapping it and laid it next to her on the bench. "That's it, then. The sum total of what we have left of him."

Her lips began to tremble again and Valerie embraced her. She tried to comfort, but found herself weeping as well, hopelessly, the weak sobs of one who has already cried a great deal.

Something made Auset lift her head from the embrace and look toward the fountain. She gasped audibly and froze.

Feeling her grow rigid, Valerie looked over her shoulder. "No!" she whispered. "Don't move. Don't frighten it."

"Oh, my God," Auset whimpered softly into the air, not taking her eyes from the horror. "Please, please don't hurt her. Oh, please."

Nefi sat upright on the ground by the fountain, her eyes half closed, as if in infant sleep. Coiled once around her body, with its head hovering next to her face, a full-grown king cobra swayed back and forth.

Auset whispered, "Please, oh, please" over and over.

The snake tilted its head downward and for an instant gently touched Nefi's cheek.

Auset jerked violently and tried to lurch forward, but Valerie held her back. "It's not a bite. Look. She's smiling."

The snake arched over Nefi's narrow shoulder and slid down her back, then along the ground into the underbrush of the garden. On the stones where it had crossed, a line of pale green light glowed for a moment, then faded.

Auset threw herself toward her and snatched her up. But Nefi curled forward and struggled to be set down again.

"Leave her where she was. Something's going on." Valerie took hold of Auset's arm and pulled her back onto the bench.

The birds that had been feeding came back. They were joined by others: warblers, doves, and quails. When the fountain rim was covered, they lit on the brush beside the path. They were unperturbed when a cat, slender and sleek, crouched just in front of Nefi's feet. She sat, as if in a trance, her mouth slightly open, and stared dreamily toward the wall on the south side of the garden where larger birds gathered: kingfishers, egrets, and ravens.

"What's going on?" Auset's voice had gone from terror to wonderment.

Then on the north side, on the roof above the private apartments, ospreys and gulls landed on the one side; on the other, a small white vulture and a falcon. Last of all, as if all others had prepared the way for him, a splendid male ibis flew over the wall and lit on the ground. Beside it, a smaller yellow bird with a dark head flickered briefly into visibility, then flickered out again, like a sputtering flame.

"What does it mean?" Auset stood up.

Before she had taken a step, the entire menagerie fell silent. Nefi looked around at them, her face suddenly radiant, as if she had been waiting for an audience. Slowly, she raised one fist toward them, swept it in an arc, then opened it. On her palm sat a large dung beetle. Its iridescent carapace shone greenish-black in the sunlight. It turned on her palm, as if to look at her first, then extended its little wings and flew off, leaving behind a piece of soil it had rolled into a perfect ball.

"Khepre, creator of the world," Valerie murmured. "It's a visitation. But what are they trying to tell us?"

"*Minfadlik,* Madam." Suddenly Fahd was on the the garden path rushing toward them. The whole flock of winged creatures took flight, and the cat too slunk away. The houseman paused a moment, clearly bewildered by the flurry of wings everywhere, then continued, greatly agitated. "Mahmoud al Fakhir is not home and there is a visitor. The American. Mr. Derek's father, and two others. He says it is important and he insists to come in."

28

International Law

Valerie rushed through the narrow alleys of the souq again, as she had been rushing for a week. She reached the Shari al Badustan, then slowed for a moment, to catch her breath.

Carter had been pale. At least he mourned, she thought. But he had had his lawyer at his side and minced no words when he announced that he was canceling his missionary tour to "take his family home." By his "family," he meant the mortal remains of his stepson—and his granddaughter.

What a coup, she thought. If the Aton was a conscious and deliberate adversary, and it appeared now that he was, then he had achieved a brilliant masterstroke. In a single week his mysterious agents had eliminated the guardian ancestor and the two fathers and had brought a fanatical cleric to claim the Child of the gods, to be raised in a God-fearing monotheist home away from Egyptian influence.

The irony was exquisite. The prophecy was indeed fulfilling itself, and the Sun Disk Aton, in his Christian form, was "rising in the West." But if the Egyptian gods were powerless to defend their own messenger against monotheist fanaticism, one thing still protected them: the secular law. She hoped.

The Blue Nile hotel was located at the end of the Shari al Badustan. A notch above Sammed's place, it had a front desk rather than the counter of a coffee house. There was no air conditioning, and everywhere she heard the whirring of fans. A word with the man on duty and she went upstairs.

Najya Khoury stood in the doorway, and her expression of confusion lasted only a moment before it evolved into warmth. She had obviously just washed her face in cold water. Ringlets of hair still held droplets, and her partially open shirt showed a V of moisture from the middle button up to both shoulders.

"I'm sorry to just appear this way, but you did say that I should look you up if I needed anything. I do, and it's sort of urgent."

"What's happened? Forgive me, but you look terrible." Najya led her into a hotel room only slightly larger than the room at Sammed's, but better furnished. "Can I offer you something? A cold beer?" She nodded toward an ice chest in the corner of the room. "Harry always has a supply."

"No. No, thank you. I just need to talk, ask a few things." She half smiled. "And who better to turn to than a complete stranger you met in a hammam, right?"

"For God's sake, talk to me then. Come, sit down. Tell me what's going on."

Valerie looked around. The one chair in the room was piled with photographic equipment. The only free surface in the room was the bed. She sat, smoothing out the bedcover on both sides of her. Her throat was dry, and for a moment she couldn't think of a suitable opening remark. She coughed. "Can I have a glass of water?"

"Of course." Najya took the bottle of water from the nightstand and poured some into a paper cup." Sorry, paper is all you get here."

Valerie drank it and held the empty cup tapping it nervously on the bottom.

Najya took the cup from her and waited patiently, still standing.

Valerie rubbed the side of her mouth to keep her lips from trembling and spoke, finally, when she was composed. "A...uh...a close friend of mine...a sort of brother...an American...opera singer..." She felt suddenly foolish trying to establish the details of his identity before she even began. "He was killed a few days ago in a sort of religious riot."

"You mean the shooting at the Evangelical Church? I reported on that. That young man was your friend? Oh, I'm so sorry." She was silent for a moment, obviously drawing connections. "But didn't you also know one of the victims in the Luxor train wreck?"

Najya sat down next to her on the bed. The ringlets of hair were dry now.

"Yes. The first one was Yussif Nabil and the American was Derek Ragin. They were part of the same family. That is, they were the adoptive and natural father of a child, the child that I need to get your advice about."

Najya leaned in solicitously. "Of course, but—"

"It was unusual, I know," Valerie continued, "that the two men should be friends that way, but that's not why I'm here."

"Yes, I understand. But I'm wondering how you're connected with them."

Valerie closed her eyes. This wasn't where she wanted the conversation to go. "Through Derek, the natural father with whom I was very close."

Najya was already elsewhere. "Two sudden violent deaths in one 'family,' as you call it, just weeks apart. That's more than suspicious. Are the police involved?"

"Yes, of course. But what I came about is the baby. I need to ask about international law. You said you studied—"

"I did. Many years ago. What do you want to know?"

The frown of concern that settled on Najya's face was comforting. The look of someone who understood life's complexities and who could be confided in.

"Well, Derek's father—stepfather actually—is an American preacher, and he arrived in Cairo with him. He's still here. Now that his stepson is dead, he wants to take his grandchild back to the United States, to be raised as a Christian. And he has a lawyer with him."

"A lawyer? A man's son is killed in a melee, and the first thing he does is set his lawyer on a custody claim?"

"Well, he's investigating the death, of course, but it was clear even when he arrived that he wanted the little girl back in the US. Since Derek was shot, he's claiming that the child is in danger here and would be safer with him outside of Egypt."

"He sounds dreadful."

"He is, and I can usually stand up to men like him. But when it involves the law and the courts, I don't know. And after everything else that has happened in just a few days, I'm sort of at the end of my rope."

Najya touched her lightly on the shoulder, as if considering an embrace, then stood up. She walked away for a moment, then returned with the paper cup, this time containing a shot of whiskey. "Here, drink this. I know it's a cliché, but it does take the edge off. I want to hear more."

Najya was next to her again, wonderfully close. Valerie could smell the soap she had just washed with. She nodded silently and downed the whiskey in a single gulp. She coughed from the first shock, then felt the warmth spread through her chest. Najya was right; it blurred the pain.

"He was all I had for family, for almost ten years. He saved my life once, brought me back to life, at the risk of his own. He was the purest soul I ever knew."

Najya brushed a strand of hair out of Valerie's face, her deep brown eyes sweeping over her like velvet. "I know what you're feeling. My brother was killed in the street during the first intifada for the crime of throwing rocks at a tank. I know the hole it rips in your chest, and I'm so sorry. If it's any consolation, the pain is all yours, not his. And you can do a lot for him—in his memory. What do you think he would have wanted?"

Valerie tried to chuckle, but it came out a brief snort. "He would have wanted a full chorus and orchestra, at least. And an opera if I could manage it." She wiped her nose again. "But I know for sure he would have wanted his daughter to be raised in Egypt with her own mother. Right now both of them are living here with Auset's parents."

Najya took the cup and set it aside. "Under any law I know, a mother has the right to raise her own child as long as she's competent. She is competent, isn't she? I mean she doesn't talk to ghosts, does she?"

"No, of course not." Valerie looked away, thinking not any longer, anyhow. "So what should she do?"

"Well, I never actually practiced law, and international treaties generally deal with states, not individuals, except as to what state an individual belongs. The child could be considered a US citizen due to her father, but she's also, of course, an Egyptian. It will be very difficult for a stepgrandfather to claim custody of a child in the care of her mother and real grandparents. I think this man is all bluster. Still, stranger things have happened, so you'd better check with someone who's actually a practicing lawyer."

She sifted through objects in a large canvas shoulder bag at the foot of the bed and fished out a thick calendar. From a pocket at the back of it she shook out several business cards. "Here. Try this guy. Nitzan. He's good. A Jew, so he'll be a disinterested third party. Plus he's smart." She copied the information onto a scrap of paper.

Noting two numbers on the paper, and only one of them with a Cairo area code, Valerie folded the paper into her shirt pocket.

"If I were staying in Cairo, I'd go with you to see him, but I have to leave tonight for my home office. I'd like to follow the case from there, though, so please keep me informed. My telephone number is also on the paper."

Valerie studied the splendid Arab face. The narrow, forward-set nose, the slightly oval eyes from Mongol genes that floated through the northern Arab population, warm black-brown eyes lined by thick lashes. A fine line of dark hair also grew down in front of her ear. Details she hadn't noticed when Najya was half naked. "I'm grateful for your help. I don't know what I would have done—"

"Please, it's nothing." Najya said quietly and extended a slender hand toward her, slowly.

It seemed to take minutes, but finally the errant hand was at Valerie's face, and the fingertips brushed lightly along her chin line until her thumb touched the corner of her mouth and rested there. All she had to do was move her head the tiniest bit and the thumb would sweep over her lips.

Keys clattered behind the door; one slid into the lock. Najya's hand jerked away as if scorched. She stood up as the handle turned and the door opened.

"Hello, Harry." Najya was composed. "We've got a visitor, but I believe you've already met."

Valerie saw a smile flicker over his face for an instant, though it could also have been disdain. Or maybe he was one of those men who got excited at seeing women together.

He set his backpack down on the bed and hooked his thumb over the edge of his pocket. "Good afternoon, Ms. Foret. Have you come to claim this room too?"

Valerie stood up calmly and focused on him for the first time. He was well muscled, like a man who worked out obsessively, but his manner and bulk seemed at odds with his pale face and too-pretty almond eyes. Something about the overall man was off-putting, not the least of which was the knowledge that he was having sex with Najya Khoury.

Valerie glanced around as she moved toward the still open door. Her sweep took in his camera equipment, beer chest, their luggage, and finally Najya herself. "No, I know that all this belongs to you."

She patted the shirt pocket where the scrap of paper was. "Thank you for the information, Najya. I'll keep you posted."

Valerie walked through the doorway, passing Harry. "It's all yours now."

29

Muslim Widow

The door opened once again to Fahd's stony face.
"Is everything all right?" Valerie asked spontaneously, then felt foolish. There had been two deaths in the family, and a foreigner—a complete stranger—was threatening to take away their grandchild. Nothing was all right.

They were halfway down the corridor then, and she could see into the garden. It was peaceful, as before, and the usual garden birds still lit on the fountain rim. A few swooped back and forth between the fountain and the table, apparently waiting for crumbs. Auset was busy serving tea to her father and to a cleric.

The mullah was an imposing man. Even sitting he seemed large. He wore a loose abaya, the same shade of dark gray as his full beard. Both were offset by a white turban. He was saying something to Auset as she filled his tea glass, although he didn't look directly at her. She said something in reply that Valerie couldn't hear and then returned to the kitchen.

Valerie touched Fahd's arm. "If you don't mind, I'd like to go and help Auset."

"Yes, Miss. As you wish." He led her past the surprised men to the open doorway, then withdrew.

Auset looked up from her tea tin. "Oh, I'm glad you're back. I could use someone to talk to."

Valerie set her backpack on the floor. "I've got good news. My journalist friend gave me the name of a lawyer who can help us. But she said your case sounds strong anyhow."

Auset took the paper, appearing sullen.

Valerie sat down at the work table. "Who's that cleric?"

Auset poured tea into two new glasses and handed one to Valerie. "A mullah from my father's mosque. I'm surprised he'd even come here. He disapproves so strongly of my Jewish mother."

"He's here because of Carter?"

"Yes, to give the Quranic solution. Everything, of course, has a Quranic solution."

"Why is he advising your father?" Valerie held the hot glass by the top and bottom and took a sip. "You're the one who's threatened."

Auset's lips slid sideways. "That's the way they do it. 'The man is the shepherd of the family.' That means my father is in charge of everything, even my children."

"So what do you suppose he's advising? It might be good to know." Valerie realized her tone was as cynical as Auset's.

"Well, I'm damned sure going to find out." She drew Valerie to the corner of the kitchen where a side window looked out toward the tea table. The wooden slats of the shade could be tilted downward, as they were today, both to keep out sunlight and to block visibility from the outside. Sitting close to the window, however, they had a partial view of both men, though only from the chest down. They could hear their voices clearly, but see only the bottoms of their two gray beards moving up and down in conversation. Though the mullah was younger by a decade than his host, his longer, fuller beard seemed to signify a superior authority, and his word was, in the literal sense, the law.

The beard of al Fakhir was talking. "I speak only to you and to no one else of my shame. I trust in your confidence as well as your knowledge."

The longer beard nodded assurance, and al Fakhir continued. "Yussif, may his soul rest with God, was not the father of my grandchild. The father of my grandchild was a foreigner, an American, but like Yussif, he was killed. Now the father of that American lays claim to the child. What does the Quran say in such matters? Which claim is the greater in this case? That of the mother's father or the father's stepfather?"

The mullah tapped softly on the table with large fingers. Dark hairs curled on both sides of each knuckle. "Both Quran and Hadith declare women to have primary right to custody of children if they are of sound mind and good character, if they are good Muslims and their children are Muslims. But if she keeps the company of non-believers, there is an impediment and the woman may forfeit the right to custody."

"This only confuses the matter, for my daughter does keep the company of non-believers, as I do myself, and the father of the father is a Christian."

The dark-haired hand lifted to the gray beard, stroking wisdom from it. "The claim of a non-believer on a Muslim child is, on the face of it, inadmissible. But if the father of the child is a non-believer, the secular courts may disregard Islamic law. That would be unfortunate. You must protect your daughter from this taint. It would be wise to find a Muslim husband for her as soon as possible."

"She is of an independent nature," al Fakhir said. "Even before she went to New York to study. And the child, although she is the joy of our house now, will make it hard for her to remarry."

"A child is always blessed in the eyes of Allah, must be cared for, and must never suffer the sins of the parent. But if the mother is wanton, there is always the surgery."

"No." Al Fakhir answered quickly. "That was suggested many years ago, but it is not my way. And she is too old for that now anyhow."

"Then she must be made to marry again as soon as possible," the mullah said.

"But she is in mourning. And she has a strong will. I have never imposed my will on her in these matters. Perhaps I should have."

The clerical fingers still tapped. "It is the man's duty to lead the woman, and certainly his daughter. She has already proven herself reckless."

"How long must she mourn before she can remarry?"

"The Prophet, peace be upon him, has spoken clearly on the *iddah,* 'Such of you as die and leave behind them wives, these shall wait, keeping themselves apart, four months and ten days.'"

He paused, letting the obstacle become obvious before he offered a strategy. "But it is not a sin for a man to declare his intentions during that time, to wed her afterwards." He paused again and let the logical next question arise by itself. He clearly already had the answer.

"There is a good man in the mosque, older and a widower. He has children who need a mother, and I think he would agree to the marriage."

"I am not sure I can convince my daughter to accept a husband whom she does not know."

"You do not need to 'convince.' It is your duty to give your grandchild a father to protect her from the claims of this foreigner."

One of the garden birds, the size of a robin, but yellow, suddenly landed between the two men's hands. The mullah covered his tea glass with one hand and with the other swatted the bird away with enough force to knock it from the table and out of view of the window.

As if the intrusion of the bird had concluded the conversation, the mullah stood up from the table. His hands were still visible, hanging paw-like at the side of his dark gray robe. "You have your solution," the gruff voice said. "I will approach the man and inform you of his answer. You can then make the arrangements."

He moved away from the table and his last audible words were "Four months and ten days. This is God's will and God Almighty knows best."

Al Fakhir followed the cleric away from the table and out of sight.

Inside the kitchen, Auset stood up as well and leaned against the window frame. "I can't stand it," she said finally out loud. "I'm surrounded by wolves."

30

Retribution

He stood in front of the glass case that held the Barque of the Sun. In the midst of the jostling crowd he occupied his own sphere of concentration. His hands lay flat on the glass top, in spite of the Do Not Touch sign. He stared, full of loathing, at the parallel rows of animal-headed gods that flanked the orb of gold. Every sigh of admiration from the crowd was like a barb that prodded him, reminded him of their ignorance and of his mission. In their childish oohing and ahhing, they did not know they looked on the time of the beast, did not appreciate how it threatened them.

To grovel before beasts again and set humanity back thousands of years. Who but perverts would come up with such a religion? He would not put it past them to even copulate with dogs. They were an abomination—he savored the Biblical word.

The call had come to him to set aside his job, where he was unappreciated anyhow, and his family, which was nit-picking him to death, to rid the world of them. His decision to answer the call had hardened his will, purified him somehow—and given him a vast patience. He had waited a long time before acting, had carefully followed each of them until he knew their ways. He was their shadow, their nemesis, their just executioner.

A tiny part of him also felt that he was evening the score, achieving a final revenge, if not on the boys who had once used him, then on others just like them. He had long since forgotten the boys' names and even their faces. All he remembered was the humiliation as they made him play the whore. Perverts, all of them—even if they did later marry—and they had tried to make a pervert out of him. Well, he was a man now and had already dispatched one of their kind. He would soon get rid of another, to both punish a crime and eradicate a dangerous cult.

The blood of his heroic ancestors pulsed through him and warmed him.

31

Egyptian Museum

The last thing Valerie wanted to do was business, but she had to at least make a gesture of it. No matter that she had lost three loved ones and the rest were in jeopardy. She couldn't walk away from "The Priest's Collection," as the museum called it. She had already surrendered much of the glory of the discovery to the university as a whole. She had felt guilty despoiling Rekemheb's tomb until she realized he himself didn't care. The artifacts had served their purpose, assisting him into the underworld. Since he had a sort of new life watching over his living family, he was finished with them.

The days of discovery were a warm but distant light somewhere at the back of her bereavement, and she ached when she recalled them now. What life Rekemheb had, as a ka, was now snuffed out, just like that of the descendant who carried his image. She had lost them both in a day: the sweet man who had been called with her into the treasure-filled tomb, and the odd, slightly stiff ancestor who had welcomed them.

Bereavement numbed her as her own sudden orphaning had not, for at six, she hadn't understood what death was and had kept waiting for her parents to reappear. By the time she grasped that they never would, the wound had covered over, and she had learned how to be solitary. While the few nuns who were kind to her saw to her physical needs, she transferred her emotional needs to the figures in her imagination.

She exhaled slowly, as if to expel the dreadful feeling of abandonment, and climbed the stairs to the Cairo Museum. She would take care of business for an hour and then return to Auset, who seemed to have a strength she herself lacked.

"Ah, Doctor Foret. How nice to see you again." Chairman of Antiquities Fuad Rashidi strode toward her just as she walked through the door. The two years hadn't been kind to him, for he had lost even more of his hair and had developed jowls. Jameela, his errant wife, was almost certainly directing all her favors elsewhere.

"We have added a few new things to the exhibit since you were last here." He extended his arm to lead her to the collection along a corridor of which she knew every centimeter. They had gone scarcely ten paces when a man called out from the other side of the lobby.

"Sayyid Rashidi, I am sorry. The curator is on the telephone. He said it's urgent."

Valerie was relieved. "It's quite all right, Dr. Rashidi. I know my way, of course. I'll wait for you there."

As he hurried away, she looked at her watch. Six thirty. The public would be gone by now anyhow, and she would have the place to herself.

She entered the familiar high-ceilinged exhibit hall and strolled around the periphery, eyeing the funerary treasure that she knew in every detail. Strange how it now seemed both precious and worthless. Precious because it was all that she had left of them, priest and man, and worthless because it was not them.

There were the familiar objects: the statue of Osiris; the gold-painted wooden bed on slender animal legs and with lion heads at the upper end; chests of wood and ivory; fans, newly fitted with ostrich feathers; alabaster vessels of a dozen sizes and shapes.

The exhibit was well done, the four walls expertly painted with copies of the tomb illustrations. On the north side was the calendar with its twelve thirty-day months ending in July. On the east, a seated pharaoh received the kiss of wisdom from the god Amun. The south wall held a scene of Pharaoh Meremphah bestowing a gift upon the kneeling Rekemheb, and on the west wall the Great Balance weighed the heart of the deceased in the underworld.

She strolled toward the center of the hall. Encased in glass was the centerpiece of the collection that drew the visitor's eye like an icon. The breathtaking Barque of the Sun *was* an icon of sorts.

Gold leaf was hammered over wood nearly a meter in length from swanlike prow to the high, curved stern. At the center, the naos-cabin housed a sphere of solid gold. The sun god Ra in his essence and glory. Ten painted wooden gods sailed in state with him. She remembered the overseer's boy, Ibrim, who had been slapped for touching the barque, and Volker Vanderschmitt, who had been the one to slap him. Vanderschmitt, who had killed her and then died a terrible death himself.

Something about the display annoyed her, and she moved to the right angle of light to see it. Some fool had left handprints on the top, she noticed, and she wiped them off with her shirtsleeve.

She pivoted away from the display toward the left. Ah. This must be what Rashidi was so proud of. The empty sarcophagus was set along one wall, its cover removed and replaced by a sheet of Plexiglas. She recognized the elaborately ornamented coffin, of course, but what took her by surprise was the gauze-wrapped dummy within it. She would have laughed at the theatricality had it not been for the painted mask on the mummy's head—painted with the face of Rekemheb, which was also the face of Derek.

She felt her eyes pool again, and alone in the quiet hall, she could almost hear the voice of Rekemheb, reciting once again the words of the scribe god's prophecy:

A child of your line will bring you forth into the world again in the hundredth generation. Then you shall be witness to these things: the Balance, the Book, and the bearing of the Child. This is our hope against the Aton, rising in the West.

She whispered back, "Rekemheb, what's happening to us, old friend? I've done all those things. I've stood before the Balance, written the Book, and we both were there when Nefi was born. So if we're the hundredth generation that the scribe god was talking about, we're just about wiped out. I guess the gods will have to start looking to the hundred and first."

It was a bitter joke, but then the thought itself gave pause. A vague realization began to take form, like a dull light in her head that began just then to burn more brightly. She held up ten fingers, each for a century, and counted forward from Rekemheb's generation in New Kingdom Egypt.

Valerie calculated. If each generation is twenty years, and five generations are born in a century, then fifty generations would make up a millennium, and a hundred would be roughly two thousand years. But two thousand years after the reign of Pharaoh Meremptah would be about 1000 AD. The realization was staggering.

The familiar face looked impassionately at her through the Plexiglas as she whispered the revelation. "You lived a thousand years before the birth of Christ. We *can't* be the hundredth generation after you. You knew it all the time, but you never told us. The Child of the hundredth generation was born in the Early Middle Ages."

She made another circle of the room, breathless, ordering her thoughts. She had to talk to Auset.

Then she saw it.

A small display case against the wall near the entrance. She knew its contents because she had put them there herself. A collar of gold and turquoise, hammered gold bracelets, slippers, finger and toe covers lined up in order of size. But next to them, in the corner, lay something that did not belong there.

Rekemheb's amulet, the amulet that Derek had brought back to Egypt and which Auset had taken from his suitcase. It could not be a copy, for Antiquities did not even know of its existence. And it could not possibly be the original that she had seen in Auset's hand the day before. She stood in front of it, paralyzed.

"Dr. Foret, please forgive the interruption." Fuad Rashidi stood in the entranceway.

"Oh, I'm sorry, Dr. Rashidi, but I was just on my way out. I can't stay long today. But please, take a look at this." She directed his attention toward the display case. "Can you tell me what this is? The amulet, I mean, there in the corner. It wasn't part of the collection."

He stood at her elbow, and she could sense his bewilderment.

"I confess, I don't recall it, and I certainly should. That's strange. It has no tag either. I must look in the catalog."

"Yes, yes, please do that. In the meantime, I'm truly sorry. I have a very important meeting," she said over her shoulder to the baffled man. "I'll telephone you." She quickened her pace until she was almost running.

Her head pounded with questions. Who or what had brought the amulet from its hiding place to the museum? Were the gods toying with them? And most importantly, had the gods sent forth another chosen Child a thousand years before Nefi?

32

Jerusalem

Amhara shaded Reni's face with a cloth as she herself squinted toward the Kidron valley.

"There it is, Sayyid Husaam," Sharif said unnecessarily as they reached the top of the hill. "Al Quds. The Holy City."

Husaam stroked his beard. "I should be relieved, I suppose, but I would rather be in Damascus." From their elevation, he surveyed the landscape. "The Kidron valley is greener than I remember it. They must have had good rain this year. We can camp just down there between the wall and the brush." He looked toward the western end of the wall. "There's a pool not far from the southern gate. Siloam, they call it. The men can water the animals this evening and be done with it."

The Cairene and Negev caravans made two clusters below the walls of the city. The men unloaded the camels and separated the freight as they had every evening in the desert. The women started two adjacent fires for the cooking, then pitched the goat-hair tents around them.

Amhara unrolled the largest rug for Husaam to sit on in front of his tent. "How long will we have to stay outside the city, Father?"

"Not long. Only until I can send a message to the emir for permission to enter. I won him more than one good deal in past years, so I'm certain he will grant us quarters. In the meantime, you should keep to the tent with the other women."

Amhara looked over at the Negev women who were heating their cauldron of *fuul* beans over the larger fire. She was weary of the noise and bickering and longed for the family tent they had shared before, with Faaria on one side of the curtain and her father and Sharif on the other. But since the two caravans had joined together, the Husaam tent had become a place of business and male talk, and the half dozen women of both camps were relegated to a single tent.

The double caravan did feel safer, however, and the monotony of the daily trek was alleviated by talk, even if it was trivial. And when they camped now in the community of women, a group cared for the children, so that each woman, in her turn, had a bit of rest. Only the sleeping arrangements were tedious, for Amhara hadn't had an hour alone with Faaria.

She unfastened the sling that held Reni on her back and laid the drowsy infant down beside her father. "Here. Please take her. I'll be back in just a moment." She looked around for Faaria and saw her finally, hobbling the camels.

She joined her, standing over her as Faaria bent down to tie the sisal cord loosely above the animal's knees. "Father said we have to stay with the other women until we go into the city. But that shouldn't be long. It will be different once we're inside."

Faaria was gruff. "Let's hope the emir actually remembers your father, and this isn't just wishful thinking. Then let's hope he likes him enough to offer us rooms." She dropped her voice. "Will we ever be alone again?"

Amhara knelt down beside Faaria and said softly, "There's a place where we can go alone before dawn, the pool of Siloam. The shepherds won't go there to water until after morning prayers. Would you like—?"

Faaria dropped long eyelashes. "Oh, yes, I would."

❖

Ludolf of Tournai drew his *khuffia* closer around his head so that it covered him like a Bedouin's turban, and only his eyes showed.

The scouting party had been well organized, with four men riding ahead to survey the land for food, water, and wood. A knight was not needed to accompany them, but Ludolf had nonetheless volunteered. He had grown impatient with the bickering among the commanders and longed to reach the end of his three-year pilgrimage.

Now he would be among the first to see the precious goal of all their labor before it was transformed by battle and fire.

All afternoon it was a gray spot on the horizon, which appeared and disappeared as he rode over the hilly landscape. But then, as he crested the ridge of what he knew was the Mount of Olives, he saw it from above.

The Kidron valley was greener than he had imagined, with herds of goats grazing on the rocky plain. They would be useful to feed the army when it reached the city, he noted. A caravan seemed to have just arrived; he could see the camels being unloaded and the low black tents set up around the fires outside the city walls. He briefly resented the very normalcy of Saracens setting up their household before the city of Christ.

Jerusalem. The most precious place on earth, a place that he had carried in his heart for three years. He had studied every image of it, read every passage in the Bible, listened to every tale, and it seemed he knew it already. There on the one side was the Tower of David and, across from it, the dome of the great temple. And between them—his heart seemed to leap—were the smaller and more precious domes of the Church of the Sepulchre.

The late afternoon sun shone from deep in the west and poured a rich orange light over the city, as if burnishing it for the believer. Here is where God had descended to earth. Where His incarnation had walked and preached and been tormented for men's sins. Deep in the brickwork of its streets, droplets of His sacred blood still lingered.

Ludolf's hand came involuntarily to his heart. His chest tightened and he burst suddenly into tears. He dismounted and fell upon his knees and prayed in a trembling whisper.

Overwhelmed, he knew that he could not return to the Frankish camp that day. The other scouts would be turning back now to report where the armies could best encamp and strike the city. But he would spend the night in fasting and prayer beneath its walls.

A line of trees and low brush ran southwest and he followed it, crossing over the ruins of some ancient wall. As he approached a copse of trees around a pool, the shepherds watering their sheep ignored him. In the gathering darkness, his face and hair were covered by the headscarf, his leather jerkin concealed by loose Saracen clothing, so he felt neither threatening nor threatened.

He threaded his way through the low trees and finally dismounted to avoid being brushed from the saddle. Then he saw a piece of paradise. At the center of the copse the rectangular pool lay placid, catching the last rays of evening light. On the one side rock formed a natural wall, and on the other, wide steps of crumbling brick led gently down to water level. Yes, he recalled now; the maps the invading army carried had showed a spring on the south side of the city, but gave no indication it was enclosed in such lush greenery.

The water was sweet, as he knew it would be, and after he quenched his thirst, he brought his horse to the edge to drink. By the last light he led his mount back into the brush to avoid attracting attention. He savored the moist air and the chirping of the cicadas and wondered with a sudden shudder if this could have been the Garden of Gethsemane. But no, the Frankish maps showed the sorrowful garden on the eastern side, and he was on the south.

He loosened his saddle and tied his horse on a long leash so it could graze, then undid his bedroll. The night was gentle and the ground beneath the trees was soft. Warmed by the joy of achievement and by the sense of lying so close to the city of Christ, he fell asleep. He dreamt he guided a great boat across the waters, and at his back, the Holy Spirit burned in a sphere of golden light.

33

The Pool of Siloam

Allaaaah uakbar! The sound of the first call to prayer insinuated itself into Faaria's unconscious. As a non-believer, she shut it out at first. But something deep inside her recalled that it signaled the short precious period before daylight, the stolen time.

Her eyes flew open. She reached toward one of the dark forms that slept on the carpet around her and touched it soundlessly. Amhara jerked to wakefulness and sat up. Next to her Reni still slept, sucking her fist. The Negev women would feed her along with the other children, and she would probably be content for a couple of hours before she would begin to cry for *Ummi*. In silent agreement, Amhara stood up at the same time as Faaria, and they stepped from the tent into the transparent darkness.

The sky was still cobalt, but dawn was close and there was just enough light for them to creep among the tents. A handful of men from the caravan knelt in prayer. Their foreheads pressed to the ground, they faced the opposite direction as the two women sprinted westward.

"Are you sure there's no one here?" Faaria whispered when they reached the circle of trees.

"It's too early. The men will be at prayer for awhile, and then they'll eat. There's time, I'm sure."

"All right. Come here then." Faaria drew Amhara to a spot just beyond the stone steps that led into the pool and in front of two trees. The pool itself was still black and uninviting, and the flocks would not water there for another hour.

The wall of trees around the pool blocked the faint light afforded by the dawning sky, and each woman saw the other only vaguely.

"I have waited half a hundred days to do this," Faaria whispered. She took hold of the face she could barely see and pressed her lips on it. In the cool air of the grove, their two mouths were a center of warmth that radiated downward. They stood together in a tight embrace for several minutes, until Faaria broke the kiss and whispered into Amhara's hair, as if she could be overheard. "I know the sweet thing that's at the end. Let me touch you and take you there, habibti."

"Yes, yes," Amhara breathed, opening her abaya.

Faaria stepped back and pulled her long galabaya over her own head and undid the cord to let her trousers fall to the ground. For a moment they looked at each other, pale bodies ghostlike in the half light.

"Hurry, habibti." Amhara stepped into her arms again. "I am afraid the shepherds—"

Faaria covered her mouth with another kiss, deeper and more urgent than the one before. Then she drew her down onto the patch of grass between the trees and the stone steps. They lay side by side for a moment, warming themselves on each other, breathing each other's scent.

Faaria inched down and took Amhara's full breast in her mouth. How glorious, how dizzying it was to know her this way. If this was wickedness then she was lost, for she would not stop herself. Her hand moved down the softly curving belly to the forbidden place, and Amhara opened to her.

A wave of excitement spread through her, bringing the wonderful tight heat to her own sex, and she buried her face in Amhara's neck. A thousand times she had imagined how it would be to touch her this way, and she had been right. It was passing wonderful. What she had not imagined was how easy it would be, how they would both fall so quickly into wild abandon.

Oh sweet heaven, to feel Amhara press against her and slide her hand down beneath her belly.

She lifted slightly to let Amhara's fingers go to the forbidden place and...ohh. What delicious madness, to set two fires burning—the one she fed with her hand and the one that flickered between her own thighs from the demon serpent that slipped inside of her. Fire and serpent. In her delirium the infernal images combined, and she surrendered to perdition.

Like brushfire it caught them both, young bodies that had craved too long, and they writhed and strained until the thing erupted. Faaria felt it first in Amhara, then in her own shuddering rapture.

"Oh, habibti," Amhara whispered. "I knew it would be like that. I knew you could make me happy that way."

"You did the same for me." Faaria chuckled softly. "Shameless woman. You knew exactly what to do. How did you know?"

"What do you think, you silly person? Of course I knew. You are just like me."

"Not exactly. For example, I don't like this, but maybe you do." She leaned over and nipped at Amhara's breast.

"Oh!" Amhara yelped. "No, I don't like that. But maybe you like this."

She tickled Faaria along her ribs, causing her to giggle. Then they fell again into an embrace, silent with gratitude.

❖

Some bright sound awakened him, and he opened his eyes to the first light of dawn. He listened, perplexed, thinking it was birdsong, then realized it was girlish laughter. He threw off his blanket and stood up.

There at the corner he saw them, two Saracen women. He crept closer, concealed by the foliage and the pre-dawn dimness, to a vantage point where he could see them clearly. One was slender and boyish, her hair scarcely reaching her shoulders, and the other more voluptuous.

He peered through the brush, rapt, trying to make sense of the spectacle. For they were lying on the ground, naked and locked in an embrace. The short-haired one lay half over the other one, and their mouths were pressed together.

He'd heard stories back in Flanders that the Mohammedans copulated with animals. This, he concluded, must be another form of that perversion.

The boyish one lifted herself up, resting her weight on her elbow, and the voluptuous one who still lay on the ground became fully visible. His heart pounded at the sight of the woman's full breasts and the triangle of hair between her thighs. Three years it had been since his oath of celibacy, three long, blood-soaked years, and he knew he should withdraw or lechery would undo him. His Christian conscience told him he looked on wickedness, yet he could not tear his eyes away.

He watched, both thrilled and horrified, as the taller one slid her hand between the legs of the other. He thought he heard her moan, and he wanted to look away but could not, so powerful was the grip of sin. The offense was both to God and nature, a stone's throw from the Sepulchre of Christ. Not only did they desecrate a holy place, they polluted him, for he felt his resolve weaken, as if a witch's hand caressed his sex.

"Abomination!" Outraged, he burst from his hiding place.

The two defilers leapt to their feet and stood quaking as he advanced. Then the taller one stepped in front of the other and barked something at him in their vile language.

"Satan's whore," he spat back, and knocked her on the side of the head with his fist. She felt to the ground stunned and moaning.

The other woman clutched her black robe around herself and backed away.

Savoring the game, he cornered her between the branches of a tree, and their two bodies touched. Her eyes were wide with fear, but she did not struggle as he encircled her throat with his hand. He might have heard the faint sounds of movement behind him, of something being pried from the ground, but he did not care.

His pulse racing, his manhood hard against the Saracen witch, he croaked, "A pity you are not a Christian. I would fill you full of children and you would serve me while you bore them, one by one." Oh, he could smell the spices in her hair. He thrust against her, his head swimming with lust. He could hear his own breath and hers, and closed his eyes for one delicious moment.

White-hot pain exploded in his head as the rock crashed against him from behind and knocked him sideways. The woman slid away from him and he collapsed against the tree. It took several moments for him to regain his senses, to realize his khuffia had slid off his head and his hair had sprung out. When he could stand up again, the two witches had vanished.

He would have chased them down and killed them, but the sound of shepherds returning with their flock prevented pursuit. He knelt quickly at the pool's edge, splashed water on the cut behind his ear, then set the khuffia back in place.

He tightened his saddle and rode off, back to the Flemish bivouac at Asur. Seething, he recalled the pair of witches that had been found in his own woods. Wild women, unbaptized, who lived in squalor with their animals—a pack of foxes and rabbits and cats, and even a crow that did their bidding. They confessed under torture to fornication with the devil and were given to the fire, but the event had unnerved him. He had their house burned, along with such of their cats and rabbits as could be caught. It was shortly afterward that his wife had died in childbirth, and he was certain something of the witches' spell had lingered.

Evil was persistent. The Christian lands themselves were ever threatened by it. All around them savages and infidels pressed in, and the evil seeped ever through the cracks. One had to be on guard against it always—and when possible to strike before it manifested.

The pope had called them to defend the Byzantines, but for Ludolf this crusade was a private thing. He drew a connection between the witches' spell that killed his wife and the evil that they marched against in the Holy Land. And he could not abide to see a cat.

34

Flight

At the entrance of the museum, Valerie peered down the length of the street looking for a taxi. Then she saw Auset's parents, at the foot of the stone steps. They saw her too at the same moment and climbed toward her, obviously upset.

Her heart sank. Was there some new disaster?

Mahmoud al Fakhir stood in front of her, panting from the sudden climb. Hannah came up behind him more slowly, looking no less anxious.

"Is everything all—?"

"Doctor Foret. Do you know where my daughter is?" He showed no emotion, but his hand trembled until he gripped the metal banister.

"No, I don't." Her excitement and confusion about the museum revelations gave way to alarm. "I left her at home. Didn't she leave a note or anything? How did you know where I was?"

Al Fakhir scowled, clearly in no mood to be questioned in return.

"We went to your hotel first," Hannah volunteered. "They said you might be here working. We thought she might have decided to join you for a while, for a trip perhaps."

"A trip?" Valerie was speechless. "What kind of trip?"

"I don't know, but our granddaughter is missing too." Hannah clasped her hands together like a school teacher, but the anxiety on her face was anything but prim. "Are you sure you don't know—?"

"You were with her yesterday," al Fakhir persisted. "Did she tell you of any plans?"

"You mean with respect to Reverend Carter? I gave her the name of a lawyer to contact and told her that her legal position was strong. She was angry when I left, but that's all."

"Angry? Why?"

"Sayyid al Fakhir. It's not my place to discuss your relationship with your daughter. But surely you were aware that she was furious about being pressured to marry someone from your mosque."

Al Fakhir's anxious face became stone. "You are quite right, Dr. Foret. It is not your place." He turned around abruptly and descended the stairs again. At the bottom, he glanced up and waited for his wife to follow.

Hannah laid a hand on Valerie's forearm. "You do not understand our family. If my husband could not force Auset to marry when she carried her child, he cannot force her to marry when she is a widow. He knows this, and it is difficult for him. He must balance his faith on one side and his family on the other."

"I'm sorry. Auset may have overreacted, but she didn't tell me anything. I really don't know where she is."

"We found this." Hannah held out something toward her, something wrapped in linen and tied with a cord.

Valerie held it for a moment before she realized that it was Rekemheb's statue.

"What is it?" Hannah asked. "Why would she leave this note on top of it?" She held out a postcard with a picture of the pyramids on the front, and on the back, in hurriedly scribbled Arabic, "Don't worry about me. I'm fine. Please give this to Valerie."

"A doll with the face of Derek, dressed as an Egyptian priest? What does it mean?" Hannah unclasped her hands, imploring. "Please, we are very worried. So many terrible things have happened."

"It's just…a souvenir," Valerie lied. "It has no special meaning." She unwrapped it and felt, to her surprise, that it was warm. From Hannah's hand or pocket? It seemed too warm for that. Then she saw the tiny piece of paper tucked under the wooden arm and withdrew it.

She frowned. "It says, 'I'll call Derek,'" Valerie read out loud.

Hannah's face registered relief, then confusion. "Derek? How can she call a dead man?"

Valerie rubbed the side of her face for a moment. It made no sense to her either. Then she slapped her hand to her belt. "Of course! His phone. I keep forgetting to turn it on." She opened it and waited. After a moment the phone light shone, and a few seconds later, the message signal sounded. She held it to her ear.

Her chest tightened as she heard her own desperate messages to him, messages that he had never erased and probably never even heard. Then, at the last message, she sagged with relief.

"Auset's all right. She's gone to the one place she knows she'll be taken care of, even without money—and where Reverend Carter can't lay hands on her." *Or anybody else*, she thought to herself, but didn't say out loud. Valerie clapped the phone shut. "She's on her way to Jerusalem."

35

Proof of Faith

W hat have you done? *What have you done!*"
Valerie felt rough hands shake her shoulders and yank her
out of deep sleep. Struggling first with dream panic, she finally reached
consciousness.

"Nekhbet!" She shrugged off the hands and sat up. "What are you
talking about?" She went on the offensive. "What do you mean, what
have I done! What have *you* been doing? Rekemheb is lost, Yussif and
Derek are dead. Auset has fled to Jerusalem. And what have we heard
from the gods? Nothing!"

Nekhbet would not be interrogated. "Al Quds. Jerusalem!" She
spat the words. Whatever the name, it is the worst possible place. A
malevolence follows her. You must fetch her back immediately."

"Of course there's a malevolence. Even *I* figured that out. So tell
me who or what it is? You're a goddess, you must know!" She almost
said "for God's sake," then realized the absurdity.

"I know only the past, which accumulates in endless memory. But
in your world and time, I see only what I set eyes on. Surely this thing is
inspired by the Aton and will have even greater power in Jerusalem."

"Well, this 'malevolence' doesn't need any more power than it's
got. It's already succeeded in killing two of us," Valerie retorted. "So,
what really happened to Derek and Yussif? They died for the gods,
didn't they? Because the chronicle is finished?" She realized that all her
questions already held the answers.

Nekhbet nodded. "In part. The Aton struck first at the ones who
were not protected."

"Not protected? What the hell does that mean? Who *did* you
protect, then? I must be one of the lucky ones. Or am I the next one
out? What about Auset? Are you planning to raise the baby by your
godly selves once they get her?"

"Be silent. These are childish words. Did you think it would be
easy to defy the Aton, who dominates half the world? Did you think He
would stand by while you plant the seeds of the old religion? The Child

is under my wing, but we did not anticipate harm to the rest of you. We were mistaken."

"Mistaken." Valerie said the word with contempt. "Yes, so it would seem. Well, now that Yussif and Derek are taken, will they live as kas? It's the least you can do."

"Sarcasm does not become you. And neither do your idle flirtations."

"Flirtations?" Valerie scowled at the non sequitur. "You mean Najya Khoury? What's she got to do with anything?"

Nekhbet looked at her darkly, and Valerie remembered her kisses that she had misread as desire. But they had had nothing to do with passion and had merely torn her apart and scattered her all over Egypt. She felt both cheated of what she longed for and like a fool for longing for it in the first place.

"Najya is none of your business. Besides, you're changing the subject. I asked you about Yussif and Derek."

"The subject is Jerusalem. The Aton is strong there. Though he is divided against himself, every brick and stone contains him, and we are powerless. You must bring her back."

"The Aton is strong everywhere, and there are more immediate threats here. Surely you are aware that Derek's father is claiming custody of Nefi."

"He is harmless. Bring her back." Eons looked out through her eyes.

Valerie wavered. The very presence of the goddess took hold of her and excited her, vastly more than any woman had. But what in mortal women was inebriating, was in Nekhbet a toxic dose. She stood her ground. "You'll have to tell me why."

Nekhbet exhaled exasperation and pressed her exquisitely curved lips together. "Because the kas of Yussif and Derek depend on it. They stand before the judges even now, but cannot pass into the underworld."

"You mean because they don't know the incantations? But no one's going to know them. They're antiquated, meaningless spells."

"It is not the incantations. That is the least of it. The scales have weighed their heavy hearts, and the judges know that Auset has gone to the city of the One God."

"You're saying that if I bring Auset back to the fold, the judges will let them pass? Is that the deal being offered?"

Nekhbet moved, lithely, in an arc around her, feet not actually touching the floor. "Nothing is being offered. It is not a transaction." She opened her hands. The gesture reminded Valerie of paintings she'd seen of female saints.

"See it from our eyes. Our two living believers are full of doubt, and the mother of the Child has thrown off our protection and fled to the city of the Aton. You are the last one, and you quarrel with me. If you are so embittered that you cannot win over a single new believer, we have nothing to hope for."

"I wrote your chronicle. Isn't that enough? You also want me to proselytize?" Valerie thought of Jehovah's Witnesses, knocking on front doors and handing out pamphlets on the street.

"This one thing would show the judges that the words of Jehuti live." Nekhbet fell silent for a moment, then took another tack. "Perhaps you will better understand if you see for yourself where they are now." She held out a dark, white-nailed hand as if inviting her to dance.

Valerie remembered the hand and its pale fingernails, and she understood the invitation. Nekhbet was offering the god-kiss, the embrace that had opened her soul and given her the vision of all Egypt. Foolish mortal that she was, she had learned too late that the kiss, for all its stunning effect, was emotionless. Nekhbet did not love her—did not love anyone.

"No," she said softly. "I don't need to see them. Derek saved me from death once. If you tell me this is the condition of their rescue, that I must bring a new believer, I'll try. I owe him this."

"All right, then." Nekhbet seemed unprepared for the refusal of the kiss. "I'll leave you to it."

"All right," Valerie repeated and waited for the goddess to disappear, as usual, after making her point.

Instead, Nekhbet leaned forward and lightly pressed her lips on Valerie's mouth, for a second only, not enough to spark the vision or stir desire. A brief, bewildering kiss, like some awkward, inexperienced girl. Then she did disappear, leaving in the empty place where she had been, the sound of her command.

"Go to Jerusalem."

36

Al Quds

Archers stood atop the wall, and below them a phalanx of guards lined both sides of the Eastern gate. Only one of the heavy doors was open, and the entryway was packed with people trying to enter. Donkeys brayed and men shouted within the swelling mass at the gate that oozed as a thin trickle into the city. Husaam and his household stood before the guard, waiting to pass scrutiny.

"Let them enter!" An impressively accoutred officer and a standard bearer rode across the courtyard toward the gate. Behind them, a groom led a string of two horses.

Faaria pulled Amhara and Reni away from the hooves that clattered on the stone pavement.

The officer drew up before the sergeant of the guard. "These people are the guests of the emir," he announced as the line of horses swung around behind him. After an acknowledgement from the guard, the officer assisted her, Amhara, and the baby onto one of the horses and signaled that Husaam should mount the other one.

Faaria glanced anxiously back at her brother, who was still held along with a white camel at the checkpoint.

"What about that one, sir?" The guard pointed with his thumb toward Sharif. "We are under orders to send them to the Dung Gate."

Astride the emir's horse in his new status as guest, Husaam appealed to the officer. "*Minfadlak,* sayyid, we have obeyed this most reasonable of orders. Our drovers have taken the rest of our caravan to the southern gate. This beast carries gifts for the emir."

"Admit them," the officer ordered, and Sharif led the camel inside. With surprising speed he couched the camel, mounted it, and brought it to its feet again. Meanwhile, the officer drew his horse alongside Husaam. "On behalf of the emir, Idris ad Dawla, I am here to escort you to the Citadel."

"I thank you and my family thanks you. I look forward to speaking with the emir." Husaam appraised the officer's rich costume and seemed pleased.

Faaria knew why. The prosperity of the host always reflected favorably on his guests.

The officer led them through a tunnel-like archway into a street just wide enough for two horses to walk abreast. "Do you know Jerusalem, Sayyid Husaam?" the officer asked.

"A bit. I was here when the Turks were masters. I remember the plentiful souqs and craft markets. Much better than we have in Cairo."

While the men talked amiably, keeping their horses close, Faaria glanced back again to assure herself that Sharif was still behind them. He swayed serenely on his white mount, occasionally running his foot over the square shapes in the red woolen camel bags.

She turned back again to watch the standard bearer who rode next to them and seemed to struggle to keep a dignified bearing while his standard kept catching under the window screens that jutted from the walls.

Suppressing the urge to laugh, Faaria studied his costume. Over a linen undergarment he wore a wide silk coat patterned with geometric designs and tied at the waist by a sash. A short sword in a silver scabbard was tucked into one side of the sash and a smaller curved dagger into the other. On his rather pretty head, a short conical cap was wrapped with swaths of silk in yet another color, and a long section of it was draped across his chest and thrown over his shoulder.

"We do not know this city, sayyid. Can you tell us, for example, what that is?" She looked toward the enormous wall that ran parallel to the road they traveled.

He finally tilted his banner permanently forward in line with the horse's neck and turned his attention to them. "That is the north wall of the Temple Mount, which held the Temple of Solomon. What you see above it is the Dome of the Rock." He pointed with his free hand, so that the silk of his coat sleeve hung down handsomely. A band of embroidery around the upper arm held some inscription in calligraphy, though she couldn't read it. "Holy places for both Jews and Muslims. But the road we ride on is the path on which our savior bore his cross."

"Our savior? So you're a Christian," Faaria observed. "The emir has a Christian in his service?"

"Several. And his physician is a Jew. I cannot say the brotherhood here is all that warm, but we manage. It must be so. The city is sacred for all of us."

"Are there any sites of the old religion? Of the many gods?"

The standard bearer laughed. "For the pagans? No, of course not. Though there are stories about a temple to Venus deep under the Church of the Sepulchre."

They reached the corner of the mount and he pointed left again. "Down there is where the Jews pray. In a moment we will cross the Al Wad and go past the Church of the Holy Sepulchre, and behind that, on the opposite wall of the city, is the Citadel, where my master awaits us."

Faaria shook her head, puzzled. Believers of three faiths, worshipping within sight of each other, each one convinced the other two were in error. Didn't anyone find that comical?

❖

Subdued by awe, Faaria and Amhara followed the servant to a bench at the end of a long dark corridor. The narrow space was unpleasant until they saw they sat before an elaborate grillwork. The pattern of carved arabesques was in fact cut through the wall so that, sitting in their darkness, they could peer unobtrusively into the stateroom on the other side.

Faaria was uncertain why they had been allowed to witness the audience rather than kept waiting outside as she had feared. It appeared that Husaam al Nouri carried such authority that his women, too, were accorded certain privileges.

The audience room was impressive, suggestive more of a palace than a citadel. It was lit at all four corners by multi-ringed candelabra that hung on long chains from the ceiling. A long L-shaped divan filled the corner of the state room opposite the grillwork wall. Wide, flat cushions were placed in a row at the back of the divan, and cushioned stools stood in front of it.

As they watched, a servant carried in a brass tray with a tall snorkled coffeepot, glasses, and a dish of sweetmeats. A boy dragged over a round wooden table for him to set the refreshments on, and they both padded away soundlessly.

A moment later, the emir arrived with his ministers. Idris ad Dawla was a striking man, though none would call him large. The height of an average man, he had the demeanor of one accustomed to command. He walked close by the grillwork wall and faced it briefly, as if he did not know they were behind it. Ridiculous, of course, Faaria thought. What commander would keep a spying room without full knowledge of who was in it?

She liked his face. The deep grooves that ran from the side of his nose diagonally into his full black beard gave strength to his mouth and lent him an air of authority even when he was silent.

He dismissed his ministers and greeted his guests standing. With genuine warmth, he gripped Husaam's upper arms and held him at arm's length.

"Old friend. I am pleased to see you again. How fares your trade in times like these?"

All three sat down as the servant poured coffee from a high-spouted copper ewer.

"*Alhamdullilah*, Emir," Husaam replied. "Every caravan investment brings the risk of ruin until delivery, but for the moment we prosper enough to offer you this gift."

Sharif presented a slender leather volume to the emir with a slight flourish, while Husaam took a polite sip of his coffee.

Husaam set his cup down. "I know the emir's love of verse, though this will certainly not be the usual fare. This Persian mathematician Khayyam has made a name for himself in two languages. You will find his philosophy daring, but I believe the emir appreciates daring, in his poets as in his officers."

Ad Dawla ran his hand over the cover of the book with a smile and set it aside. "Thank you. I will read it at my leisure, though I fear I have little enough of that now. You know, of course, about the scourge that sweeps down from Europe. We must consider that they will soon arrive in full force before our gates."

"More than soon, sayyid," Sharif interjected. "My sister was fetching water at a pool just outside the city wall and was set upon by a man with yellow hair who spoke a strange language. There is great likelihood that he was a scout from the Frankish army."

Ad Dawla crossed his arms over his chest. "That the Frankish kings are already sending spies...that is alarming. We sent emissaries to them and offered complete freedom of religion in Jerusalem. All men may visit, as pilgrims, unmolested, as long as they are unarmed. And still they send spies."

"But Jerusalem has been open to pilgrims since the Fatimids have reclaimed it. Do you think they will accept your offer?" Husaam looked sceptical.

"It is unlikely," ad Dawla replied. "I anticipate a siege, although I had hoped it would be longer in coming. In any case, we are bringing in all the grain we can and will burn what we cannot. We will block or poison the wells outside the city—all but Siloam, which feeds our own cisterns. I will dispatch the catapults where we are most vulnerable and prepare the Greek fire."

"A great pity, isn't it?" Sharif set down his coffee. "The Franks have marched all this distance to reclaim what they essentially already had."

❖

There was a frenzy of activity in the souq, as people rushed to buy food to last through the siege that all knew was coming. Though carts of grain and livestock still trickled in from the surrounding villages, the freshly slaughtered meat and new produce were bought immediately, and olives, which kept indefinitely, were soon impossible to find.

Sharif accompanied the women on what they feared would be the last day to shop.

"Ufff, Sharif. You smell of camel." Faaria linked her arm in his. You've been visiting the stable again."

"For the books," he said under his breath. "I hid them under the camel straw. If we ever get out of this, they're our fortune." He perused the sparse and rotten produce that remained on the market cloths.

"Well and good. But for now, we need things like this." Faaria held up a large bundle of dates tied in a cloth. Is anything left at the grain merchant?"

"No, but ad Dawla's men have taken several barrels of it to the Citadel. If it comes to that, we'll have grain to eat, though nothing else."

"Can we try to find flatbread?" Amhara asked. "It'll keep a long time and Reni can eat it. She's been so good. She never cries, even in all this strangeness." She shifted her from one arm to another. "Look, the poor child's in rags. I'd planned to buy her a shirt in Damascus with our new money."

Faaria grinned. "I was waiting for you to say just such a thing." From under her shirt she produced a gauze-wrapped package and handed it to Amhara.

"Oh, habibti, what a beautiful thing." Amhara unfolded the brick red smock and held it up against Reni's chest. "It'll fit her perfectly!"

Her face lit up, and she pressed a damp finger on the embroidered panel in the front. "Burd!"

"Yes, darling. It's a bird. A yellow bird. Say thank you to Auntie Faaria."

Sharif took the bundle of dates from her hand. "You may have a child of your own soon enough. Idris ad Dawla has spoken with Husaam about taking both of you as his wives."

"Idris ad Dawla? She snatched the dates back, suddenly truculent. "But we've known him for only ten days, and besides, I don't want to marry anyone."

"You couldn't do better. He's an Egyptian and wants both of you. At a time like this, women need a strong man to take care of them. There is no one stronger than Idris ad Dawla."

❖

Faaria and Amhara sat on cushions in the corner of the spare upper chamber of the tower.

"Are you afraid?" Faaria asked.

"Of course I am. Terrified."

"I'll protect you, you know, if it costs me my life."

"Oh, habibti. You're just as weak as I am. You know what happens to women after a battle." She drew the blanket over the shoulders of her sleeping baby. "And children."

"I know, but I trust Idris ad Dawla. He's a fine commander. At least Sharif says so. But whatever happens, I want to be with you, even if we die."

"Samek says that lovers can be together in the afterlife if they have likenesses. You know, carved in wood. If we come though this, I'll have such things made of us, of Sharif, and of my father and Reni, too, so that we can be together forever."

Faaria offered a weak smile. "A good idea. I even know a wood-carver in Cairo. Now we must only survive Jerusalem."

Amhara stood up respectfully as Husaam and Sharif entered through the narrow doorway.

"Sit down, sit down. We'll come and join you." Husaam dropped onto the cushion next to her and raised one knee to lean on. "I have looked to our goods, but I think they are lost," he said, wan. "If ad Dawla can negotiate surrender, they will no doubt be part of the ransom. If he cannot, and the Franks attack, it will all be lost in any case." He gazed mournfully up at the opening in the stone wall through which sunlight poured in milky beams.

Sharif raised a slender hand. "Ad Dawla's Sudanese are superb archers, and the city walls are strong. The Franks will surely negotiate. And I've hidden our most valuable things."

Husaam shrugged. "If God so wills it."

At the other end of the room ad Dawla entered with two lieutenants. In the days since they had seen him he had let his beard grow, as if to add another layer of protection before a great hand-to-hand battle.

His green surcoat, of embroidered leather, hung to his knees over his linen britches. A sash of embroidered silk wrapped twice around him covered his breastplate and held a sheathed dagger. A diagonal strap held a sword on his back, its elegantly finished hilt just visible above his shoulder.

His helmet was peaked, as if it had been poured molten and cooled before the last drop at the center had fallen. The steel was engraved with Quranic phrases, and the helmet itself was held in place by a bright blue-green turban. By his colors alone, he would be seen on the ramparts.

He approached them, laying a hand fraternally on Hassaan's shoulder. "Take heart, old friend. Jerusalem is well prepared. We have troops on guard at every corner of the city, and the food supplies are ample. In any case, the Citadel remains the center of our strength, and no matter what happens, your two women should stay here."

A loud knock came from the narrow door, and then it flew open. The handsome standard bearer rushed in, breathless. He handed a message to ad Dawla, who read it silently before he crumpled it.

"The Franks have refused conciliation," he said grimly.

The messenger still stood at attention, and ad Dawla asked him, "Is there something else?"

"Yes, sir. You must come and see."

Ad Dawla followed him, and his officers filed out behind him. Weary of the long confinement, Faaria and Amhara followed them out onto the platform where ad Dawla's archers stood along the parapet. In the momentary hush, Faaria could hear the banners fluttering.

Then she looked toward the north, and her breath caught in her throat. Black along the distant horizon, like a swarm of locusts, the Frankish armies flowed toward them.

❖

Five weeks it had been, five weeks in which the Franks had attacked again and again, and each time been thrown back. Finally it seemed that they had given up, for they had drawn back into their camps and been ominously silent for days.

Faaria stood behind the merlon and gazed at the Frankish camps scattered through the Kidron valley. They were building more siege towers to replace the ones they had lost to the fierce resistance.

Sharif came up behind her. "I'm sorry, sister. It's time for you to go inside again. They're bringing up the pitch and straw."

She drew back against the wall and watched as four soldiers, two in the front and two in the back, labored up the stone steps carrying an enormous cauldron suspended between them. The pitch was cold and viscous, but she knew it would be set over a fire on the platform until it bubbled and could cook a man.

Behind them, two other soldiers carried bales of straw, and a line of boys followed them with wooden dowels and spools of cord.

"They're going to make throw-torches, aren't they?" Faaria grasped her brother's arm. "Let me help."

"No," the sergeant who guided the cauldron-bearers said. "No women on the walls. She'll be in the way."

Husaam al Noori appeared from the other side. "Let her be, sergeant. I know this woman, and she can tie a knot faster than any of these boys. She'll free up a man for the heavy work."

The sergeant nodded and drew her by the arm over to the cauldron. "Soak the straw in the tar, like this." He demonstrated, sweeping a bundle of the dry stalks into the syrupy pitch and wrapping it like a skirt around a wooden dowel the length of his forearm. "Then tie it up good like this."

"Yes, yes, I know." She took the roll of cord from him and began to work.

Husaam gathered up several spools of twine and set to work at Faaria's side. "This is my cord, you know. Good twisted flax, for Damascus carpets." He unwound a length of it and cut it with a small curved blade. "Too good to be thrown burning at the Franks."

Faaria wrapped the cord twice around the straw at the head of the wooden rod and tied it fast. "We're all too good to be thrown away in this stupid battle." She swiped the straw torch once through the pitch and laid it on the platform at her feet.

Husaam cut off another length. "I don't mind dying so much myself. But I worry about my family. Sharif was going to make us all rich."

"Well, we're together, sayyid." Sharif laid down another bundle of wooden dowels. "If any survive, they'll tell the story of the others."

"Yes, stories." Husaam shook his head. "A pity, my friend, that we could not deliver the stories in your manuscripts."

"They're not lost yet, sayyid. They're in the saddlebag under the straw of your own camels. Let's hope that whoever reclaims them knows their value."

Husaam shrugged. "Pray God they don't fall into the hands of the Frankish barbarians, who know nothing of science or poetry."

Sharif looked up at the indifferent sky. "Pray God? At the moment God doesn't seem to favor our science or poetry either. Do you suppose He favors the Franks?"

"You have to wonder what kind of God would—" Faaria stopped. There was something ominous in the air. Something more than the sound of wind and the low buzz of men's voices. She peered over the wall again and was appalled.

Sharif came to her side and leaned on the parapet wall. "Unbelievable. They're singing, and marching barefoot—in the middle of a siege. They're mad!"

As the Frankish soldiers in the thousands circled the city walls, the murmur of their voices wafted upward on the breeze. To the defenders the words they sang were unintelligible, all but the constant refrain of "Hallelujah."

Faaria murmured to herself, "A madness that will destroy us."

37

Jerusalem

Valerie descended the wide stone steps of the Old City to the Damascus Gate and threaded her way through the lines of tourists. The noise, a buzzing cloud of Arabic hawking and polyglot tourist chatter, was familiar. The souq was much like the Khan al Khalili in Cairo, but for the omnipresence of Israeli soldiers.

She checked the instructions that Hannah had given her. Auset's mother knew the Old City intimately; it had been her playground during her youth. Auset's grandparents had been shopkeepers in the Jewish quarter, but Hannah had suggested Valerie might be more comfortable in a hostel called Funduq Farisi, in the Arab quarter. Not that any place was more than a few minutes away from any other place through the winding medieval streets. But the Arab quarter was livelier, she said, had more fresh-food stands, more shops. Hannah could be forgiven for thinking she would spend much time shopping.

Funduq Farisi. There it was. A narrow doorway in the Khan el Zeit, the Olive Market, barely visible between two densely packed market stalls, one with a thousand varieties of candy and the other with coffee mugs and plates and other household minutiae stamped with the icons of Jerusalem.

A staircase led up to the reception area of the hostel, and when she walked through the second door she stopped for a moment, impressed. She stood on the ground floor of a caravanserai, or rather a remodeling of one for modern expectations. Rising in a quadrangle around her were two galleries, one above the other, punctuated by archways in the medieval style. Clearly the hostel had been adapted—with the addition of plumbing and electricity—from the skeleton of an ancient merchants' inn, a caravanserai. What was missing, she noted, smiling inwardly, was the smell of camel dung in the courtyard.

"It's about time you arrived."

Valerie spun around to see Auset lounging against the registration counter. "Be glad I arrived at all!" Valerie dropped her backpack to the floor with relief. "I'm glad you got my message. But this all would have been much easier if you'd warned me, or *anyone*, of where you were going."

"I'm sorry. It all happened too quickly" Auset gave her a quick hug. "I didn't want my parents to know. I was afraid they'd call the police, or that my mother would even come herself to try and bring me home."

"Well, you ended up scaring the hell out of them."

"I was depending on you getting the message on Derek's phone."

"I did, finally. But you scared the hell out of Nekhbet too. She showed up suddenly again and insisted I come here to get you out of Jerusalem." Valerie spoke over her shoulder as she signed the register and took her room key.

Auset picked up the backpack. "Why should I leave? What was Nekhbet's problem?"

They walked side by side up the stairs. "She didn't explain much, just said that the Aton was powerful and the Egyptian gods couldn't protect you here."

Val's room was a modest cubicle, sparsely furnished and already stifling hot at mid-morning. Valerie opened the single window and saw to her pleasure that it looked out over the city toward the golden Dome of the Rock.

"They couldn't protect us in Egypt!" Auset snapped back. "Where were they when Yussif and Derek were killed, and when Rekemheb's mummy was smashed?" Auset dropped down on the one simple wooden chair in the room. "Look, I get it. I know that the gods get strength from their believers, like…who's that little fairy creature who flits around in Peter Pan?"

Standing in the slight breeze from the window Valerie unzipped her rucksack and unpacked toiletries. "Tinkerbell."

"Yes, like Tinkerbell. But no one believes in them anywhere. They were very flashy at Dendara when they swarmed in overhead at night, but for taking care of us, they *are* useless."

"I think we're supposed to take care of *them*. But listen, we have more important things to talk about. The amulet, for example. Did you give it to the Cairo Museum?"

"Of course not. How could you even ask? It's hidden in my room."

"I saw it at the museum. In a glass showcase."

"Impossible. Maybe it's a second one that you didn't know about."

"There's nothing in the tomb I don't know about. I cataloged every item in the collection. The amulet was on Rekemheb's mummy. There can't be a second one."

"Then I don't know. And I'm sorry, but right now, I care much more about Yussif and Derek. Did you ask Nekhbet about them?"

Valerie rubbed her neck and felt the trickle of perspiration run down the center of her back. A shower was going to feel good. "That was the first thing I asked her. She said that both men are in the Hall of Judgement, but the judges won't let them pass until we get more believers to replace them."

"What?" Auset's face darkened. "They're blackmailing us now too? Those men were murdered because they got roped into this prophecy thing anyhow, and now they're denied the reward of the new religion unless we get more converts? To hell with that!"

"I think—"

"And the new believers?" Auset was on her feet now, the better to vent her fury. "Are *they* going to be blackmailed too, blocked from the afterlife unless *their* relatives bring in a few more souls?" She blew out a long breath and leaned against the wall, her arms folded under her bosom.

Valerie nodded tentative agreement. "When you put it that way, it's pretty outrageous, isn't it? But Nekhbet knew we'd be outraged and pointed out that the deaths of the men are a blow against them too. All that's left now of the prophecy are you and me. Two bitter, cynical women who are *this* close—she held up thumb and forefinger a few centimeters apart—to renouncing the whole thing."

"Closer than that," Auset groused.

"So they're desperate too, and the kas of the two men are their only leverage to get us to act. I've already agreed to try a little proselytizing. I know a few urban pagans in Brussels who would be open to their religion, even enthusiastic. But I can't contact them until you leave Jerusalem."

Auset sprang up, hands on hips. "That just sounds like another kind of blackmail. Nefi's happy here, and before I drag her back to Cairo, and to the claims that everyone's making on us, I have to know it's better there than here."

Valerie had no good answer ready and knew when to stop arguing.

At the sudden lack of pressure, Auset softened. She reached for the doorknob.

"Look, my creepy uncle and his wife are visiting tomorrow, and I have to help my grandparents get everything ready. You know: shopping, tidying up. I'll try to get away tomorrow afternoon to give you a tour of the city. We can talk about Nekhbet's worries then."

"All right, but I'm warning you. I'm not leaving without you. In the meantime I need a shower."

"Yes, you do." Auset smiled for the first time and let herself out.

❖

The bathroom, Valerie saw, was typical of the accommodations she'd enjoyed lately—that is, miniscule. But as long as there was warm water—there was—and the drain wasn't blocked—it wasn't—she was satisfied. She showered blissfully, noting however that the ten-centimeter chip of soap was wearing thin and would serve for one wash only. Fine. She had no plans for the rest of the afternoon and could buy more.

In clean clothes and with the warm air drying her hair, she ventured back into the dense activity of the Khan el Zeit. The sheer volume of its merchandise displayed on every wall and surface and dangling overhead, the bombardment of colors and sounds, all were a comfort, a reminder of vitality in the face of bereavement. She let the sensations wash over her like a wave: the cacophony of hawkers calling in Arabic, Hebrew, and English; the haggling customers; the smells of sheesha smoke and cigarettes; the oils for sale in the next shop.

A shuffling street-sweeper pushed refuse in front of his broom along the center of the street toward the block of harsh sunlight where the tunnel opened to a square. She startled as a cart rumbled past her drawn by a single man, no different from its biblical equivalent except that its tires were rubber. Grit dropped from it onto the street he had just swept and fell back into the cracks between the bricks. Two thousand years of grit.

Derek, she thought with a wan smile, would have hated it. No matter. She would have dragged him here, made him appreciate what the souq was—civilization's first hub of commerce.

She studied the people: the swarthy faces of the Arabs, the slightly paler ones of the Jews, the—by contrast shocking—whiteness of the Western tourists, and she knew none of them would be Derek.

A hand touched her back.

38

The Holy City

She flinched from the touch and spun around, one hand lifted in defense.

"Oh, I'm sorry," Najya Khoury said. "That was stupid of me, considering what you've been through."

"That's all right." Valerie laughed nervously. "I'm just a little jumpy. I never expected to run into you in the Old City."

"But you told me you were coming in this morning, and I was on my way to your hotel. I wanted to give you a tour of the Old City before anyone else does. Have I interrupted anything?"

Valerie felt reprieved. "Yes. A day of morose wandering. A tour is just what I need to take my mind off things." She grew serious again. "I'm really glad to see you."

❖

Najya cleared her throat as she pointed with an open hand. "And this, mesdames et messieurs, is the Eastern Gate, which has had five or six names over the centuries: The Lion's Gate, Jehoshafat's Gate, St. Stephan's Gate, Mary's Gate. It has been knocked down and rebuilt, closed and opened up, but is in all cases the entrance to the Christian quarter."

"So, what's that wall there?" Valerie played the tourist.

"The north wall of the Temple Mount. What you see above it is the top of the Dome of the Rock, from which Mohammed visited heaven." She pointed with her entire arm, the enormous size of the wall seeming to require an equally large gesture.

Then she pointed toward another lower structure built around a pool of water. "And over there is the Bath of Bethesda, where Jesus healed the sick. Oh, and the road we are walking on is the Via Dolorosa, where Jesus carried his cross."

"A lot going on in one place."

"You have no idea. Every brick and stone has got something

'going on.'" Najya touched her sleeve, guiding her to the left. "Come on, we'll start with the Jews."

❖

"So, that's the western Wall. It's higher than I expected." Valerie stopped behind the fence that separated spectators from active worshippers, who seemed to enter from under an archway at the side. She scanned the yellowish granite blocks that rose high overhead. Each block was about a meter high, and tufts of grass grew in the spaces between them.

"It's part of the Temple of Solomon, isn't it?"

"No, only a part of the wall that supported the hill under the temple. This wall, by itself, had no religious importance. The whole mount is essentially a Jewish shrine, and over the centuries, Jews prayed next to the southern Wall, eastern Wall, and even on the mount itself, wherever the authorities allowed them to."

On the one side, several bearded men in black coats and wide-brimmed hats were lined up facing the Wall. As they rocked back and forth murmuring, the long curls that corkscrewed on both sides of their heads swayed in countermotion. On the other side, a lone man read from a small leather-bound book. A black leather strap held a little box against his forehead and wound around his left arm to his middle finger. A fringed shawl covered his head and shoulders and hung down his back.

"What's that little black thing on his forehead?" Valerie squinted, trying to make out the tiny object.

"They're called tefillin. Little boxes with rolls of parchment with quotes from the Torah. There's another box on the left arm also tied with a strap that winds around his arm to the middle finger."

"Kind of like the rosaries we had to hold when we prayed in my convent school. You had to hold them a certain way and recite the Hail Marys and Pater Nosters in the right order."

"Yes. Everyone has their magic." Najya glanced at the Wall again. The man in the shawl was leaning forward now, his head pressed against the stone. "And their sorrow," she added. "It's a schizophrenic city."

Najya touched her arm again and led her away. Valerie followed, noting that this time it was not just her sleeve that Najya touched. The spot on her arm still felt warm.

A few minutes later they stood under the colonnade and gazed across the court toward the entrance of the famous octagonal structure. "The Dome of the Rock," Najya announced. "Seventh century. One of the most important Muslim shrines. It was built by Byzantine Christian architects, and the Temple Mount beneath it is Roman-Jewish, but who's counting."

At the entrance they took their shoes off, pulled their scarves over their heads, and entered the cool semi-darkness. The dome rose high overhead, drawing the eye immediately upward. Below it, piers and pillars formed a circle around the rock and marked out inner and outer ambulatories. At the center stood the Rock, a heavily pitted granite formation. Najya leaned on the stone balustrade that encircled it. "According to tradition, this is the rock where Mohammed leapt off to visit heaven, along with Moses and Jesus."

Valerie looked around at the circle of archways. "Wouldn't it be wonderful if *that* were the tale that everyone celebrated. Think of how different history would have been." She peered upward, as if through the ornamental tile work of the ceiling she could actually see the three prophets ascend together in a shaft of light. "A nice image. A shame no Muslim Michelangelo ever made a fresco or oil painting of that!"

"Muslim sacred art, such as it is, doesn't portray people, and certainly not the Prophet."

"I understand, but you have to wonder what happened between *that* peaceful image in the Muslim mind and the deep seething anger that's there now?"

"You know as well as I do that the creation of the state of Israel on land that was Palestine created the current rage. But before that colonialism caused it, and before that, the Crusades."

"Crusades? They were eight hundred years ago."

"Don't underestimate ethnic memory. If Christians get emotional about the Crucifixion and the Jews about the destruction of the Temple, how much more should Muslims be bitter about the Crusades, which are historically documented in detail?"

Valerie looked into the middle distance for a moment. "I dreamed once about a crusader. He killed a man in front of me, and I even remember the dead man's name. A merchant, Husaam al Noori. It probably helped that I was dozing in his mausoleum in the tomb of his scribe Sharif al Kitab. Strange that after two years I still remember both names."

They had circled the Holy Rock and wandered outside of the shrine. At that moment, loudspeakers in the courtyard sounded the call to prayer. Valerie glanced at Najya. "Should we leave?"

Najya shook her head. "It's all right. The ones who pray worship mostly at Al Aqsa mosque."

A few men remained in the courtyard. They stood in place facing southeast, with their hands to their ears, and began to murmur. The words were blurred, but Valerie had heard them a thousand times and knew them by heart: "*Bismillah Arrahman Arraheem.*"

They strolled to the middle of the square, away from the praying men, and Valerie took up the theme. "I don't know much about the crusaders. The nuns in my convent school taught that they were heroes and martyrs."

Najya's voice was scornful. "I don't think so. Your own historian, William of Tyre, gives a hair-raising account of the slaughter. I can give you a copy of it, if you like."

Valerie studied the somber, distant expression on Najya's face. The golden dome behind her caught the midday sun and sent it back in a sudden blinding flash. Awash in the reflected light, Najya Khoury was for an instant surrounded by gold, an icon of Muslim women, aggrieved and mourning.

"No, you don't have to do that. But on behalf of my European Christian ancestors, I apologize."

Najya smiled gently. "On behalf of my Jerusalemite ancestors, I accept."

"*Jerusalemite* ancestors? I thought no Muslims survived."

"A few did. The emir, for example. My family insists we are his descendants."

"Very impressive. But how—" The "Hallelujah Chorus" sounded in a high, tinkly register. "Oh." She slapped her hand to her belt. "I can't get used to this thing." She fumbled the object off her belt loop as it chimed "and he shall reign forever and eeeeever…" She flipped it open and held it to her ear.

"Auset? Oh, of course. It would have to be you, wouldn't it? Lunch tomorrow? With the whole family? Oookay. What time? Should I bring something? Uh-huh. Well, then…all right. Yes, that'll be fine. Bye." She clapped the phone shut with the same flick of the wrist she'd seen Derek use, smiling to herself for an instant as she remembered it.

She directed her attention back to Najya. "So, what's next? Have we seen everything important?"

Najya laughed. "You really *aren't* religious, are you, or you couldn't ask that question. Everything in Jerusalem is important." She looked to the side down the Via Dolorosa. "We haven't seen the Church of the Sepulchre yet. But you know, it's a big church." She glanced at the sky. "And it's getting late."

Valerie touched her forearm. "Oh, I'm sorry. You've given up your whole afternoon for me, and I haven't even thanked you. Well, I'll let you go then. I'm sorry to assume—"

"No, that's not what I meant. It's just that instead of dragging you to yet another holy place, where neither one of us will worship—I thought we could have dinner. I actually live pretty close to the Old City, on Sama'an al Sadek, five minutes by taxi."

With a twinge of guilt Valerie wondered if she could be doing something useful that evening to convince Auset to leave. She couldn't think of anything.

"I'd love to."

39

Najya Khoury

It was a small apartment, Valerie thought. No, she amended, it was more an ordinary apartment made small by the floor-to-ceiling cliff of books on one wall and the clutter of heavy objects hanging on the other one. On the third wall, in front of the windows, a desk was covered with a computer monitor and piles of papers. An equal number was in and around the trash bin.

Najya walked into the kitchen while Valerie perused the library. One whole bookcase held law books: treaty law, Ottoman law, Israeli law, directives of the British Mandate. The adjacent case was more appealing. Half a dozen histories of Jerusalem, in Arabic, Hebrew, and English. Art books, studies of the pharaohs, of the Babylonians, of Fatimed Egypt, of the Crusades.

"Do you read anything past the twelfth century?" Valerie called into the kitchen.

"Yes, on the bookshelf by the window. I hope you like tabouli and babagenouj. It's what you're getting. I also made a salad," Najya called back.

"Sounds delicious." Valerie examined the current reading material: D.H. Lawrence, Finkelstein, Mandala, Reinhart, Chomsky, Pappe.

Najya stood in the doorway with two bottles. "Red or white?"

"Red, if you don't mind. Looks like you're pretty political."

"You think?" Najya poured out a large goblet of merlot, handed it to her, and returned to the kitchen.

Holding her glass, Valerie moved to the opposite wall. An elaborately woven red camel bag hung on hooks, its tassels nearly to the floor. Next to it was a collection of antique weapons. At the top was a Moroccan musket, its stock inlaid with silver. Under its barrel, a hammered metal powder flask hung on a silver chain. Below it was an impressive inventory of blades and scabbards, from full-sized scimitars to sleek daggers and sharply curved Yemeni jambiyas. She took a drink of the wine. "I've never had dinner in a terrorist's apartment before," she joked.

Najya came in carrying bowls of dips, tomatos, pita. "Oh, you like my wall? There's a lot of family history there. The musket, for example, was my great-grandfather's, and the scimitar on top is one of the things my brother brought back from Saudi Arabia. He claimed he got it from a desert sheikh in exchange for his best hiking boots, but with Saïd, I was never sure how much of his stories was fiction." She offered warm pita.

"Your brother. You said he was killed. I'm sorry. That must have been hard for you." Valerie took the bread and a generous helping of each of the dips.

"It was much worse for my father, who had made his peace with the Israelis. He felt completely betrayed."

"What happened? To Saïd, I mean. Tell me about him."

"He was a teacher, you know, at Al Quds University. Middle Eastern history. That's why he traveled so much. He had already published a few things, mostly translations of medieval works. He even found documents that support our family's assertion of being here since the First Crusade."

Valerie began to appreciate Najya's somber nature. What she'd misread as humorlessness was really a too close familiarity with life's brutalities, a familiarity she'd recently gained herself. "How was he killed?"

"He went to Nablus one weekend for a wedding. An IDF tank rolled in for some reason or another while they were celebrating, and the men threw rocks at it. It was a reckless thing to do because the IDF shot back with real bullets. The groom was killed too."

"Gods, I'm so sorry. I know what that feels like. The anger and sorrow together, you just choke on it. All for religion."

Najya cleared away dishes. "Not only religion. After thirty years of wars and intifadas, I don't know anymore where religion ends and greed and vengeance begin. Not to defend religion, mind you." She returned with the wine bottle and directed her to the sofa.

"Well, we've established what kind of Muslim *you* are." Valerie held up her wine glass.

"That's what happens when you let women go to school." Najya laughed softly. "Actually I do know Quran fairly well. My father made us study it. It never seemed to have anything to do with me, though, and the last straw was when I read Sura 53."

"The so-called Satanic verses, about the goddesses Lat, Uzza, and Manat. Yes, they are something of an embarrassment to the infallibility of scripture. A bit like Leviticus."

"Oh, I *am* impressed. A European Catholic who knows Quran. What other surprises do you have?"

Valerie smiled to herself. *You have no idea*, she thought. "Ironically, the last time I talked about those verses and those goddesses was with Yussif, the man who was killed in the train explosion. He was still Muslim then and was troubled because he'd seen what seemed like a goddess in the night sky. We all did."

"You saw a goddess in the sky. I wish I'd been there with you. I told you I thought human beings naturally craved moral direction. Maybe we crave sentience in nature too."

"Have you ever thought how you would react if you saw one? I mean a goddess in the sky, or anywhere?" Valerie asked, cautiously.

"Uh, no. I can't say I have. It would play havoc with my atheism though, wouldn't it? Let me know the next time your goddess appears, and I'll tell you then what I think."

"There's more than one, actually. You know, in the nature religions, divinity is everywhere." She could feel her face getting warm. It might have been the difficult subject and the risk of sounding demented, or the wine, or even the proximity of an attractive woman she had once seen naked.

Valerie had taken pains all evening to keep from staring too long at any one part of Najya's person, most particularly the golden-tan color of the skin of her neck, or the fine bones of her face, or even her narrow hips so flattered by cotton trousers. She glanced around the room. "So many books. Law, history, politics. Some pretty heavy meals here. What do you read for pleasure? Or for solace?"

Najya poured out the last of the wine into both their glasses. "Well, for pleasure I read Arabic poetry. While for solace, I read…" She reached past Valerie's shoulder and pulled a slender volume from the shelf. "Persian poetry. I'm sure you know Omar Khayyam."

"Of course." Valerie leafed through the Persian-English volume. "I only know him in French though. My favorite quatrain is *"Étrange passe la caravane de la vie."*

Najya sat down next to her as she turned the pages and studied the illustrations. "Yes, I like the ones about the caravan and the caravanserai too. Maybe you're thinking of this one." She reached across Valerie's arm, the heel of her hand lightly brushing the fingers that held the book open at the edge. She leafed through several pages until she found what she was looking for. "See if this one sounds familiar."

Valerie was feeling the effects of the wine now, and the sphere of light in which they sat seemed to detach itself from the rest of the world. The *Rubaiyat* was at the core, drawing them together. Valerie held the narrow volume from below with her palm, and she felt the weight of Najya's hand that rested on it from above. It was almost as if, through the pages of the *Rubaiyat*, they were holding hands.

She licked her lips, tasting the residue of the wine, and began to read out loud.

> *Think in this batter'd caravanserai,*
> *Whose portals welcome and send forth each day*
> *How merchants, scholars, lovers, and their creeds*
> *Abode their precious hour and went away.*

Najya nodded faintly with the rhythm. "It's a nice image, the passing of generations, hundreds of them, from nowhere to nowhere."

"Not to nowhere," Valerie said. "Sometimes the later generation, the hundredth, say, or the two hundredth, may be expected to accomplish something. I, for example, am expected to accomplish something," she said dreamily. "I was supposed to have accomplished it already today."

"How very mysterious you are." Najya was sitting on one hip now, an arm thrown along the back of the sofa. "To accomplish what?"

Valerie already regretted having spoken. She'd been too anxious to interest Najya, who sat so close and smelled so wonderful. But it was a story that she couldn't tell her. "Look, I don't know you very well—and I don't want to involve you in something dangerous."

"Dangerous?" Najya looked perplexed. "How did we get from Omar Khayyam to dangerous all of a sudden?"

"I'm sorry. It was a leap, wasn't it? I just meant, I'm here in Jerusalem because of some generational obligation. And when it's done, I have to leave."

"I hope it won't be soon."

"I'm afraid it will. In just a few days, I think. But maybe we can see each other again." A crasser voice in her head said *Idiot. Why drag this out? Just reach out and kiss her.* She felt herself staring again, obsessively, at the muscles that swelled so wonderfully around Najya's mouth, drawing attention always to her lips. *No, too soon.* She looked past Najya at the objects behind her.

On a table at the end of the sofa lay something she hadn't noticed. An expensive-looking Nikon with telephoto lens. "That's quite a camera you have there. Do you photograph much?"

"It's Harry's. He lent it to me for a few days. Actually I'm not a very good photographer at all. I just take snapshots to help me remember details. Harry's the professional."

At the mention of the man's name—twice—Valerie felt something inside her collapse and be replaced by...she wasn't sure what. A mixture of embarrassment, anger, even nausea. The cozy flirtatious dinner, the whole afternoon changed meaning. It was all just sisterly friendship, a girls' night out, everything she didn't want. And she had almost made a fool of herself. She looked at her watch.

"I'm sorry if I seem rude, but I have a lot to deal with in the next few days. And I'm sure you do too, so I won't keep you any later this evening." She stood up.

"Oh, it's not at all late." Najya looked at her own watch. "But I can understand that you might be tired from travel and stress." She stood up next to Valerie. "Look, what about meeting tomorrow evening? I'd like to show you the Pool of Siloam. My grandfather was part of the team that renovated it."

Valerie hesitated. What was the point? Najya belonged to a man and Valerie was on his turf. In another life, before the bloodshed, she might have taken up the challenge, but not now. Now she was under threat and in a hurry. It would only make sense to say no.

"I'd love to. I have a lunch in the afternoon, but we could meet about six."

"Six would be perfect." Najya seemed unusually pleased. "You're going to meet Auset's family?"

"Her grandparents, who are orthodox, so the lunch will be kosher. Is there anything special I should know? I mean besides not asking for pork chops?"

They were at the door now. "Yes. Don't kiss the host. You Belgians do a lot of that kissing thing, but it's strictly taboo here. With men, I mean. So don't kiss any men, ever."

The word "kiss" on Najya's lips seemed provocative; each time she said it, it was a tease. But Harry's things were in her house. And Najya was one of Harry's things.

"I'll try not to," Valerie murmured and walked dazed and confused into the corridor.

By the time she was on the street she remembered why she was in Jerusalem, and bereavement settled over her again like a fog.

40

Let My People Stay

At the last moment, Valerie wondered if she should have brought flowers. And now it was too late. She knocked.

Sephora Ibrahim opened the door. A woman somewhere in her seventies, she bent forward against the door jamb and squinted amiably through thick eyeglasses. Valerie's first thought was Golda Meier, but no, she amended. Sephora had a certain gentle sadness in her face, like a woman who had expected life to turn out differently.

Dr. Foret, please come in." She stepped backward, supporting herself on her cane. "So nice to finally meet you."

As she walked in, Valerie smelled onion and garlic. "Can I help in any way?"

"Thank you, dear," Sephora said. "We have a girl who cooks, and she is taking care of everything." She hobbled ahead down the hall to the dining room.

A man met them at the end of the corridor. Stooped and completely bald under a white kippa, he laid a palsied hand over his heart in greeting. "Itzak Ibrahim, Auset's grandfather," he said in thickly accented English. "Good afternoon, Dr. Foret. Auset has told us about the tragedy of your friend in Cairo. I am very sorry for your loss."

She was touched by his sincerity and by his bringing the subject up at all. He had to have known that Derek was the father of their illegitimate grandchild.

"Thank you, Mr. Ibrahim. I am pleased to be here." She laid her hand on her own heart, hoping that the rest of the evening would not be as awkward. She knew the taboos of conservative Islam, but not of Judaism, and wondered how soon she would blunder.

They entered the large dining room where another man and woman waited.

"This is my son Yehuda, and his wife Hadassah." Itzak's open hand trembled slightly as he pointed with it.

Itzak Ibrahim, with his short well-trimmed white beard and wizened eyes, was as engaging as his son was not. There was a family resemblance in the eyes, and Valerie could see a hint of Hannah in all their faces. Though both men had declined to shake her hand, Itzak had sparkled warmth, while Yehuda's eyes slid off her and glanced elsewhere.

Hadassah was opaque; her expressionless eyes suggested a woman who pronounced no opinions, although a look of disapproval at Valerie's trousers had fluttered quickly over her face, then disappeared. She resumed unwrapping a large bouquet of cut flowers from a cone of wet newspaper. She had, Valerie noted, the perfect coiffure of an expensive wig.

Yehuda, for his part, wore the same black suit as the men at the Wall and had the same curled *payes* in front of each ear.

Valerie smiled toward her host and exhaled audibly when Auset appeared with Nefi in hand.

Nefi held out her arms. "*Khalti,*" she said as Valerie knelt down and kissed her on both plump cheeks.

"Habibti!" Valerie lifted the giggling two-year-old into her arms while Auset brought a high chair to the table from the corner of the room.

The kitchen help brought in the meal and Valerie saw she was not a "girl" at all, but a woman in her fifties, Arab or Druze or—less likely—a poor and secular Jew. Valerie's first instinct was to assist her, but the demeanor of the others—including Auset—suggested they had a long established ritual, not to be interfered with.

With practiced efficiency, the woman swept repeatedly from kitchen to dining room carrying soup tureen, salad bowl, platter of warm pitas, and a wide tray with half a dozen sauces and pastes.

When the table was complete, everyone stood up. Itzak pulled himself up from his chair and spoke the prayer. "*Baruch atah Adonai Ehohenu melech ha-olam hamotzi lechem min ha-aretz.*"

Valerie lowered her head in respect and tried to make out the meaning of the Hebrew words. It seemed a simple blessing on the bread.

Itzak lifted his glass of wine to his guests. "To family and friends. It is a blessing for an old man to have so many people at his table."

All sat down again and Valerie said to the host, "It is an honor for me to sit at this table. You are the second Jerusalemite I've met whose family has deep roots in this city."

"Who was the other one, dear?" Sephora asked as she handed around the bread. "Maybe we know him?"

"It is a woman. A Palestinian," Valerie replied, wondering if her remark counted as a faux pas. "Her family name is Khoury."

"Khoury." Sephora was silent for a moment. 'I do know that name. Yes. Someone named Khoury worked on the renovation of the Siloam Spring tunnel a few years ago. It was in the newspapers."

Itzak nodded agreement. "A few families here, Jews and Arabs both, have been in Jerusalem for centuries—maybe a millennium. The historical records say that crusaders murdered everyone in 1099, so the farthest back we can claim to date ourselves is the twelfth century."

Itzak's impish smile reminded Valerie a bit of Yoda.

"I like to think that my ancestor and the ancestor of my neighbor Abdul returned at the same time afterward and have been ignoring each other ever since."

Valerie laughed. "That would have been during the time of Salah-al-Din, wouldn't it? He took back the city from the Christians about a century later."

Itzak twinkled Yoda-like again. "Actually some Jews and Muslims managed to migrate back only a few decades after the fall under the brief reign of Baldwin III. You know, Semitic tenacity—on both sides."

"I should have warned you," Auset said, cutting up chunks of chicken for Nefi. "My grandfather adores medieval history and can match facts with anyone in the field."

"Semitic tenacity. Do you mean of Jews, or of Arabs too?" Valerie risked.

Looking up through remarkably thick eyebrows, Itzak tapped a finger on the table next to her hand to make his point. "Both are Semites, and equally stubborn. That's why neither side backs down. And I know the Arabs have their Jerusalem songs, just as we do. There is quite a nice one, by that Lebanese woman, Fairuz. 'Al radabu…' He hummed a few bars of a lively tune. Do you know Fairuz? You look a little like her, you know." Sephora cleared her throat and he lowered the wattage of his twinkle. "Just to say I know the Arabs have their dreams and their roots too."

"Roots?" Yehuda took issue. "The roots of the Jews go back over two thousand years."

Valerie felt Auset tense next to her and changed the subject. She turned to Hadassah. "I noticed the bouquet you were unwrapping. Where do you get such beautiful flowers in Jerusalem?"

"Oh, they are from our own garden," Hadassah said with obvious pride. "My husband grows flowers, mostly roses and carnations. We also have a vegetable plot. I love it that we can grow things on our own land—'make the desert bloom,' so to speak."

"Yes, I can understand that. Cultivating the land makes you feel part of it," Valerie replied politely, though she'd never planted anything in her life.

Yehuda's expression warmed slightly at her remark. "Absolutely. You feel a connection with your ancestors who worked the same soil." His eyes took on a distant look. "And when you feel close to the soil of Israel, you feel close to God." He stared off into space for a moment. "Sometimes I just stop and hold a clump of soil in my hand and say a prayer of thanks that God has brought us back home."

Valerie heard the ardor with which Yehuda had said "soil" and "home." It was a sentiment she would never feel, but could respect. She could imagine him standing, humble, in his garden, and for a moment she liked him. "Where do you live?" she asked.

"In Hebron," Hadassah replied and looked ready to be asked more about flowers.

"Hebron, in the West Bank," Auset interjected. "My uncle's lovely large garden and orchard that were given to him by God used to belong to Palestinians. Apparently God hadn't given it to them, but only lent it for a few centuries."

Valerie lowered her eyes and felt her face warm. Five minutes into dinner and she'd already opened the gate to a minefield.

Yehuda wiped his mouth and beard and laid his napkin down with ominous care. The warmth was gone now from his face. Valerie wondered if she should ask to use the bathroom and stay there until it was all over.

"It makes me sick to hear you always whine about Arab land," he said. "You should be damned glad your mother's family is safe in Israel. Six million others were not so lucky. If you hate your Jewish blood so much, go back to Egypt and put on the veil."

"Yehuda, mind your manners," Itzak said, raising the hand that held his fork.

A small voice in Valerie's head cried, *Shut up! Do not get into this!*

"I'm sorry," she said. "It was Germans—Europeans who committed the genocide. Not the Palestinians." Valerie looked at the pained face of Sephora and immediately regretted becoming involved. It was obviously an old family argument.

Yehuda tried a new tack. "They left a desert and we have made it into a garden." He pointed to the salad. "How do you like our Jewish tomatoes and artichokes?"

"Well, of course you have," Auset returned fire. "But not because of God. Billions of American dollars have allowed you to introduce agro-industry, using water from Palestinian wells. With that much money, the Palestinians could have done it too."

Yehuda opened his mouth to speak, but something clattered on the windowpane like gravel and distracted him.

Obviously relieved to get away from the argument, Itzak got up from the table and went to the window. "My heavens. It's hail! How strange."

"Hailstones? In September? Well, it must be one of those odd summer storms," Sephora said from the table. "It will be over in a few minutes."

Itzak opened the window. "Oh, no!" He shut it as fast as he could, but it was too late. Flies and mosquitoes swarmed in, settling on everything.

Auset waved them away from Nefi's face and plate.

Hadassah laid her napkin over her plate, but flies had already landed in the serving dish, and she tried to spoon them out.

Yehuda ignored the buzzing pests. "You had the blessing of being Jewish, but instead of marrying a Jew and having a family like a decent woman, you went your own perverse way. Don't think this family isn't embarrassed by the dark-skinned bastard from a foreigner you have inflicted on us."

Itzak stood up. "Silence! I will not have that talk at my table. All of my family are welcome in my house and in my heart. Where did you learn such hatred, Yehuda? Hatred is not Jewish."

"Please, everyone, sit down." Sephora raised both hands in supplication.

A cry of horror came from the kitchen.

Itzak jumped up again, and Valerie followed him into the kitchen, where the serving woman stood at the sink.

"Blood. Blood came out of the faucet!"

Trickling from the faucet was a thin steam of reddish brown liquid. From a space under the window, flies and mosquitoes continued to find their way in. Itzak turned off the faucet. "Blood cannot get into the pipes. It is rust, or some growth in a broken pipe."

Clearly unconvinced, the woman backed away and seized a broom to swat at the tiny brown frogs that appeared under the sink.

"Come, come. It's only a summer storm." He led them out of the kitchen and sat down again at the table. "Please, children. We are four generations here. Let us have peace together."

With a clap of thunder, the lights suddenly went out. "An eclipse too?" Hadassah asked into the air. The lights flickered for several moments and then came on again. "It's like the plagues of Egypt!" she exclaimed. "What's next, I wonder."

Auset laid her arm over the high chair that held her first-born child. The expression on her face showed that, pious or not, she remembered exactly what came next.

❖

"You were a little hard on your uncle, weren't you?" In the doorway to the building, Valerie slid her arms into the straps of her rucksack. "I should think by now you'd know how to avoid quarreling with him. He's obviously passionate."

"They're all passionate. Israel could have had peace a long time ago if not for their passion. My grandparents are so loving, and all they ever wanted was a nice Jewish family that went to temple, ate kosher, and had lots of grandchildren. Bad enough that my mother married a Muslim. It took them years to get over that." She shook a tiny frog off her shoe and continued.

"But Yehuda has gone in the opposite direction. He's always been self-righteous, but now he's more Jewish than Jehovah. He thinks God gave all of Palestine to the Jews and wants the Arabs to be driven out, end of story."

"Funny, I know a Christian minister who believes the same thing." Valerie glanced up at the sky. "Well, the hail cooled things down a little. And the vermin are thinning out, too. Strange storm, wasn't it?"

Auset shivered. "With everything that's happened, I get nervous at every little oddity like that and wonder if it's directed at us. I mean, it was right out of Exodus."

Valerie scraped a bit of red-brown mold from the threshold. "Here's your 'blood in the water.' Itzak was right; strange weather, but not a plague from the One-God. Besides, if anything, shouldn't the natural forces be more on *our* side? Maybe it's a sign from *our* deities." She slid her foot along the sidewalk and chuckled. "If it is, then all they've done is made everything a little slippery."

Auset laughed softly. "So much for being saved by Rekemheb's gods. They couldn't even get plagues right." She reached over Valerie's shoulder and zipped up one of the pockets on the rucksack, an older sister gesture, although she, in fact, was the younger one. "Look, I've been thinking about what you said—about the judges, I mean, refusing the underworld to Yussif and Derek. It still sounds like extortion, a death threat to their spirits. I don't want to find out that the Egyptian religion is no different from the dogmas that are around here now—that it will make us act like Yehuda."

"I think the Egyptian gods are far too disorganized to inspire passion in anyone. And there's no dogma in animism."

"I suppose you're right, but I still keep imagining Yussif and Derek just waiting—like hostages—for us to do something to help them. So if Nekhbet says it depends on our leaving Jerusalem and finding people crazy enough to join us, then, okay, I'll leave."

"You mean all I had to do to get you to leave was suffer lunch with your uncle?"

Auset chuckled. "Thank you, dear. That *was* a real show of loyalty. But I also called the lawyer, the one whose name you gave me. He said there was no reasonable case Reverend Carter could make to have Nefi removed from her own country and her own mother. So I think we're safe."

"Your parents will be relieved, not to mention the gods of Egypt. When can we leave?"

"Well, my grandmother has to go to the clinic for her leg tomorrow, and I promised to take her. I'll fly to Cairo on Sunday. But if Nekhbet really is worried, you can leave ahead of me and take Nefi. My parents would meet you at the airport and take her from there."

"One day shouldn't make that much difference." Valerie glanced at her watch. "Oh, I have to go now. Are you sure you'll be okay? I mean, I didn't start a new intifada upstairs, did I?"

"No, it's still the old one. Anyhow, Mr. and Mrs. Sunshine will be leaving for Hebron in a little while anyway. They've got nine screaming children waiting for them at home. My grandparents go to bed like birds, at sunset, so Nefi and I'll have a nice quiet house all to ourselves. Go and meet your friend. We can talk more tomorrow." She embraced Valerie a second time and went inside.

In a shop doorway at the bottom of the street, a man watched the two women separate and checked his watch.

41

Siloam

Valerie hesitated on the stairs that led down to the ancient pool. Her mind felt like a room crowded with people arguing past each other: anxious, indignant, bereaved, and all of them filled with a sense of dread. It was definitely not the right time for this.

And what was "this" anyhow? A passing acquaintance, a straight, apparently coupled acquaintance was showing her the Old City. There was no "this."

At the foot of the steps, a handful of people in Bermuda shorts stood around the pool. Then, from behind them, someone waved. Valerie waved back and descended the remaining stairs.

"Hello." Najya Khoury glided toward her both radiant and down-to-earth in a loose white shirt with sleeves rolled to the elbows. She touched Valerie's arm and guided her to the far end of the pool.

Valerie studied the shallow pool, no more than six meters wide and some fifteen or sixteen meters long. At its head, a high archway covered the beginning of a tunnel, and on the far side from where she stood, a stone wall rose several stories.

"I invited you here because my grandfather worked on this tunnel a long time ago, repairing the clay seams. I've always thought of it as ours. My family has been involved in maintaining a lot of the city's sites. I've got keys to just about everything."

"What particular miracles supposedly took place here?"

"None, actually. This was the city's main water source in biblical times. It was surrounded by trees up through the Middle Ages and must have been lovely." She glanced back at the Bermuda shorts group taking pictures. "The tourists will leave in a little while and we'll have it to ourselves. Sit down over here where the stones are flat." Najya brushed off imaginary dirt from the stone next to her. "So, how was lunch?"

Valerie sat next to her facing the pool. "Rather unpleasant, as a matter of fact. By the way, Auset says thank you for the lawyer's name."

"What happened?"

"Oh, it was Auset's uncle. A settler. From Hebron."

"Umm. The ones in Hebron are the worst. Really aggressive."

"He sounded just like Derek's stepfather. Come to think of it, he also sounded like the mullah that Auset's father goes to for advice. They all say the same thing."

"I think we had this conversation before, with fewer clothes on." Najya laughed softly.

In the late afternoon it began to grow dim in the canyon of walls that surrounded the pool. Najya's voice was as velvet as the light. "Have you accomplished what you came here for?"

Valerie took a deep breath. "Yes. I've convinced Auset to leave, so we'll be flying out right away."

"Whatever for? Didn't she also just get here?" Najya leaned forward, setting her elbows on her knees. "Is this connected with the two deaths? Please tell me if I can help with something. I thought we'd gotten to the point where you knew that."

As she spoke, the sun dropped behind the city walls, and for a moment, the cavern they were in was plunged in gloom. Then a row of lanterns flickered on along the four sides of the pool. They bathed the area in a soft orange glow that created an atmosphere of trust and intimacy, a place where one could say anything.

Valerie studied the dark, intelligent face. "Look, if I told you something bizarre, something that flies in the face of your knowledge and common sense, would you be able to suspend disbelief long enough to hear me out? I mean before you decided I was a madwoman and ran for your life?"

"Hmm. Excellent opening line. Well, to be honest I couldn't imagine running away from you under any circumstances. Besides, you're a well-known scientist, accomplished, brilliant. I could trust you quite far."

Valerie stared into the dusky tunnel and chose her words. "In the tomb," she began cautiously, "for which I am so 'well known,' I uncovered...well, forces. Entities that you would never expect, that don't fit in with anything you know."

"Are we talking about the supernatural here?"

"Well, I suppose... Let me start again. Certain elements of the ancient Egyptian theology are in effect, although we tend to see through them. That is, nature itself, on occasion, manifests itself in personifications, and the Egyptians recognized them. They gave them names, portrayed them as half human and half nature, mostly animals." Valerie stopped. "This is the point where you get up and leave, right?"

"No, no. Still suspending disbelief here. Please go on." Najya's expression was studiously neutral.

"Well, I thought at first I was hallucinating. Believe me, I'm an atheist and a scientist. If anyone did *not* want to acknowledge the supernatural, it was me. But the four of us—a Christian, a Jew, a Muslim, and an atheist—all saw them. Anyhow, they want to come back, those gods, and they enlisted Auset, me, Derek, and Yussif to make that possible."

"And you learned all of this in the tomb?" Najya asked in a neutral journalist interview tone.

"No. It took a while to piece it all together, and in fact, we had hints much earlier, when Nekhbet began appearing."

"Nekhbet? Who's that?" Najya was leaning on one arm now, lightly brushing against her, and Valerie felt the warmth between them. She frowned, perplexed. She was being mocked, of course, but only gently. She was also being listened to, and she desperately needed to talk.

Valerie took a breath. "I guess I have to start further back. Nekhbet is the Vulture Goddess of Upper Egypt and one of the two divinities. The other one is Wadjet the Cobra, who protected the royal line. You can see their heads jutting from the front of the double crown of the New Kingdom pharaohs."

"And what is Nekhbet's connection with you?"

"Apparently, I'm supposed to be the chronicler, and so at the behest of the scribe god, Nekhbet was supposed to protect me. However, she hadn't shown up for two years, that is, until Yussif was killed."

"I see," Najya said slowly. "So you came to Egypt and now are in Jerusalem, basically on behalf of these polytheistic forces. And these forces are connected in some way to the deaths of Yussif and Derek?"

"It seems that way. And these forces, or rather the single force that stands to lose from the return of the nature gods, is the sun god. The ancient Egyptians called him the Aton."

"And the Jews called him Jahweh."

"Yes," Valerie said tentatively, then frowned. "You're taking this very well. I can't believe I convinced you so easily."

"Oh, I'm not convinced at all. It's total madness. But it *is* possible to have a rational conversation about the irrational. Even if this is all pure dementia, it's consistent, and interesting. But going along with your story so far, I see that you have a problem."

"I have lots of problems."

The velvet voice laughed softly. "The one I mean is your choice of city. If you're trying to escape the One God, the one who gets to have His pronouns capitalized, you've fled to the mouth of the wolf. From the time that the temple mount was simply Mount Moriah, this city has been full of One Gods, all forms and permutations of Him, in every brick and stone. There was a short period under Tiberias when the Romans built a few pagan temples. But under Constantine, it was the One God again."

"You know a lot about Jerusalem."

"I told you, my family has been here for a thousand years, give or take a few. Remember, the family legend has it that one of my ancestors was here at the time of the First Crusade."

"That's right. The emir, you said." Valerie felt the conversation leading off on a tangent, but at least they were talking.

"Yes, Idris ad Dawla was allowed to leave with a small contingent. My family descends from him, and a lot of the men in the family carry the name Idris." Najya tilted her head toward her. In the cooling night air, Valerie could smell the faintest hint of perfume. Najya had put perfume on. For her. The full lips, a handsbreadth away, moved, and finally their sound reached her ear. "You were saying? About the Aton?"

"Well, that's it, basically. The Egyptian gods want to be recognized again, and we four were supposed to let the world know about them. Except that two of us are dead because of that mission, and if I tell this to anyone but you, I'll be laughed out of the profession. Even you're barely holding back a laugh. I can sense it."

Najya leaned back a fraction, leaving a space between them. Valerie felt the cool evening air on her suddenly exposed skin. "You can't sense *anything* about me," Najya said.

"No. I'm sorry. I guess I don't. It's just that I care…about you." She avoided the dangerous word 'for.' "I don't want you to run off until you know everything."

Najya leaned in again. "Listen to me. I know all about you. I covered the story of your discovery. I know it took you years of research because I read your articles. I know that while you were mysteriously absent, your supervisor was killed in a sandstorm, and when you just as mysteriously came back, you oversaw the cataloging of Egypt's greatest find of the century. One does not laugh at someone like that."

She paused, the touch of her arm underscoring her support. "Besides," she said brightly. "There's a fantastic story here. And there's no way I'm leaving you until I find out what it is."

"And you don't think it's 'famous archaeologist loses mind'?"

"Could be. But whatever it is, I'm staying around for it."

"What about Harry?"

"Harry?" Najya seemed perturbed by the leap in logic.What's Harry got to do with anything?"

"Well, you have his things. You're sleeping with him," Valerie blurted.

"Slept with him. After a few beers on a hot day. Why do you care? Besides, if he hadn't gotten me the assignment in Cairo, I wouldn't have covered the train wreck and I'd never have met you. Being with him meant nothing. That sort of thing never means anything."

Valerie leaned back against the tunnel wall. "You're not in love with him?"

"In love?" Najya shook her head. "Romantic love may be a Western myth. How would you know it's love, anyhow, and not just sex?"

Valerie closed her eyes, remembering. "He…she…would be an obsession. Every event would be colored by the thought of them. Everything you saw or did you'd want to tell them about. Everything *they* did you'd want to know about." Her mouth curled up on one side. "Although it sounds a little stupid when you say it all in the plural."

Najya's voice was barely audible. "I've only ever felt that about you."

The remark was so matter-of-fact that Valerie almost missed it. "Me?" She studied the enigmatic Arab face. In the low light of the pool, it reminded her of a Bedouin woman.

But Najya Khoury was nothing like the Bedouin. "Since you found us in your room in Cairo, I've thought about you," she said.

"You knew who I was then, didn't you? Did you also know my… disposition?"

"Yes. Rumors of that sort spread quickly in journalistic circles. And then when I saw you in the hammam, well, of course I couldn't help but think about…that."

"As I recall, we talked about religion."

"Did we? I don't remember. I kept trying to imagine you. With a woman."

Valerie leaned away in mock horror. "So while I was waxing philosophical, you were playing a dirty movie in your head."

"No, not exactly. I wasn't quite sure what women did, I mean beyond kissing. It was a sort of idee fixe, but I could imagine it only so far."

"Idee fixe," Valerie murmured. "How charming to hear French spoken with an Arabic accent."

They had run the subject to its end and both fell silent, looking away from each other. The orange ground lights reflected off the water of the pool and flickered like candlelight below their faces.

Najya chuckled softly. "If you were a man, you'd have kissed me by now."

"Please don't tease me, Najya," Valerie whispered. "I've got all the uncertainties I can handle right now."

"I'm not teasing. For the first time in my life I'm deadly serious. I just don't know how to do it."

"Do what?"

"Make love to you."

The words hung in the evening air like a fragrance. Valerie let them linger and settle around them. For a moment the declaration blocked out everything else in the world and created a precious private space. Then she breathed out softly, "Come back to my room with me and I'll show you."

"I think it begins something like this." Najya's mouth suddenly covered hers.

Valerie responded tentatively, with little explorations of lips and teeth and tongue. She stopped and broke away for a moment, for the sheer excitement of starting again, this time more ardently—offering, taking, giving back again.

Valerie touched the warm face, let her fingertips drift down to the pulsing throat. Their mouths began a sort of wordless dialogue, and they grew to know each other by degrees, each venturing a bit, then opening to the other.

Najya's hand slid over her ribs and up her back, enfolding her, and she felt Najya's breasts press against her own.

Valerie waited for the familiar rush, the sudden hot tightness in her sex, and the urge to take, quickly, before opportunity passed. But something unfamiliar happened. something drew her in, to a gentle back and forth in which she seemed to slowly lose the outline of herself. Like being underwater, in the embrace of something that was scarcely different from herself, drawing breath from it and giving it back.

She ceased to care about the danger and the dread, and surrendered to the thing that summoned her.

It was, a small part of her recalled, a little like the time she died.

42

Deus Lo Volt

L udolf stood next to Godfrey of Bouillon on the highest platform of the siege tower. Still outside the range of Saracen arrows, he watched the battering ram roll up against the southern gate. Under the hide-bound wattle that covered them from arrows and flames, the rammers warmed to their task. Ludolf saw the end of the log as it swung back for each blow. The ironclad head, he knew, ate away at the wood with every thrust, and each deep thud seemed to reverberate through the ground and up to his own body.

"Like deflowering a virgin, isn't it?" Godfrey quipped.

Ludolf chuckled softly. "A Saracen virgin."

"We'll make her Christian soon enough," the duke said.

"Yes, and on this day above all. Friday, when they crucified our Lord. This could be the very hour of His death. How fitting that today we make the heathen answer for that sin."

"Well spoken, Ludolf. I will remember that," Godfrey said before his attention was diverted to the Muslim prisoners being dragged past them. "You know what to do, sergeant," the duke called down to the men below.

"Yes, my lord." The soldiers knocked the two captives to the ground and trussed each one compactly, knees to chin and arms around their shins. While they thrashed uselessly, the Frankish soldiers lifted them into the baskets of the catapults. At a signal from the duke, the counterweight was dropped and the men thrown high into the air. They tumbled as they arced, and if they screamed as they crashed onto the city walls, the sound was covered by the cheering of the Franks.

Then the siege tower was pushed forward. When it came into range, flaming arrows rained down on them, but the water-soaked hides kept them from igniting the tower.

It seemed like hours but was only a fraction of that when they reached the wall. Arrows flew at them like locusts and soldiers fell on both sides, but miraculously, Ludolf remained unscathed, though sweat and smoke stung his eyes and he could scarcely see. The wall was close, so close, yet too heavily defended to permit a foothold.

Then finally it happened. "Look! Praise God. They're ablaze!" Ludolf pointed to the nearby tower on the wall where heavy smoke had caused the defenders to fall back.

"Who will be the first Christian on the wall?" Godfrey shouted, his heavy sword over his head, poised to strike the first Saracen within reach.

"Ludolf of Tournai!" He called out his own name as he leaped onto the wall. Euphoric, he slashed left and right as he ran, and neither arrow nor blade touched him. In a moment, the assault ladders were thrown against that part of the wall, and scores of Franks joined him on the parapet. Jerusalem was breached.

❖

Praise God! The Holy City was free!

Every Saracen man, woman, and child fled weaponless toward the Temple Mount, and Frankish soldiers struck them down at will. But Ludolf knew a city does not surrender until its ruler does, and Idris ad Dawla still held out within the Citadel.

Archers and knights were on the Citadel wall, but Raymond of Toulouse had told them to stand down. Ludolf threaded his way through the fighters to the cluster of knights at the forefront. At their center stood Godfrey of Bouillon and the white-haired Raymond of Toulouse.

"Ah, here is the first Christian knight to enter Jerusalem." Godfrey clapped him on the shoulder. "Have a care, my friend. Ad Dawla and his guard have retreated to the safest spot in the city and are shooting arrows from the tower. But don't worry. My Lord Count of Toulouse will have them cleaned out in no time." Then he turned and, to Ludolf's surprise, descended the stairs again with his knights into the city.

An arrow whizzed downward past Ludolf's head and struck a soldier on the wall behind him. He lifted his shield to his shoulder and waited for the count to reply. But Raymond was watching the streets below where troops under the other nobles were pillaging freely. One by one they seized the houses, great and small, and set the standards, banners, and shields of the new owner upon them to mark the claim.

"We're wasting our time here," Raymond said as a second arrow flew over his head. "I'm for leaving them in their tower to starve. What do you think?"

Ludolf looked up at the impregnable structure. Vultures wheeled around it as they circled now above the entire city. He shook his head. "If what I've heard is true, that will take months. The tower holds vast stores. And as you can see, those archers' openings look down on all four sides. I don't think you want your men shot at every day."

"We can't leave him there and we can't force him out. What's left?" The count leaned his back against the crenellation in obvious frustration. "I suppose we can offer him safe passage in exchange for surrender. I doubt he'll trust us, though." He crossed his arms across his blood-soaked tunic. "I wouldn't."

Ludolf took a step forward. "He should. On this glorious day for the True Faith, let us be men of honor."

"Of honor?" For the briefest moment Raymond's brow furrowed at the word, while below the platform on the streets the armies rampaged. Then it passed. "Well said, Ludolf. Now, let's get this over with." He signaled to his sergeant. "Make the offer."

The sergeant shouted up to the tower and in a moment a voice came back. "For all of us? On your soul before Christ?"

Raymond shouted back, "Yes, on my soul before Christ. We are men of honor. Come down to the platform and we'll talk."

For a long time there was silence, and the vultures neared. One flew down to light on one of the merlons and would not be driven off. A soldier swung his blade at it and it fluttered away, only to light again on a ledge midway up the tower.

Then the narrow door at the base of the tower opened and four archers appeared, weaponless. When it was clear there would be no attack, they called back and four more joined them.

Finally, Idris ad Dawla, the Emir of Jerusalem, stepped out, and the Franks murmured among themselves. He had obviously fought on the ramparts, for his green satin sleeves and the tail of his bright turban were splattered with blood, and his face was sooty from the smoke.

He held his sword by the blade out in front of him, its ornate hilt tilted toward the victor, and he looked around to see to whom he should present it. Raymond of Toulouse stepped forward and received it with a slight dip of the head. With the brief surrender done, the last of the Saracens stood in the doorway, one woman in boy's clothing and another in a dark abaya carrying an infant.

Ludolf drew a sharp breath. It was the witches from the shepherds' pool.

"Your Lordship." Ludolf was suddenly hoarse. "Would you grant me one small boon, for being the first man on the wall?"

Raymond looked perplexed. "This is a strange time to ask, but all right. A boon. What would you have?"

Ludolf pointed toward the more voluptuous of the two, the one who carried the child. "I want the woman. That one."

❖

Faaria blinked against the harsh light as she stood in the tower doorway. The blurred figures silhouetted against the low afternoon sun slowly came into focus. Soldiers in chain mail and tunics bearing the dreadful blood-colored cross stood in a semicircle around the door. One of them, white-haired and gaunt, and far too old to be in an army unless he led it, already held the emir's sword. She did not know his name, only that now he held their lives in his hand.

She studied their alien faces. Under their unkempt beards, their faces were ruddy, at once pale and burnt by the sun. One of them, with yellow hair, stared more intently than the rest—and she recoiled.

It was the man who had attacked them at the pool of Siloam. Behind her, Amhara seized her arm at the same time.

The Frankish leaders spoke among themselves and reached some agreement. Ad Dawla stepped back and laid his arm around Amhara, who clutched Reni closer to her chest. Faaria realized that they were being negotiated for.

The white-haired one said something with the wave of a hand, and the blond knight seized Amhara's arm. She jerked out of his grasp and he reached for her again. Husaam lunged at him, Sharif directly behind him, but before they could take more than a step, two arrows flew with a sudden sharp sound. One pierced Husaam through the back, the arrowhead jutting out through one side of his chest, and he twisted sideways. Sharif cried out as the second arrow pierced his upper arm. Both men fell in front of her, Sharif to his knees and Husaam onto his back.

Husaam lay between brother and sister, gasping in shallow blood-frothed breaths. He whispered "Remember me," and his eyes rolled back in his head. Wounded himself, Sharif leaned sobbing over the merchant's chest.

The knight had once again claimed Amhara and held her by her hair. Suddenly something large and black flew in his face. A vulture from the tower attacked him, curling its claws into his chain mail. It hung tenaciously for several minutes and pecked at his face.

Faaria and Amhara huddled together against the tower wall, awestruck. Someone shot the vulture with a crossbow and it flew away again, the iron bolt protruding from its body.

Then Faaria watched, paralyzed, as the knight reached in front of her face and snatched Amhara's baby by the arm into the air.

In a terrible long moment every perception struck her with crystalline precision: the orange afternoon sun, the acrid smoke that wafted up from the street, the distant savage sounds of the pillaging army, the closer voice of the Frankish commander that called out "No!" and the sight of the terrified baby dangling in the air over the battlement wall.

43

Countdown

He stepped out of the shower, his skin tingling pleasantly from the harsh scrubbing he had given himself. He dried his legs and feet so that he would not track water on the rug in the other room, then took another towel to finish the job in front of his bed. The clock on the nightstand read 10:30 p.m. He was right on schedule.

He glanced around as he toweled his back, making sure he hadn't forgotten anything. The room was spartan in the extreme, the way he liked it. That made it all the easier to scrub clean, which he paid extra to have them do every day. He hated dirt, which seemed to encroach on him at every unguarded moment.

He'd laid out his clothes on the bed and stood naked before the dresser mirror admiring himself. A real man's body—no doubt about that now. He was slightly aroused from the shower and from anticipation, and he knew he'd stay that way until the job was done. It would be his best performance. All three of them at once, if everything worked out. But the first two alone would be all right too. That would give him the chance to hunt the worst one of all, his prize, and she'd know the whole time that he was after her.

His clean socks and shorts emitted a faint scent of chlorine, reassuring him they were clean. It felt good to pull his shorts over his semi-erection, as if they were holding in his rage that he would soon release. He put on spotless khaki trousers, sharply creased, and a new white shirt. Tonight would be his tour de force, after all, and he wanted to look good.

He lifted his valise from the floor and emptied it of the tools he had used the previous night to break the lock on the iron gate. He replaced them with a flashlight, lengths of cord, paper, and pencil. Clean white paper. He debated for a moment whether to write the message himself. No, it would be much more convincing if the stupid woman wrote it. Her own shaky scribbling would be a powerful lure.

He was pleased with his choice of location. Would she appreciate the irony, he wondered. A dawn sacrifice to both the sun and the Son.

Too bad that everything would be wet from the pest-filled rain. He hoped he wouldn't catch a cold.

Last of all he laid his automatic pistol inside and zipped the bag shut. His shoes were polished, but he wiped them once more with a tissue before he put them on.

He left his room and bounced down the stairs with the light step of a cheerful man. The lobby was empty, he was pleased to see, except for the owner's cat, which jumped up on the counter just as he arrived. It raised a paw, maybe to scratch him and maybe not; he didn't wait to find out but swatted it with the back of his hand. The cat flew backward with a yowl and caught him with a single claw on his knuckle. A tiny bubble of red swelled from the puncture wound.

"Shit!" he yelled as the cat bounded away. Now he'd be off schedule. He hurried up the stairs to his room again and kicked open the door. He took his shirt off carefully so as not to stain it. Then he lathered his hand halfway up his forearm and held it under water as hot as he could stand. The last thing he needed was a damned infection.

Hurrying again through the lobby that was empty now of man and beast, he resolved to kill the cat when he returned. That would teach it.

44

Ecstasy and Agony

Valerie lay with her head next to Najya's shoulder and watched the rise and fall of her breasts as she slept. Stunning breasts, full and bronze, that swelled upward from the curve of her armpit and tilted outward, inviting caress. She studied the long muscle of Najya's neck that extended up from the collarbone to her ear, holding the gorgeous head that faced away from her. A swath of jet black hair lay across it, individual strands of it quivering each time Valerie exhaled.

Awestruck, she recalled the moment before climax, when she understood the meaning of "blood like wine," for every cell of her had been intoxicated. Then the airless peak when she had no words or even breath, only the heart-stopping rush when flesh seemed to ignite and all else disappeared.

But lovemaking had not stilled her desire, as it should have, as it always had before. It made her hunger more for Najya, for ever greater closeness, until she could inhale her, drink her in. Even now, after they had brought each other to ecstasy again and again through the hot night, she longed to press her mouth once more over the soft slippery places and to hear Najya moan with need and pleasure.

What was it then that percolated through contentment and still troubled her? How could a night of unebbing passion not make her happy, except that it demanded more of her than she was used to? It was as if something precious had been given to her, and now she had to guard against losing it. Something precious. Yes, that was it, she grasped in the last moments of consciousness. Her lips close to Najya's ear she whispered, or perhaps only thought, "*Je t'adore*" and slid again into the warm pool of sleep.

❖

The fluttering of wings penetrated her unconscious. Then the sound of her name called out—unmistakably—in anger. She opened her eyes—and sat up abruptly, holding her sheet to her chest.

"Nekhbet!"

The goddess took form beside the bed, so close that she had to look down. She was sheathed, as always, in a dress of countless minute black feathers that shimmered ominously. "You are ever following your appetites," she said coldly.

"And you are ever invading my privacy when I am satisfying them," Valerie countered. She glanced at the sleeping Najya, then questioningly at Nekhbet.

She shook her head. "She should not waken yet."

Valerie frowned. "Why not? Why don't you reveal yourself to her? Then you'd have your convert. She already half believes." She looked again at the sleeping Najya, who lay facing her on the pillow, as if she listened.

"No," Nekhbet said a bit too abruptly. "The gods cannot live on revelation. Not even the One God does that any more." She watched Najya for a moment. "Only what comes from the believer with its own force can sustain us, not her groveling before a spectacle. But you turn me from my purpose."

"Your purpose? Would that be to explain why you've abandoned us?" She lifted her watch from the nightstand and saw it was a little after 10:30 p.m.

"I warned you to take them away from here."

"I did what you wanted. I convinced her to leave. But it takes a few days to arrange."

"A few days is not soon enough. Every hour threatens. You must get her to leave immediately."

Valerie saw Nekhbet's glance travel down from her face to her exposed shoulders and chest. For two years she had hungered for just such interest, but now it confused her. "Why is Jerusalem any more dangerous than Cairo, where Yussif and Derek were killed?"

Nekhbet's expression grew cool again. "Because the Aton is all-powerful in this city. He can harm you only through his agents, but the worst of them is here. We do not know who that is, but we sense the malevolence that stalks you."

"You only sense it? Hell, I sense it too." Valerie snorted. "You really don't know any more than I do."

Nekhbet's lips pressed together slightly, as if unwilling to release the distasteful words. "About your world, no. That is our weakness. The workings of this age are…bewildering. We only know the past, in its vast depth, and in painful detail."

"Well then, you might have told me more about it. I had to figure out myself that we aren't the hundredth generation of the prophecy. We aren't, are we? Who *were* they, anyhow? *When* were they?"

A wave seemed to pass through the shimmering blackness that covered the goddess. "It is true. The prophecy has failed—repeatedly. You are only the newest attempt. We no longer count them. But the hundredth generation was the first attempt, and it failed in this city. It failed *because* of this city." She paused as the announcement sank in. "If you have the stomach for it, I will show it to you."

"Show me? Oh, you mean the way you showed me Egypt once." For a moment Valerie held Nekhbet's glance and felt a shiver of excitement.

"With the god's kiss, yes." She glanced again at Najya and her eyes darkened. "Though you seem to prefer the more carnal sort."

Valerie looked back and forth between goddess and the woman sleeping by her side. "You don't like her, do you?"

"She is nothing to me. Leave her for a moment and come here. I will give you the vision."

Valerie hesitated, then drew the sheet up on her chest. "I don't think so."

Nekhbet said nothing, but exuded exasperation. "Do not be coy. This is a truth you must see."

Valerie pulled the sheet higher. "Can't you just *tell* me what they did wrong?"

"They did nothing wrong. It was *my* error, a disastrous one, born of the belief that revelation alone would be enough." She gazed out the window into the Jerusalem night. "It is not."

Then, astonishingly, Nekhbet knelt beside the bed. Valerie drew away. As much as she resented being abandoned, she also did not want to surrender again, to be emotionally overpowered by Nekhbet and hungry for her all the time.

"Please. Just tell me," Valerie repeated softly. She felt Najya's shoulder press against her back, but still the other woman did not wake. Not even when Nekhbet's arms rose and the white-nailed fingers caressed Valerie's face for a moment. Then, with what almost seemed like passion, the divine mouth pressed hers again urgently and without tenderness. Valerie felt sudden scorching desire rush through her like flame through tissue, and she slipped into unconsciousness.

❖

She circled high overhead, held aloft on shafts of air warmed by the fires below. She saw that the walls had been breached and columns of smoke were scattered throughout the city. The invading armies poured inside, first through one opening and then from all sides. The blue or white tabards of the foreigners streamed like flecks of pigment along the narrow streets, confronted and then mingled with the motley colors of the defenders before advancing farther. The cries of clashing armies, of victory by one, for mercy by the other, rose up to her.

The smoke blew eastward and she dropped lower, sweeping in a wide arc over the western end of the city. Though the cries of slaughter rang from the streets below, on the Citadel walls there was a curious calm. A group of knights stood below a tower, and one of them called up to the defenders within. Soon they came out: eight men, their leader, then common folk: two men and two women with a baby.

She understood in an instant what she saw. It was the gods' Child, long prophesied and now manifest and surrounded by her family. But the gods had known too late of the malevolence that would sweep down from the north, and now the Child was caught in the sea of its rage. Did the invaders know what they had stumbled upon, or could the Child still be saved? Already a knight had seized the mother, but she resisted him. If he took her, both she and the baby were lost. Something had to be done instantly.

Surely, she could enlighten him as she had done countless dynasties of pharaohs. She was a goddess, he a mortal, no matter the force of his inspiration. She plummeted, catching her talons in his chain mail. The force of her fall drove him to his knees, and he thrashed until she found an opening to give him the god-kiss. It needed only the briefest touch of her beak. She showed him everything in a single vast landscape, letting the truth wash over him, and she knew he had the vision; she could feel him shudder with it.

On the one side wooded hills rose from a fertile valley cut by a river; on the other, savannah gave way to tundra and windswept dunes.

From one end to the other, the land teemed with life. Buffalos and gazelles grazed near spotted leopards, and even in the dry lands, rodents and reptiles crept among the tenacious brush. Overhead, birds swooped and cried out, their plumages of every color the eye could know, and below them, insects swarmed with their own melodies. Everywhere was sentience, and nature in its plenitude breathed welcome.

Framing the tableau like sentinels, the sister goddesses watched, the snake Wadjet and the vulture Nekhbet, each one with a woman's face and each one upon her tree. Between them on the shore stood Rekemheb, and the Child in his arms grew from baby to radiant womanhood. She stood for a moment with open arms, encompassing all around her.

The knight shuddered again, and the vulture waited for him to grasp that she had shown him paradise. Yet he resisted and his spirit thrashed, and she could not fathom why.

Valerie saw through Nekhbet's eyes and also through her own, tainted by the bitterness of the father's line, and Valerie understood. The embrace of nature held no comfort for the Christian knight. In his eyes it was not epiphany but nightmare, and when he dropped to his knees, flailing, his soul was not enlightened, but appalled.

Before him, rising up from a shore, the landscape seethed. Every soulless creature of the fallen world—horned beasts, great spotted cats, and countless wild things—crept toward him. Snakes, lizards, toads slithered among them, while overhead crows and predatory birds circled and shrieked. Even the trees hissed threats, while the wind and the water over which he floated were full of menace.

At the forefront stood a dark-skinned man, nude but for a white kilt and shorn but for a single braid on the left side of his head. The devil surely, and the creature that sprang from his arms and grew to womanhood before his eyes could only be his spawn.

Then revelation came. Yes, it was the devil's portal; there was the proof. On his left side stood the forbidden tree, the woman-headed serpent twisted in its boughs, and on his right, the black-winged Angel of Death.

It was the garden of temptation, and the creatures calling to him were the enemies of God. Yet they were beasts, and God had given him dominion over them. As if in confirmation, the sphere of light behind him gave forth the one command: "Silence them that rise up against me."

Then Nekhbet/Valerie felt the iron bolt shoot through her, and she was torn loose from the howling knight.

She fluttered upward away from the other arrows and, aghast, saw the knight lurch to his feet and snatch up the Child. He held her for a heartbeat out over the wall. Then, while the mother shrieked he let the infant drop onto the stone pavement to be crushed under the horses' hooves.

Convulsed with horror, she ascended again above the Citadel and flew over the city in the spasms of death. She hovered over the Frankish knights as they slaughtered every creature in their path: Saracen, Jew, and Byzantine, everything that was not like them. Small groups huddled in the doorways or fled into the houses, mosques, and temples, but always they were found and hacked to death. In the narrow passageways where the blood could not escape, it gathered into pools from the dismembered bodies and stained the horses' hocks and the stirrups of the knights.

Then finally it was dusk and the Frankish men could no longer see friend from infidel. They sheathed their swords and set to looting what had not already been claimed.

The vulture looked again to the Citadel and watched, choking with sorrow. On the ground where the Child had been trampled, jackals had gathered. They did not eat, but took the broken infant body in their jaws and trotted off. Then, by evening light, the victor and the last defenders crossed the same stone courtyard.

They passed before her in a brief cavalcade, black forms against the blood red sky. The Frankish general led them, his protective banner over all the others. Behind him, the emir led the refugees: eight weaponless guards and the two women, who rode together on one horse. The one in front rode silently; the other sobbed, collapsed against her back. Last of all, in angular silhouette, a man perched high on a camel, its white coat, even in the darkness, outlining the bulky camel bags that hung on its side.

45

Allies

Defeat, expulsion, night. She thrashed, wracked by silent sobbing and by the iron bolt that pierced her chest.

The innocent Child, their hope for all the world, was crushed in an instant because of her. She had misjudged the immutability of his rage and had provoked him to infanticide. Her heart broke at the realization.

The vulture's kiss had killed the Child.

❖

"Valerie. Wake up. What is it?" A familiar voice penetrated the pain. Hands caressed her face and she opened her eyes.

Najya reached across her and switched on the table lamp by the bed. "You were crying in your sleep, habibti. What's wrong?"

Valerie sat up, shaken, and ran a hand through her hair that was clammy with sweat. "I saw it," she said hoarsely. "It was awful."

"You had a nightmare, that's all."

"No. It wasn't just a dream." She rubbed her forehead and looked inwardly for a moment, then took a long breath. "She was right. If I had known, I wouldn't have had the stomach for it."

"She? Who? What are you talking about?" Najya was sitting up next to her now. With the sheet across her waist, she looked as she had in the hammam. How much had happened since then, ten terrible days ago. Valerie was still reeling.

"I'm so glad you're here." She leaned her head on Najya's shoulder.

Najya kissed her hair, then her eyes. "I'm glad I'm here too. I told you I'd follow you." She stroked damp hair out of Valerie's face. "Talk to me."

Valerie pressed the heels of her hands over her eyes, piecing together the images. "I saw…" She stopped, then started again. "Jerusalem had fallen. The last Saracens were fighting from the tower in the Citadel, and the crusaders convinced them to surrender. The emir of the city, his guard, and two women came out. Two men also, but the crusaders killed one of them. The baby too. Oh, Najya, they killed the baby."

Najya was silent for a moment. Then, she spoke quietly. "You can't have known that. History books only talk about ad Dawla and his guard. Nowhere do they mention the women or the baby. How could you have dreamed what only my family knows?"

Valerie drew her knees up and rested her forearms on them. "I keep trying to tell you. It wasn't a dream. It was from Nekhbet. She was here, while you slept. And if you accept a dream that's impossible, why can't you accept the possibility of Nekhbet? At least for the moment."

Najya leaned against her. "All right. For the moment. I'm sorry. I promised to suspend disbelief. Tell me more about the…scene. We'll figure this out."

Valerie stared blankly into space, letting the images emerge from memory. "There were the crusaders: Godfrey of Bouillon, Raymond of Toulouse, I think. I remember *their* names from history books, though. And I read about the emir, though I don't think I ever knew his name. The ones who surrendered, does your family story tell who they were?"

"The emir was called Idris ad Dawla, and he is the ancestor I was telling you about. We don't know the name of the two women, but they were his wives, one of them presumably my maternal ancestor. The other two men were merchants, at least the one who was killed."

Valerie took her shirt from the end of the bed and pulled it on as she stood up. She pushed the hinged window out as far as it would go. A slight evening breeze blew in, relieving the stuffiness of the room.

"There was another scene, at dusk." Valerie stared at nothing and tried to recall the details. "All of them were leaving the city, all but the one who was killed. The emir, the women, and another man behind them riding a white camel and carrying…I don't know. Something large and bulky in his camel bags."

"Yes, he appears in my family story too. A merchant, or scholar, and what he carried out of the city—stolen or rescued, I don't know—were books, precious manuscripts. They made him rich when he returned to Egypt. If you dreamt all those details, it is beyond coincidence. What else was there?"

Valerie closed her eyes. "The slaughter." She shook her head to try to dispel the memory. "Jackals had gotten into the city somehow, and they were carrying away the baby's body. She brooded a moment. "Of course," she whispered, "that's what she meant."

"Darling, you've lost me again."

"The Child of the gods was killed here in Jerusalem, by fanaticism, and by…a misunderstanding. And nothing has changed today but the degree of bloodshed. We have to send Nefi back to Egypt immediately. I'll go and get her tomorrow morning." Valerie took Najya's closed hand and brought it to her lips. "Habibti, I swear to you…on what we shared last night, I'll be able to prove all of this to you eventually. But for now, you have to trust that what I tell you is real, however bizarre it sounds. Lives depend on it!"

Najya covered Valerie's hand with her own. "Because it's you, and because of last night, I believe you."

They both startled at the sound of knocking at the door.

46

Malleus maleficarum

Itzak Ibrahim stood in the hotel corridor, eyes directed toward Valerie's feet in apparent embarrassment at standing before a strange woman's bedroom. One hand lay over his heart in a gesture of apology; the other held a rolled piece of paper.

"Forgive me, Dr. Foret, for disturbing you in the middle of the night, but my granddaughter is missing. I wanted to call the police, but I found this." He unrolled the paper with palsied hands and she took it from him.

Alarm struck her at the first line. She struggled to keep her own hand from shaking as the various possibilities flew through her head. One thing was certain though; it wasn't a police matter.

"No, it's not necessary to call the police. Everything's fine," she lied. "I'm sorry that she's caused this unnecessary concern. It looks like a mutual friend of ours has had an emergency and she's gone to her. She probably didn't want to disturb you."

Itzak raised his eyes from the floor for a moment, registered shock at her scant covering, and dropped them again. "But why didn't she leave a note in a language I know?"

"I…uh…I'm sure she didn't expect you to find it until the morning. She must have thought you'd simply telephone me and didn't imagine it would cause you so much worry. It was foolish of her, and I'll tell her so."

Appearing to be reassured, he made a slight bow and backed away, his hand once again over his heart. "Then I'm sorry to have bothered you, and thank you for your help, Dr. Foret."

"That's quite all right, Mr. Ibrahim. Please don't worry. I'm sure everything's fine. Good night." She shut the door and listened until she heard no more sound of him outside. Then she spun around. "Najya, this is it. This is the test of how much you trust me. Gods, how I need you to trust me."

"Test? What's going on?" Najya stood by the bed, the sheet wrapped toga-like around her. "The note. What does the note say?"

"She wrote it in French or, more likely, someone forced her to write it. I don't even think she speaks French." She unrolled it again under the table lamp.

"*Ils seront sacrifiés—lorsque Aton sera dans les cieux. Là ou le Messie un jour apparaîtera. Là même, la décendance de Rekemheb s'éteindre à jamais.*"

"I'm sorry. My French isn't that good." Najya leaned over her shoulder.

"They shall be sacrificed—when the Aton rises in the sky. There where the Messiah will one day appear. Thus is the line of Rekemheb extinguished forever." Valerie sat down on the bed and read the note again to herself. "It's an announcement of an execution, just what we were talking about a while ago."

"I don't understand."

"Auset and Nefi have been kidnapped. Whoever has them is going to kill them when the sun comes up. And they forced her to write this note specifically for me."

"How do you know it's not an ordinary psychopath?" Najya began to get dressed.

"He calls the sun the Aton, a term that hasn't been used in three thousand years." She read the letter for the fourth time. "'There where the Messiah shall one day come in.' What does that mean?" She clenched and unclenched her hand.

Najya stared out the window that overlooked the dark city. "This city has got messiahs and prophets everywhere," she muttered. "Via Dolorosa, Church of the Sepulchre, Bethesda—"

"But wait." She turned around. "The Messiah is supposed to enter the city one day through a double archway called the Golden Gate. All three religions see it as the place of Last Judgment. The Messiah is supposed to open the Gate of Grace for the Righteous and the Gate of Mercy for the repentant sinners."

"Can you get us through it? You must know how."

"No one can go through it, and you can't even see it from inside. It's a big hollow block. It's got a flat roof, an interior with nothing but columns, and the outside wall has been bricked up for centuries."

"All the easier to hide someone there, then." Valerie pulled on her trousers and tied her shoes while she talked. "We'd better hope they're there. We haven't got time to search the whole city."

She reached into the bottom of her knapsack and lifted out a small holstered revolver. She opened the cylinder, confirmed that it was loaded, and closed it with a flick of her hand. "I hate carrying this," she said, hooking it onto her belt. "The last time I took it out, terrible things happened. Still, there's no way I'd confront this madman unarmed, whoever he is."

Najya took a step back. "A pistol? My God, Valerie. Why can't we just call the police?"

"I told you this was a hard test. The police can't help. It's bigger than that." She fished out a small flashlight, clicked it on to test it, and slid it into her pocket.

The corridor was poorly lit, the hour late so that only the night lights were on. "It's not a simple kidnapping by a lunatic. Yussif and Derek were killed by the same person who smashed Rekemheb—and for the same reason."

"Rekemheb?" Najya stayed at her side as they descended the main stairs to the empty souq. "Isn't that the name of the priest whose empty tomb you discovered?"

The door to the hotel swung shut behind them and left them in the midnight alley.

"It wasn't empty. He was there. Not just his mummy, but also his ka—his spirit. I told you this was going to require a lot of suspended disbelief."

"No more than the rest of the Egyptian theology that you've already gotten me to suspend it for. So what has destroying Rekemheb got to do with the kidnapping?"

The tin shutters that covered every shop in the tunnel-like Souq Khan al Zeit gave back a faint echo to their footfall and voices.

"He's the link. When he was alive, as a priest in the court of Meremptah, he heard the prophecy that his descendants would bring the gods back. The sequence of attacks—first on his mummy, which killed his ka, and then on the two fathers—shows that someone, something, is set on wiping out all his descendants."

They emerged from the tunnel onto the Via Dolorosa.

"Wait. Descendants?"

"Derek, me, and ultimately Nefi, the Child. And I'm sure now that Nefi is at the heart of it. Someone is removing the rest of us, one by one, to get to her."

Rats scurried along the sides of the narrow street just ahead of them as if to clear the way of obstacles. They quickened their pace.

"But why Nefi? She's just a baby."

"No, she's not. She has a connection to the wild things that the rest of us don't have. More importantly, she inherited some kind of mission that we don't understand yet. Nekhbet presented her to the gods the night of her birth and said the Child would always be under her wing. But I can't see what good it's done. It hasn't kept her from being kidnapped."

They were almost running now.

"I know a way to the gate that won't attract any attention. This way." Najya pivoted right onto the Al Wad and left on the Aqabat Tekeyah. "We have to go across the Temple Mount."

Inside the grounds of the Dome precinct, Valerie felt less visible. Though the vast open court off to their right was bathed in light, and the golden dome itself shone, the row of trees along the north wall behind the lamps afforded them cover. Where they ran on hard-packed soil they made speed, but where they met stone, they had to slow to keep from slipping. The rain and infestations of the previous day had made every exposed surface slick with slime.

Then they were on open ground again, grass-covered, exposed, but no one apparently bothered to guard empty space. Somewhere a dog barked but, mercifully, not for them.

"There it is." Najya halted suddenly, panting. "The double portal," she said between breaths. "Still waiting for the Messiah."

It rose high and dark overhead, more a massive stone tower than a gate and scarcely welcoming, for man or god. Its two inside portals were covered by rusted iron gates that stretched from ground to archway.

Valerie shone the flashlight beam through the bars into a cavernous space. Two rows of columns supported the roof, and nothing inside moved. "There doesn't seem to be any place to hide people. Is there a warden's room anywhere that I can't see?"

"No, only a stairwell to the roof."

Valerie ran the flashlight over the entire gate. "Look, the lock's been cut. I guess that gives us our answer. They're here."

Najya tugged vigorously on the iron rim. The gate swung toward them with a metallic groan, scraping along a groove that had been made earlier.

Inside the gate chamber the fluttering and squeaking in the darkness told them that small creatures fled from them along the floor and overhead. The columns cast ominous shadows that moved like wheel spokes as the flashlight beam swept across them. Against the far wall, the outline of the exterior gates curved over their two walls of bricks.

Valerie tried to imagine the hall filled with joyful celebrants shouting and throwing palms as the Messiah entered. The pretty image was difficult to sustain in sight of the grime on the walls and the smell of mold. The whole city smelled musty now, she noted, since the vermin-filled rain.

"There's nothing here...and no place to hide," Valerie concluded.

"Except in the stairwell, over there." Najya pointed toward a narrow door in the farthest corner. They shone the light beam through the doorway and, pivoting around, up the stone staircase. Then they heard it. Laughter.

"So. You solved the puzzle," a male voice called down to them in English. "Well, it wasn't a very difficult one. Come on up." The faintly accented voice sounded familiar.

As they climbed the stairs, Valerie drew her pistol and held it behind her. She stepped out onto the rooftop, her foot slipping out from under her for a second on the slimy surface so that the flashlight beam went wild. Then she caught her balance.

For a moment she saw only a black form silhouetted against the paler night sky. Valerie swung the light beam on him.

"What the hell?"

47

Ils sont Sacrifiés

Najya walked toward the hulking figure in the flashlight beam. "Harry? What is this? What are you doing?"

"Hello, Najya. You're looking good. How's your new girlfriend treating you?" He moved slightly to the side of Auset, who was tied up at his feet. Nefi squatted petrified and silent next to her mother, clutching her arm.

Najya stopped, her eyes seeming to measure the distance between Harry and herself, between him and the edge of the roof. "You haven't answered my question."

Slightly ahead of her, Valerie also stopped, acutely aware of the fact that she and Harry both had guns. But hers was pointed at him from a distance while his was pressed directly against Auset's head. "What's this all about? What do you want?"

He laughed out loud. "So many questions." He turned his face into profile for a moment, like a preening film star. "You still don't recognize me, do you? Well, I always was the handsome younger brother. Volker was the odd one, and ten years older."

"Brother?" It took Valerie a moment to absorb the information. "Volker Vanderschmitt had a brother?"

"Yes, I'm surprised he never mentioned me." For a second, the sarcasm left his voice and he seemed disappointed. "Well, no matter. The important thing is that he knew what you were—and how dangerous— and he died trying to stop you." He raised his free hand to shield his eyes. "Take that light out of my face or I'll shoot it out."

She dropped the beam to his chest, and by the ambient light she could still see both his face and his crouched victim.

Auset sat effectively immobilized, her hands tied under her knees. A cloth gag covered her mouth, though it looked as if she'd managed to work her jaw halfway free. She watched the exchange between Valerie and Harry, but made no sound.

Valerie concentrated on his face. He *was* better looking than his

Akhnaton-faced brother, but his cold, dead expression seemed far more ominous than Volker's aloofness.

"But you must know, he died in a sandstorm outside El Kharga. There was an investigation afterward. It was in all the papers."

"He was eaten by vultures," he answered in a monotone.

"I'm sorry about that. But it's what happens in the desert."

"He followed you there, but you came back, and he didn't. Don't lie to me like you did to all the others. I know the real strory. You were under his authority, but you didn't like it. Instead you went on a rampage, and when he tried to rein you in, you killed him and left him for the vultures. Did you think there would be no consequences?"

"Rampage? What are you talking about? It was nothing like that."

He seemed only then to take note that she pointed a pistol at him. "Put that stupid gun down. Kick it off the roof, or I'll put a bullet through her the way I did Derek." At the word "her" he pressed the tip of his automatic to the side of Auset's head.

Jolted by the murder confession, Valerie searched for alternatives and found none. No matter how accurately she aimed, it would not be good enough, while *his* shot would be deadly. She laid her pistol down in front of her and nudged it over the edge of the roof with her foot. She heard Najya exhale in a sigh that spoke for both of them. Now all they had were their wits.

"He was killed in a sandstorm," she persisted. "I wasn't even there. And besides, what have Auset and her baby got to do with what happened to Volker?"

He snorted. "Did you think this was all just a little vendetta? Revenge for the family honor? Oh, no." He expanded his chest and set his pelvis forward like a gladiator stepping into the arena. *Morituri salutant*, she thought, ironically, but he was there to do the killing, not the dying.

"I know about this sick little religion you're trying to get started. Animal worship. Something we left behind us thousands of years ago."

"How do you know about that?" Valerie was astonished. "Your brother didn't know anything about it. Nobody does."

He smiled coldly, obviously pleased at being able to surprise her. "Volker wrote me about you stealing the mummy. He was sure something strange was going on, and he was getting close. That's why you killed him, isn't it?"

She shook her head. "You've got it all twisted around."

He continued, ignoring the remark. "After I found out about it, I began to do a little research. About the excavation, about you, and one thing led to another. I've been following you for two years." He tilted his head back, to deliver the last blow. "I even read your demented manuscript."

"My chronicle? That's not possible."

"Of course it's possible. How many drafts did you go through and discard before you submitted it?"

"You went through my garbage?"

"Never mind how I got it. But it revealed everything about you and your filthy cult."

His words hit her like a blow to the chest. He was the first person, the only person, to read her revelation. He was the test case. "But if you read the manuscript, then you know how your brother died. You know everything! You know about Rekemheb and the coming of the gods!"

Her head began to swim. Was her chronicle so inept that it could convert no one—just another fantasy novel on the market? She would have been humiliated if fear had not taken up all the room in her mind.

"Yes, your lunatic fantasy. It made my skin crawl to read it. I smashed your mummy just to prove nothing would happen, and I was right. You didn't even notice. To get you here, I had to move down the list to the next one in your little family of perverts. Two of you queer, and *this* one…" He pushed Auset's head again with the gun barrel. "Fornicating with a black man. And your talking animals. Do you think anyone is going to believe that crap?"

She tried another tack. "If it's such crap, how is it harming you? Why are you so worked up about it?"

"Because it's evil, and somebody will always fall for it. For generations my family has fought for the right—in the military, the government, even in the church. I may have been slow to accept the family mission. I was a weakling, a pretty-boy. But Volker's death changed everything. It made me a man—a man who had the courage to deal with you and your sort."

"My sort?" She tried not to look at Auset, but out of the corner of her eye she could see that she was slowly changing position, preparing something. Harry didn't notice.

"Yes, all of you 'rights' screamers. Immigrants, feminists, eco-terrorists, homosexuals. Now your little cult wants everyone to become atheists and worship animals. You won't be satisfied until you've dragged us all down. Someone has to stop you."

"Stop us from what, exactly? We haven't done anything." She was stalling now, letting Auset do whatever she was planning.

"From increasing your disgusting little cult. No more children of Rekemheb—no more cult. It's as simple as that."

He glanced toward Najya. "Sorry you had to get mixed up in this, but you were a very good lure. And now you've gone and become a believer, haven't you?" He shook his head. "Women are so gullible."

Najya seemed dazed. She stared at him, engaging him. Nothing in the world seemed to interest her at that moment but Harry. "Yes, it *is* a pity. We had something good there in Cairo, didn't we?"

Auset, meanwhile, had drawn up one leg until her knee touched her chest.

Najya's voice went dark and velvety, and the still night air carried it to him. "All I believe in is my work. You should know that by now. But Cairo *was* good. I'd hoped we could do another assignment together." She edged sideways, causing him to pivot around and put Auset directly behind him. "It's a shame we can't…"

Valerie saw the ploy and edged to the right as well, holding his attention.

He was clearly flattered, just enough to be off guard for a moment, and as he tilted his head again for his reply, the gun barrel dropped a few centimeters. "I guess there's something about a real man. Women always like—uff!"

Auset's foot had shot out suddenly, knocking his leg out from under him. He caught himself right away and only went to one knee, but in the few seconds it took him to refocus, they were on him.

Their combined force threw him backward onto the ground. He still held the gun but could not raise his arm. Valerie lay across the right side of his chest and grasped his wrist. She pounded it on the brick until he lost his grip and the pistol slid off his palm to lie between little pink shoes.

Furiously, he arched his back and managed to roll toward the left, but Valerie and Najya still held him flat to keep him from scrabbling back toward the weapon that lay at the feet of the child he planned to kill.

Auset thrust her chin out and freed her mouth from the gag. "Pick it up, darling," she said, sounding both soothing and urgent. "Ummi says it's all right to touch. Pick it up, habibti."

Timidly, Nefi grasped the gun with two hands by the barrel and held it in the air like a tomahawk.

Harry was on hands and knees now, dragging himself toward her. His outstretched hand was a few centimeters from the little feet. "Throw the gun over the edge, darling. Throw it away. It's nasty. *Bisurah*! *Bisurah*!" Auset urged.

Thrown off balance by the weight of the gun, Nefi toddled awkwardly toward the edge. "Be careful, don't go too far," Auset called after her "Put it on the ground, habibti, and push!"

Harry rolled onto his back again and managed to free one arm. He delivered a powerful punch to the side of Valerie's head, stunning her, then slid out from under her and Najya and flung himself toward Nefi.

He snatched the pistol by its handle with a grunt of triumph, but his momentum carried him to the edge. He tried to crouch again to slow himself, but the mold-covered bricks gave him no purchase, and he flailed as first one foot, then the other slipped over the edge. In a last desperate movement, he grasped Nefi's arm and pulled her with him into dark, empty space.

48

Heartbreak

Nightmarish. They hurled themselves down the stairwell to the inner gate, then dashed along the inside of the city wall all the way to the next opening at the Lion's Gate. Hysterical, inconsolable, Auset staggered behind them, gasping, her incoherent sobs reduced to a desperate wet breathing. The run seemed to take forever.

From the Lion's Gate they doubled back along the same wall on the outside of the Old City, stumbling over the irregular ground. Valerie rushed ahead with the flashlight, pushing all thought from her mind.

At the foot of the double gate was a Muslim cemetery surrounded by an iron railing. Valerie cleared it, barely breaking stride. The others followed a minute later, and the three of them ran stumbling among the ancient tombstones.

They found him immediately, at the foot of the wall, the hollow at the back of his skull revealing how he died. Valerie might have felt a twinge of sorrow for him if his death had not also been a murder. She swept the light in a circle around him, her chest aching with dread. But she found no small broken body near him.

"He had her by the arm. She can't have fallen anywhere else. Or crawled away," Valerie added, sickened by the thought.

Auset rushed among the stones calling her baby's name, sobbing, dropping to her knees, then staggering to the next dark spot.

Valerie saw no point in trying to hold her back. They were all living the nightmare vision she had seen just hours before. The shattering thought came to her. Were they forced actors in an ever-recurring tragedy, the casting of the gods' Child from the adversary's walls onto the rock below? Would it always end this way?

Najya leaned over Harry's body again. "Wait. Look at his right hand, the one that grabbed Nefi. He's holding something else." She pried the object out of his clenched fingers and Valerie shone the light on it.

The white plaster statue of Venus de Milo glowed up at her. She turned the bottom up and saw her own name. It was the statue that

Derek had given her, the one that should have been at the bottom of her
backpack at the hotel.

❖

"That's impossible."

Najya took her by the shoulder. "Didn't you say that Nefi was
'under Nekhbet's wing'? Couldn't she have taken her in some way—
and left this to tell us where?"

"Take her? How? Snatched her out of mid-air?"

"I don't know. But she's a goddess. Can't they do things like
that?"

Valerie winced with uncertainty. Could it be that simple? What
if they were wrong and Nefi lay somewhere, critically injured, in the
darkness? Could they leave her there while they followed some vague
promise? Valerie felt madness creeping in. "Where, then?" she almost
whined. "What the hell sort of clue is the Venus de Milo? We're in
bloody Jerusalem, not Paris."

Auset still scrabbled around in the brush, calling Nefi's name,
choking.

Every sound pierced Valerie's chest like a blade.

Najya clasped Valerie's hand that held the tiny statue. "Listen to
me. You said trust is everything. You said that Nekhbet had sworn to
protect Nefi 'under her wing.' Isn't this *your* test then, and not mine? If
you trust her and her promise, then the Venus is the message. And if it's
not, then we both go back to being atheists."

"All right. All right. So tell me." Valerie's hand was shaking.
"How is Venus the message?"

"This is a long shot, but there *is* a Venus temple—at least the ruins
of one—in Jerusalem."

Auset sat now, her arms around her knees, trembling. "What if
she's here some place? A baby's bones are soft. She could still be alive.
I won't leave her. It'll be morning soon. We'll be able to see her."

Valerie looked back and forth between them. Go or wait? Her
brain felt torn in two. Finally, she crawled over in front of Auset.

"We were made a promise, and this promise is everything. If it's
true, we'll find Nefi. You were at Dendara. You saw Nekhbet carry Nefi
on her wings. That's got to mean something. This is the test for all of

us—to remember that night." She paused for a breath and said, with a certainty she did not feel, "Nefi is in the Temple of Venus."

Auset was limp, seemingly incapable of willful response. She covered her face with her hands, her pale fingers jutting through the strands of her disheveled hair. "All right," she rasped weakly. "I'll go."

Valerie looked toward Najya, who, of all people, had argued Nekhbet's case. "And where might that temple be?"

Najya was already on her feet, brushing dirt from her trousers. "Under the Church of the Holy Sepulchre."

49

Church of the Sepulchre

I can't believe you have the key to the Church of the Sepulchre," Valerie said.

Najya stood before the wide wooden door of the portal and tried to fit an iron key into the lock. "I told you my family's been part of this city for generations. My father is one of the doorkeepers." The key refused to turn and she yanked it out.

"A Muslim with the key to a Christian church?"

"It's been that way since the Middle Ages. A Muslim porter locks the great doors at night and opens them again in the morning. The same two families have been doing it for centuries."

"Please…hurry." Wild-eyed and disheveled, Auset rocked from one foot to the other, her hands clenching and unclenching like restless things.

Helpless to assist otherwise, Valerie glanced around the courtyard, surveying the surrounding buildings for signs they might be watched. All was silent. She directed her attention back to the portal. "It doesn't look much like a church."

Najya chose a second key. "It's really a collection of chapels, sanctuaries, tombs, and shrines. And six different sects maintain them." The second key head was also too large.

"Damn." She let the second key fall back on the ring and tried a third. "It started with Constantine, who sent his mother Helena to pick a spot for a church. She chose the Temple of Venus, she said, because she found a piece of the True Cross here. A coincidence, of course."

"Please. Can we skip the history lesson and just get inside?" Auset pressed her forehead on the oaken door as if she could will it open.

The key slid into the aperture and Najya turned the lock slowly, exhaling relief. She opened the door, wincing as it creaked at every centimeter.

The interior was dimly lit from bronze lamps that hung in a row of truncated amphorae over a wide stone. The moment they were inside they heard the sound, the musical murmurings of a chant from the western end of the church.

"I was afraid of this," Valerie whispered. "All-night service."

Najya listened for a moment. "It's from the rotunda," she whispered back. "We should be okay. We're going in the opposite direction." She led them to the right, along a dark corridor. Halfway down, they passed a stone formation that jutted up through the floor to the ceiling and formed a portion of the church wall.

Valerie stopped and studied the pale, pockmarked formation. "What's this? A rock in the church?"

Najya stopped next to her. "You *are* a terrible Catholic. That's Calvary, where they crucified Him."

"Please, can we hurry?" Auset rushed ahead of them, then waited, rocking with impatience for Najya to lead the way again.

"It's that way, around the ambulatory." Najya led them past another dark chapel on the right. A narrow staircase lay just ahead at the foot of the curve.

"We have to go through the chapel of St. Helena right below us. There's a smaller chapel below that, where she supposedly found the True Cross. Any Roman ruins will be there."

"Maatha tafaalani huna?" a gruff voice called out, startling them all. The speaker stepped into the light, a black-clad, heavily bearded orthodox priest. He switched to English. "What are you doing here in the middle of the night?"

Najya recovered first. She produced a press card, which would have been unreadable in the poor light even if he had accepted it, which he didn't. She assumed a measured tone, both apologetic and self-confident. "Excuse us, Father." She added his ecclesiastical title. "I am Najya Khoury, daughter of Shafiq Khoury ibn Idris, the doorkeeper. We are doing historical research and were trying not to disturb the service."

The priest was unimpressed. "At 2:30 in the morning, the church is not open for anything but worship. Not for anyone. The doorkeeper knows that. You will have to leave—both of you."

Both? Valerie resisted the urge to look around for Auset. "Uh...we do apologize. Both of us."

"This way." He extended a black silk-encased arm in the direction they had come. "Immediately—or I will call for assistance."

Najya was the consummate professional. "That won't be necessary, Father. We were finished anyhow and can show ourselves out. Thank you for your help."

"This way," he repeated the gruff command, urging them ahead of him down the ambulatory to the portal, then out. Behind them, the bolt slid into the great lock with a thud of finality.

Valerie leaned against the door. "This nightmare just won't end. And poor Auset. She's hiding some place, half mad, and now locked in. We've got to get back to her somehow."

Najya fished out the key ring again and slid one key after another along the metal loop. Finally she held up a small one, half the size of the portal key. "I thought this was here. It's the key to a maintenance entrance on the other side. It will get us in, but we'll have to get past the service again."

"Then we'd better hurry."

❖

They crept from column to chapel to column again, trusting in the fervor of the worship service to keep attention away from them as they flitted along the periphery. Every bend and corner in the church held danger, and they did not dare to use the flashlight.

"So now, here we are, back in the corridor where we started, and without Auset," Valerie whispered. "And what if we're wrong? It tears my heart out to think we might have brought her here for nothing, while Nefi is lying outside the walls." She covered her face for a moment. "Gods. How could it have come to this?"

Najya took her by the arm. "Don't mourn yet. Down there is the Chapel of St. Helena, and it's even lit." They were on the stone staircase now, and her voice echoed slightly against the stone walls.

At the foot of the stairs they looked up into a large square crypt. Its roof was supported by four inner columns that formed another square at the center. High overhead, small semicircular windows looked out at ground level on three sides. Dozens of bronze amphorae hung on chains from the ceiling, though none gave light. Rather, a soft glow emanated from the massive glass chandelier at the center and from small lamps attached to the two chapels on the eastern side. The floor was covered with an elaborate mosaic.

"One more level down—at least." Najya pointed to narrow stone steps that dropped into darkness. She took a turn with the flashlight and clicked it on as they descended.

At the bottom, she swept the light beam in a wide curve. It illuminated a roughly cylindrical space carved in bedrock. The rough-hewn rock was covered with Plexiglas panels. Directly across from the stairs was a tiny chapel with a simple Latin altar and, above it, a large bronze statue of a woman holding a cross to her shoulder.

"No chance that's Venus, is there?" Valerie remarked.

"No. More St. Helena, of course. This is the place she's supposed to have found the cross. Grim, isn't it? But this is where it stops." She strode to the near end of the row of Plexiglas panels. "But behind this partition is an opening to yet another chamber, maybe several. Archaeologists know that they're here, but the religious groups that control the church aren't interested in excavating them. They're pre-Christian."

Najya was already wedging herself behind the first panel and shining the flashlight along the rock ahead of her.

Valerie followed and edged forward in the darkness behind her. She heard Najya's sudden intake of breath, then the clattering of the flashlight falling on stone. They were engulfed in blackness. "What's wrong, Najya. Are you all right?" Blindly, she slid along the rock face. Her right shoulder slid off the wall into a vertical opening, and she dropped to her knees. She groped helplessly in the darkness until she felt a curved back. Najya was kneeling.

"What is it?"

Valerie bumped her head on the rock, but forced herself to calm, to wait, feeling Najya, seemingly unharmed, under her hands. Then her eyes began to adjust to the darkness, and over Najya's shoulder she could slowly make them out. Finally she heard their voices. Her fear and dread evaporated in an instant, and she too broke into tears of relief and gratitude.

50

Temple of Venus

Valerie found the flashlight finally, clicked it on, and pointed it toward them. At the center of a circle of broken columns, Auset stood with her arms around both her living child and the one who held her, the ka of Yussif Nabil. On both sides of them, like best men at a wedding, were the kas of Derek and Rekemheb. They turned slowly and gazed unblinking into the light.

Derek had on his dark "church suit," though his clean white shirt was stained at the front with a wide circle of blood. Yussif was in the galabaya he'd worn on the fatal train trip to Luxor and would wear now forever. His face was expressionless, as always, behind his beard, but his eyes glistened with tears. Nefi's head was on his shoulder, though she slept, and her feet dangled under his forearm in little pink shoes.

Derek laid his cheek on Auset's head and placed a kiss somewhere in her wild hair, then looked again at Valerie. "Hi, sweetie," he said quietly.

"So, it was you after all." Valerie entered the cave-like chamber and embraced him, tingling when her cheek touched his, as from a faint electric charge.

"What did you…? How is it possible…?" she sputtered.

The ka of Derek Ragin chuckled softly and took both of her hands in his. "Calm down, girlfriend. We'll explain everything."

She stepped back to appraise him. She could see the difference now between him and Rekemheb, though the ka radiance shone from both of them. "I see you made it past the judges after all."

His mouth twitched toward the side. "Only just. The scales doomed us both for our heavy hearts. Jehuti spoke for us, but even he had to make a deal with the judges. He promised them a new believer to show the prophecy was still on, but of course that depended on you." He hugged her again. "I knew you could do it."

"You've answered one important question. No, you don't need to be mummified."

"Yes, but since we're not, Yussif and I are sort of temporary. We're going to need some statues quickly before…you know. Before we fall apart." His eyes lit on Najya, who still stood, frozen, at the entrance. "Who's your lovely friend, sweetie?"

"Oh, I'm sorry." Valerie took Najya by the arm and drew her forward. "Derek, may I introduce Najya Khoury: journalist, Jerusalemite, and…the believer who saved you. Najya, this is Derek Ragin, my opera-singer friend. And that…" she nodded toward the embracing couple. "That, of course, is Yussif."

"Hello, Najya. Welcome to our side." Derek leaned over and kissed her lightly on the cheek.

She jumped at the spark of contact with the afterlife and drew away. "A pleasure, I'm sure. But you know. I'll…just stand over here out of the way while you all get reacquainted." Her glance slid to Yussif, who still whispered comfort to Auset, then to the third apparition.

He was bare-chested, as always, with his hands behind his back, but the smile on his usually somber face was new.

"Najya, this is Rekemheb, Priest of Hathor and our ancient ancestor, Derek's and mine."

"I finally meet your mysterious priest. Hello." Najya offered her hand.

Rekemheb took the hand, which seemed to send another jolt of otherworldliness up her arm, and bowed from the waist. "We have been doubly blessed. Our new sister is also very fair of face."

Najya smiled uncertainly, then glanced sideways at Valerie. "Is he flirting with me?"

"Maybe. But I don't think he's right for you. You know…dead and all." Valerie addressed the ka again. "Why didn't you show yourself in your tomb? I was certain the statue ceremony had failed."

"I could not. I was too far gone and I had no substance. I gathered it slowly, but it was days before I could even move an object. And I had to do that, a very precious object, as you saw. That was more important than comforting you."

"The amulet. That was you, then. In the museum."

"Yes, to keep it safe for the Child. We could no longer leave it with you."

"Why not?" She dropped her eyes as the answer became self-evident. "Oh. You expected me to be killed too, is that it?"

"I'm afraid so," he said with unexpected candor. "Auset had just fled to the city of the Aton and you would soon follow. We could not protect you." Then he added, "It was Nekhbet's wish."

"Ah, Nekhbet. Of course." Then she heard the fluttering in the next chamber, and at the edge of the circle of light she saw the great black wing.

"Nekhbet."

At the sound of her name, the goddess made a faint gesture, the smallest motion of her hand, and the chamber glowed. No lantern was visible, but the walls themselves emitted a soft amber light. Nekhbet stood before what might once have been a statue, but only the plinth remained.

Valerie ventured into the second chamber and confronted the familiar harsh beauty. She understood Nekhbet now and grasped the fragility of the prophecy. It could fail. It *had* failed once; she had seen it through Nekhbet's agonized eyes.

They were like an old married couple that had come full circle. Valerie had passed through desire for the Bedouin, to abject awe of the goddess, to recriminations, and finally to a deep, abiding sympathy. She no longer needed Nekhbet to love her back.

"The hieroglyph for 'protection.' I understand it now." She let herself fall into the fathomless coal black pupils. "I wish I could have seen you snatch her out of mid-air."

"I was not always so skillful," Nekhbet replied with quiet remorse.

Najya had followed Valerie into the second chamber and now stood beside her. She stared, rapt, at the entity who seemed to stand, but, in fact, hovered a centimeter above the ground.

The moment was as intense as it was awkward, and the air crackled, with what? Jealousy? Confusion? Valerie thought of the scene in the hotel room. She shook her head, shutting an internal door on the whole painful dynamic, and extended a hand in each of their directions.

"Nekhbet, this is our first new believer, whom you have…uh… seen before. A journalist. As the Book of the Dead says, she 'lives on truth, and none may testify against her.'"

"Be careful where you walk. This is a hallowed place." Nekhbet's reply seemed a non sequitur, and Valerie was disappointed. But then the goddess dropped her eyes to look between them, and her expression changed to tenderness.

Nefi stood there, looking somber and troubled, as no two-year-old should ever be.

Valerie and Najya both made way for her, and she placed herself directly before Nekhbet. Taking hold of the black feathery garment just above the divine knee, she tugged gently, her little lips trembling.

"Netjeret nebu. Tcheni," she intoned solemnly.

"What's she saying?" Najya whispered.

Without taking her eyes from goddess and Child, Valerie whispered back, "She said 'Where is the yellow bird?' Don't ask me what it means."

"It is there, darling." Nekhbet pointed to a corner of the chamber, to a stone tablet that lay flat on the ground. Covered with dust and streaked with the damp soil of the chamber, it had escaped their notice.

"Lift it up," she said to Valerie. "Please."

Najya and Valerie knelt by the tablet and brushed the dirt away from its edges. When they had exposed enough of the stone to take hold of it, they wrenched it upward onto its side. In the hollow of packed earth beneath rested a simple wooden box.

"Open it," Nekhbet said softly.

Valerie pried up the cover with shaking hands—and nearly dropped it again.

A tiny skeleton lay curled at the center. Its skull was cracked, and the tiny bones of its hands were still closed into fists. Its tattered smock, hidden from the light for centuries, still had its rust red color. At the front, an embroidered panel showed a yellow bird in flight.

Valerie felt a wave of unendurable sorrow.

"The hundredth generation," Nekhbet said.

"I know." Valerie touched the smock with the tip of her finger. "So this is where the jackals brought her. I'm glad." She closed the coffin again and laid the tablet tenderly back in place. There would be no need to ever open it again.

Nefi stood now at the foot of the gravestone, her own fists clenched against her chest. She began to cry, with the weak, fearful sound of an abandoned baby. Behind her, Auset too looked ashen.

"Do not cry, Child." A male voice suddenly spoke. Rekemheb had entered the chamber, and his customary faint radiance seemed to increase at the center of his chest as he wafted near. He knelt on one knee before Nefi and carefully uncurled one of her fists.

"The bird you dreamt of is not gone," he said soothingly. "Look." With that he scooped his hand into his own glowing chest. Withdrawing it, he held a bird, the size of a small parrot and as radiant as he was, perched on his knuckles. "You see, it is my ba."

Nefi stared at the creature, eyes glistening, then held out a finger to touch it.

Rekemheb smiled with both his faces, on his ka and on his ba. "Now I will show you something even better."

With a deft twist of the wrist, he seemed to set his ba-bird on some perch back inside himself. He held out his empty hand for a moment, like a magician about to do a trick, then slid his fingers into the same place on her chest as he had on his own.

Enchanted, Nefi looked down as Rekemheb withdrew his hand and held it up to her. A budgie-like creature glowed at the center of his palm, lighting her face like a lantern from below. She watched it, rapt, her mouth forming an "O," then kissed its narrow head. The ba-bird opened its wings slightly and fluttered.

"This is yourself, my precious one, and this is how you will come to us one day. But not for a very long time." Rekemheb let the ba-bird slip again into the infant chest. Nefi giggled softly, as if tickled, then grew solemn again as her ancient grandfather kissed her head in turn. "Remember us, darling, and never be afraid," he said, and as he stood up again, he faded away to nothing.

Nefi sighed once and, like the exhausted baby she was, she raised her arms to be picked up by her mother.

"It is time you took her to her proper place, and we returned to ours," Nekhbet said, drawing a conclusion to the spectacle.

Auset was not satisfied. "So, what do we do now? Is this going to go on forever? The Aton can strike her a thousand ways, everywhere we go: not just madmen, but lightning, sandstorm, plane crash. I hate this and I want it to stop."

Nekhbet raised a hand. "The Aton in all his names is no force of nature. He is held aloft solely on the wind of men's belief, like their nations and their exalted offices. His power to harm is only through his believers. You must be on guard against all those who represent Him too aggressively. But we will look after you. The Child is always under my wing. Return to Egypt."

"And Derek's stepfather?" Auset added a final objection, but her voice lacked conviction.

"His threat was small, as you surely knew." Nekhbet clasped her hands in front of her in school-teacher fashion.

"And what about Nefi's father...fathers, actually. They will be all right?" Valerie knew the answer, but wanted confirmation.

Nekhbet backed away, apparently finished with the audience. "You know well you must make a likeness of them, and you must do it soon, before their forms are taken back into the earth. Now go, my patience wears thin."

She looked again at Najya, her expression unreadable. With the sound of fluttering wings, she assumed for an instant the shape of the great vulture, then a hollow of colorless air. An instant later the illumination in the chamber flickered out, and they were plunged into total darkness.

"Damn. I hate it when she does that," Valerie groused, fishing in her pocket for the flashlight. She clicked it on and saw that the others had already moved toward the first chamber.

"They've all gone," Auset said. "It's just us now." Nefi had fallen into exhausted sleep, and Auset shifted her higher on her shoulder.

Valerie touched her on the back. "Are you all right, Auset? After everything that's happened?"

"Yeah, I think so." Auset sighed. "I was a little crazy there for awhile, but I'm okay now. I have Nefi back and soon, I hope, Yussif."

Valerie swept the walls of the chamber one last time with the flashlight beam. "Then let's get out of this hole." She pointed the light beam toward the crevasse leading from the underground chambers back to the lowest chapel. Auset went ahead, and Najya walked by Valerie's side.

"The story of a lifetime, and no one on earth will believe me," she muttered.

"I know what you mean," Valerie said as they slid along the Plexiglas panels and into the stone chapel. At the top of the stairs, the chapel of St. Helena was now dark, though a dull blue-gray came from the hemispheric windows high above them.

On the second stairway leading upward, Auset took a last look at the pit from which they had just emerged. Valerie stopped with her. "Do you trust Nekhbet now, after all this?"

"I don't trust any of them. I'm so sick of religion and religions. Those gods and their priests and mullahs and rabbis. They throw you into despair from which they offer to rescue you again. I wash my hands of all of them."

"I know what you mean. As a scientist, I choose no religion, but unfortunately, religion keeps choosing me."

At the top of the stairs, Najya took the flashlight and went to offer assistance to Auset. The corridor that led to the portal was dark, as the rest of the church was now. Only the pale granite of Calvary loomed again before them on the left. Najya directed the flashlight along the stone floor of the corridor as she and Auset passed the great rock.

Two steps behind them, Valerie halted suddenly. "Oh, no."

51

Ecce Homo

S he was full of dread, yet sick to death of dreading. She should have known. There was no way an alien deity like Nekhbet could penetrate so sacrosanct a place without provoking a response. This was it then.

His long hair was matted with blood under the crown of thorns. He was nearly naked, a ragged, bloodstained cloth around his hips the only covering. His pale white body was terrible to see, bruised and lacerated, and he hunched slightly. He did not speak, but only breathed painfully as a man exhausted and broken by torment.

Auset circled back, clearly impatient. "What is it?"

"She sees something," Najya answered. To Valerie she said, "There's no one there. Only some dust from the rock. Come on, you're exhausted. We're *all* exhausted."

Valerie stepped even closer, until she stood only a meter from him, but still he did not speak. Or perhaps he did and she could not hear him, for his lips moved slightly. She waited, oblivious to the anxious voices of her friends. Finally she touched him. She flinched from the shock of the touch and the realization that he felt exactly like the pagan gods when they had touched her and opened her spirit to another place. But his place was a place of agony.

"I thought I was free of you," she said to him softly. "Now I have to believe in you again."

The man of sorrows held out his own hands which, like those of Rekemheb, held a light of their own. They trembled, and blood ran from the palms along his fingers. He rasped, "No. You only make it worse."

"I don't understand."

The Savior shook his head, feebly. "I am only a part of Him who lives also in His believers. But in his believers He is set against Himself, and His right hand smites His left." The voice was soft, but hoarse as if his throat, like every other part of him, was raw.

Valerie shook her head. Fighting between sects who claimed the same God was no revelation to anyone. "What has that got to do with us? We aren't Christians."

"You must tell them." He spoke slowly, his head thrown back slightly, forcing every word over the open sores of his mouth. "I was a teacher, a healer, a maker of wine and bread. I too was a Child in the temple." He paused a moment with closed eyes.

She couldn't tell if it was from the exertion of talking, or whether he was recalling a time of celebration rather than pain.

He opened his eyes again, and they were filled with tears. "The stories that men tell are not of my righteousness and joy, but of my martyrdom. They could have chosen the healer or the winemaker, but they pray instead to the cross that tortured me. They pray to this." The Christ touched his side where the ribs were visible under his translucent skin. Blood oozed from a long diagonal wound into the cloth around his hips.

"Tell them, please, to stop."

The stories that men tell. Valerie thought of the scribe god's warning of the power of the word. She wondered if the two forms of god could ever talk to each other, whether Jehuti could solace him. No, she realized, the One God had torn himself away from all the others.

"*Je suis désolée,*" she said, in the language of her childhood prayers, with more piety than she had ever felt as a believer. "I will try to explain to people. Though I don't think they will listen."

He seemed to slump and his hands dropped to his sides. He looked up at her one last time, and she noticed what beautiful eyes he had, with lashes like a girl's.

"No, they won't," he whispered. "They want the martyr." Closing his eyes again, he withdrew, pressing his back to the rock of his Golgotha, the "place of skulls."

"Wait," she said, recalling the anxiety of her first communion. "Please. Are my sins forgiven?"

He looked at her for a moment, as if not comprehending the question. Then he shook his head. "I am not the judge," he said, and faded back into the rock of Calvary.

Finally, she heard their voices.

Najya laid a hand on her shoulder and shook her gently. "Come on, darling."

She led her the rest of the way out of the church, and it was not until they stood before the portal that Valerie spoke. "Did you see him? Did you hear what he said to me?"

Najya laid her arm around her back. "Whatever you saw and heard, we can analyze it later. I'm so tired I can't talk any more."

Auset shifted the quiet baby to her other shoulder. "Yes. I have a wet two-year-old in my arms, and I haven't slept in days."

Grainy-eyed and dazed, Valerie stepped between them and slipped her arms through theirs. In the cool predawn air, their physical warmth on both sides of her was a deep comfort. "Yes, for god's sake, let's go home."

52

Remembrance

Faaria leaned on her stick and peered with dim eyes at her brother as he shuffled from the courtyard of the newly finished mortuary of Husaam al Noori. Though he was older than she, age had been kinder to him, she realized. Well, he had also not borne six children. She, on the other hand, now felt every one of her nearly seventy years and had been under a pall for a year since the death of Amhara.

"It's beautiful, Sharif. A pity it will stay empty though, while Husaam's bones lie some place in Jerusalem."

"Not completely empty. I've had the masons build a modest tomb in the back, a simple sarcophagus, for me. If I can't lie by his side in death, I can lie by his monument."

"Fair enough. Though I think his spirit would have been content with less splendor. Since you have no children to spend all your money on, you can spend it on mine."

He took her arm and they hobbled together, two bent figures, back to the main road of the necropolis. "Your children are doing quite well, Faaria, and do not need me. Do not begrudge this tribute to Husaam, in whose household we both found someone who loved us. Besides, the money that I've earned all these years began with the sale of his great manuscripts. When I saved them from Jerusalem, I knew they had value, but I did not know how much."

"Jerusalem," Faaria mused. "What a horror. I have almost erased the nightmare from my mind. And would have sooner if the vizier had not constantly called my husband to account for the loss of it."

"Idris ad Dawla could stand up to the vizier as well as any man, and no one would think to blame him for the Frankish savagery. He had the force of character to free us all from Frankish hands, even Amhara, whom they coveted," Sharif mused out loud. "And fate has been generous to us all since then, hasn't it? Idris ad Dawla honorably regained a place in the court and was given land for his service. That's a good ending to the story."

Faaria smiled at the stooped figure of her brother, who seemed to always harbor optimism. Perhaps the books gave him another happier world to live in. "But the story is *not* ended. It never is. You know as well as I do that the Franks are marching now on Cairo, and there will be another battle before the year is out."

"The Franks have overreached themselves this time, though," he countered. "The caliph's army is strong. Moreover, haven't you heard of the great soldier from the East? Salah al Din, he's called, and he is already on the march behind the invaders."

She shook her head. "I am too old now to worry about coming battles. I care only about my children and grandchildren now."

The servant stood by the horses, and after he handed the reins to Sharif, he helped Faaria into the saddle. When they were both mounted, Sharif took up the thread of the conversation.

"Yes, and all of them are doing well. Your sons are prosperous and your daughters have good husbands. I was worried for awhile about your oldest, Samia. She was just like you, a wild thing, and I thought she'd never marry. Idris got her settled down finally, but now her daughter is just as bad. What a lineage you have produced!"

Faaria laughed along with him. Yes, there was a sort of lineage of odd women. She had concluded as much herself when her granddaughter, at the age of eighteen, refused to marry the fiery young soldier her father had picked for her. When the reproaches began, Faaria realized they were the very same ones that had been made to her and then to her daughter, for being "wild." She knew, the way the men could never know, that all three of them—mother, daughter and granddaughter—preferred the tenderness of women.

The solution, as it turned out, was remarkably simple, once she had managed to convince the grumbling father. Given a sufficient dowry—and a dowry from the house of Idris ad Dawla was always sufficient—all they had to do was find some mild clerk or merchant who would be content to let his young wife have her way. As long as she bore him a few sons over the years and did not publicly shame him, she could have her "tender friendships" as she wished.

Faaria felt a sudden pain in her chest and could not tell whether it was ailment or simply longing for Amhara. Oh, how she missed her. She brooded on the thousand sweet nights that they had shared in ad Dawla's harem, first as passionate lovers and then, in advancing age, as companions. If their husband sensed the intimacy between them, he never resented it, content, it seemed, with their constant tenderness toward him.

Amhara had done her duty and given birth to a son soon after they returned to Cairo and began what would be a large and robust family. Motherhood became her, though she never quite lost the melancholy over her lost infant. Faaria had caught her now and again staring into space, as if looking for a sign from the gods who had promised something and then failed her. And when Amhara had taken her last breath, a year ago, they had shared the same fierce longing, that their two spirits would embrace again in the afterlife.

❖

Finally they reached the house, and the two servants came to help Faaria from her horse. She asked for some tea to be brought to her room.

Her sleeping room was cool, and she removed the hijab with a sigh. The pain that returned as she sat down was probably the indigestion that plagued her. But if it was not, then things had an urgency. With difficulty, she knelt on arthritic knees and drew two chests from under her bed, one in ebony and one half its size in alabaster.

The wooden one was full to bursting with all her family, and it pleased her to see them all together there. Amhara's sons and daughters and her own, and on the top, the layer of grandchildren. Off to the side, wrapped separately, were those of the first generation, carved in their maturity.

Samek had told Amhara of the spirit—the ka he called it—that returned to house in the image of itself. And so, in the faint hope of cheating death, Amhara had insisted that every one of their household, and everyone they loved, be carved in wood. Each one was taken upon their sixteenth birthday to the image maker to be recorded in a graven image. Sharif had heard of this practice and, though skeptical, he agreed. He insisted however that likenesses be carved not only of Husaam, but also of his old white camel that had brought them out of Jerusalem.

Idris ad Dawla was there too, of course, in the splendid armor he wore when he saved them from the Franks. She had let the image maker carve the Frankish knight as well, according to her description. Though she doubted the murderous invader would go to the afterlife where the kas of the virtuous dwelled, she wanted to record him. If there was judgement there, or retribution, she wanted him to meet it in the bloody cross-marked clothing of his army.

She closed the ebony box and tied a cord around the hasp to hold it closed.

The alabaster chest was more precious for it held the image of Amhara. In the first year of their new life in Cairo, while the terror of Jerusalem was still fresh in memory, they had officially renounced the Father God in whose name a river of blood had been shed. But of the religion of the gods they knew little, only what Samek had explained— that the spirit could live on after death as ka. What was required was simply a life of righteousness toward nature and if not a mummy, then a likeness, in which the ka could house.

Faaria couldn't remember how they had found the image maker in the souq, perhaps by accident. But once they knew his craft, they went, each one to make a likeness of the other, vying in precision and using their own hair.

She lifted the Amhara doll from the alabaster chest and kissed it tenderly. As always, it seemed warm to the touch, but then, her hands always warmed at the touch of her, even of her mere image. Faaria didn't know if a spirit lived in it, or ever would but, just in case, their two likenesses would lie together in a single casket. She placed the precious figure next to her own and closed the lid for the last time. After she pressed the hasp in place, she took a candle and coated it with wax to seal it, wondering if it would ever be opened and, if so, by whom.

"*Jaddee*, are you all right? Let me help you."

It was Leyla, her favorite rebellious granddaughter, bringing tea. Faaria allowed herself to be helped to her feet and laid on her bed.

"I'm all right, dear. Look, there's something important you must do. Promise me you'll do it right away."

"Of course, *Jaddee*. I always do what you tell me."

She pointed to the two chests on the floor. "Take those to the image maker in the souq. You know the one I mean, the one who made the little statue of you on your last birthday. Don't let anyone take them from you. He'll know what to do."

Leyla looked puzzled for a moment, then embraced her. "Oh, *Jaddee*. I know you always do what's right for us." The look she gave through lowered eyelids told how much she understood about Faaria's hand in her recent marriage, and about what the two of them had in common. "I promise."

As the door shut, Faaria closed her eyes. The pain in her chest was more severe now. No, it was not indigestion. It seemed as if something struck her so hard she could not draw a breath. She thrashed a little, but made no other sound, only the softest whisper with her last exhalation. "Amhara, habibti."

53

Of Spirit and the Flesh

Valerie and Najya lay together on the narrow hotel bed, facing outward as the midday heat penetrated sleep.

Valerie opened her eyes and licked already moist lips. She tried to lean back to let the air cool her damp throat but immediately hit the wall behind her. "Uff," she said. She rolled on top of Najya and lay for a moment in a long kiss, savoring the wicked pleasure of their two sweat-slick bodies. "Umm, I adore you, *cherie*, but I'm still going to be the first in the shower." She threw back the clammy sheet.

Najya threw an arm across the small of Valerie's back, but not fast enough to keep her from sliding off and making for the bathroom.

Valerie climbed into the miniscule shower platform and stood lathering under the spray of water while it evolved from cold to lukewarm.

Soon, Najya stood in the bathroom doorway, her bronze body glistening with perspiration.

Valerie paused for a moment and let her glance slide over Najya's body like a caress. "Gods, you're so beautiful. You make me speechless."

"Speechlessness isn't one of your qualities, habibti. Anyhow, listen. It's daylight. We're awake and rational. Now, tell me the truth. What did we see last night under the Church of the Sepulchre?"

"Believe it, *cherie*. You saw the kas of Yussif, Derek, and Rekemheb, and the Vulture Goddess of Upper Egypt."

Najya leaned against the doorjamb. "She's stunning, you know. Well, of course you know. You must be in love with her. I'd be. Although that seems like a form of insanity."

"She is, and I was, and it is. But there's more to Nekhbet, of course. And more of *them*. The gods, I mean. And when you see them all together, it's beyond anything you can imagine. Like a Bosch painting, Auset says." Valerie let the water spray deliciously into her face.

"I haven't absorbed last night's events yet. I mean, one part of my

JUSTINE SARACEN

mind has recorded it, but the other part just goes on like before, denying the supernatural. That might be a kind of insanity too."

Eyes shut, Valerie spoke into the air in Najya's general direction. "I think it's actually a kind of *sanity*. I managed to push the supernatural out of my consciousness, even after writing a whole chronicle about these gods. I went back to being a scientist—rational, empirical—just to be able to function. But then Nekhbet appeared and that whole underworld opened up again."

"Underworld. Yes, there would be one, wouldn't there? You'll have to explain that place to me."

"I have a lot to explain to you, habibti. But we have time for that. You're coming back to Cairo with me, aren't you?"

"Yes, of course. I'm not leaving you alone for a moment. There's much too much going on. But listen, now, in the cold light of day, tell me what *you* saw."

Valerie soaped herself. "What I *thought* I saw—although I'm beginning to think I dredged it up from inside myself—was the crucified Christ."

"Oh," Najya said quietly. "It makes sense though, right there in front of Calvary."

"What I can't understand is why you and Auset didn't see him. That makes me wonder if it wasn't maybe a hallucination."

"Why should Jesus be any more a hallucination than Nekhbet? Anyhow, what did he say?"

Valerie stepped off the platform, dripping wet, and kissed Najya quickly before she reached for a towel. "That was the strangest thing of all. He said, 'Tell them, please, to stop.' He wanted to be remembered as a teacher, even a winemaker, not a martyr."

Najya stepped past her into the shower. "Of course he would. Who'd want to hang on a cross for two thousand years? What did you say to him?" She turned the water full in her face.

"Nothing reasonable. I was too dumbfounded. I just asked if my sins were forgiven. Shows you how much Catholic guilt was still cemented in my head. No surprise, though. I grew up in a place where crucifixes hung in every room." Valerie toweled her hair, already feeling her back drying in the too-warm air. She snickered softly. "If he'd stayed any longer I'd have asked him where I could buy some indulgences."

"Indulgences?" came from the shower. "What's that?"

"Oh, it's a Catholic thing. Remission from hell. They're no longer on sale though. Protestants cracked down."

Najya leaned out from the shower. "You laugh, but I think seeing him really affected you."

Valerie leaned against the doorjamb of the bathroom and watched the white soap lather stream down the sleek bronze body. She ran her hand down Najya's wet back to the curve of her buttocks. "You affect me too. You bring me back to earth."

"You can wisecrack, but I think you still have to figure out where you belong."

"I know that. I've signed up with the nature gods."

Najya stepped out next to her and wrapped them both in her towel. They stood for a long moment in each other's arms feeling warm, fresh skin, coarse cotton, and wet hair.

"Well, I've signed up more or less too, but I'm not sure for what. Just exactly how are the Egyptian gods going to make life any better for people—for Palestinians, for Jews wanting to live peacefully with Palestinians, for wretched people anywhere in the world?"

"In the short term, I can't see how they'd change that at all. They don't claim moral authority or omnipotence. They're just the spirits of things, and we have to take care of *them*."

"Then why worship them?" Najya's lips were warm on her shower-cooled skin as they kissed down the side of her face to the tiny scar. "They sound pretty feeble. For gods, I mean." She leaned against Valerie, her body asking a different sort of question.

Valerie pulled them back to the rumpled bed, answering both. "You're probably right. But it's a bit like democracy versus dictatorship. I'd rather have the spirits of wind, water, and wildlife all jostle for attention than have to grovel before an autocrat."

Valerie lay back and pulled Najya on top of her, belly to belly, breasts to breasts, warming again. She edged downward a fraction so she could press her lips under Najya's throat and feel the pounding of her pulse.

"And just how do you worship these gods?" Najya murmured into her ear.

The heat between her legs drew her mind elsewhere, so Valerie summarized the lesson. "Recite the chants, carry the statues to the light at New Year, and revere nature." She felt Najya's leg slide between her thighs, which had grown moist again, and she completely lost the thread.

Najya persisted. "What a choice. Vengeance and martyrs or sunlight and sex."

"Sex? Did I say sex?" Valerie breathed dizzily, the excitement between her legs spreading now to every part of her.

"Yes." Najya rocked against her in a slow rhythm and pressed the first urgent, penetrating kiss.

54

The Shop of Graven Images

S trange, I've been to this part of Cairo a dozen times, and I never noticed it." Najya stood in front of the tiny *mahal*, tucked between a kitchenware shop on one side and a tobacco and sheesha shop on the other.

The rows of mass-produced Anubis jackals, Horus falcons, and Isis mothers still stood at the front. The layer of reddish dust that had settled on them suggested they did not sell very well.

Valerie opened the door to the shop, and they ventured into its dismal interior.

"Ah, Dr…Foret, is it?" The shopkeeper approached them. "You would like to have another likeness made." It was not a question.

"Yes, we would. Two of them. Of these men." Valerie fumbled in her shirt pocket for the wedding picture. "One of them is the man you copied last week. For the priest, remember?"

"Of course. For the priest. But this time it is for himself. He is… deceased," he added neutrally.

"How do you know that?" Valerie asked, startled

He studied the picture again, avoiding her glance. "Forgive me. I saw the picture in the newspaper. I am sorry."

Najya intervened, moving the business along. "So, we would like you to duplicate the first statue, but without the braid."

"Yes," Valerie added. "And of course you should omit the spear wound in the back." She added solemnly, "Please put a small hole… through the heart."

"And the other one?" He held the picture up close. "How did he die? Shall I include a mark?"

"A mark?" Valerie looked toward Najya for help.

Najya shrugged faintly. "I understand that he was thrown from the train, so the injury would have been internal."

The sculptor still waited for an answer, so Valerie added quietly, "No mark."

"Yes, certainly, Dr. Foret." He tilted his head then, as if he studied her, although he quickly dropped his eyes. "Would you like one of yourself as well? Perhaps both of you."

"Of us? Of course not," she snapped. Then she realized the game they both played, each withholding information. It was obvious now that he sculpted for the dead. Perhaps only for the dead. Was the question his way to show he knew they were in mortal danger? A shiver went down her spine.

She changed the subject. "The other statues that you showed me a few days ago in your back room, may I see them again?"

Alarm showed briefly on his face. "Uh...the key to the lock. I am sorry. My assistant has it." He busied himself with something behind the counter.

"Sayyid," she said first, using the Arabic term of respect, but he didn't respond. Then she tried *Chemet*, in old Egyptian, addressing him as royalty, and the suddenness with which he turned around showed her he had understood. She searched her mind for other flattering terms, but all she could come up with was "vizier." "*Tsh 'aty*," she said, and his poorly concealed smirk made it clear he knew he was being flattered— in the ancient language. "We need to see the statues."

He lowered his glance again. "It is unwise, dangerous even."

"Dangerous to learn, or to reveal?"

He looked up through furrowed brows. "It is dangerous for the statues to be seen."

Valerie edged toward the rug that covered the narrow door. "You know we aren't thieves. We come on the advice of Nekhbet."

"Nekhbet. Ah, you might have said that in the beginning."

Valerie relaxed. It was truth time. "The man whose face you copied, the one who died, he was of the line of Rekemheb. And Najya..." She extended her hand toward her. "Najya is also in the family. She knows all our stories and has met the kas of Yussif and Derek, who wait for their likenesses."

His hand went to the pocket of his galabaya. "If goddess approves."

"Of course she approves. I am the writer of the chronicle. And a child of Rekemheb."

His eyes darted back and forth between them as if looking for a family resemblance. "All right, then." He marched the three paces to the carpet-covered door. "But if you want your two likenesses, you must leave soon and let me work." He drew aside the carpet and opened the padlock.

They waited once again for lamplight, sensing the coldness of the room, in spite of the hot September afternoon. He returned and lifted the lantern at the center of the chamber, illuminating the hundreds of figures. All seemed to look down mournfully at them.

"Who are these?" Valerie asked. "Tell me the truth. What is this room?"

He looked past her, into the darkness. "They are the lost ones and this is their necropolis."

"They're all ka statues, aren't they? How is it that you have them? Is this all of them?"

"I will tell you our story. First the Greeks and Romans came with their own gods, but they let us keep our ways. But when the Christians came, the mummification stopped. Those who still believed had likenesses made of themselves to receive their kas, but no priest could be found to speak the incantation, for many had been killed."

He took down a figure and showed it to her. The limbs were intact and carved hair was still in place, but the facial features were hacked away. "And where the people succeeded in bringing ka and likeness together, the Christians seized them and smashed their noses so that they could not draw breath in the underworld."

He brushed his fingers lightly over the ruined face. "Those who were left became guardians of their empty images. They gathered up the ka-dolls, even the ruined ones, to mark our history and passed the guardianship to their children." He swept his hand in a semicircle over the array of dolls and statues. "Now you have had your explanation and you must go."

"Not yet. Please." Valerie raised a hand. "Tell me more about them. Who they are? Are any in the lineage of Rekemheb?"

The image keeper sighed. "Yes, some of his lineage and some of those who knew of it." He pointed overhead to a line of figures carved in various dark woods and took one down. It bore a strange resemblance to both Derek and Rekemheb, though its copious hair sprang out in a sphere around its head. "This one, Samek, was a believer, and in Nubia his children believed as well, and his children's children. Until they were taken into slavery and converted. All were lost, of course."

Najya studied the various shelves with obvious fascination. "I see dolls and statues costumed up to the Middle Ages, but none after."

"There were few believers, and if they made themselves statues, these were useless, for no one knew the ceremony."

Valerie raised her eyebrows at the realization. "I knew the ceremony from my research. Does that mean that I was the first—?"

"Yes. In a thousand years," he finished. "Since the hundredth generation."

Valerie shuddered. "You mean since the Fall of Jerusalem."

He nodded.

She rested a hand on Najya's shoulder, seeking support. "I saw a vision of that day, of the slaughter. And of some that were allowed to leave."

His voice was gentle now. "If you are a child of Rekemheb, then they were your family."

"One of them was Idris ad Dawla," Najya interjected.

"It was." He opened an ebony box at the back of one of the shelves and lifted a figurine from it.

Najya took it from him and held it to the dim lantern light, turning it lovingly.

"This is the Emir of Jerusalem?" Najya asked, awestruck. "The ancestor of my family?"

Age had dulled the colors and cracks had formed along the wood grain, but the detail was so fine that the face and figure still had character. Under a brown breastplate, he wore a green coat belted with a brightly colored sash. His pointed helmet was held in place by a bright blue-green turban with a tail that hung down his back and over the hilt of his sword.

"Of both your families, though, the lines descend from different wives."

"The women I saw leave the city," Valerie said. "Those were his wives, then. Are there statues of them?"

He averted his eyes. "Alas, no. But this one is also of your bloodline." He held up a mounted figure, a slender redheaded man atop a white camel. "Do you know the name Sharif al Kitab?"

Valerie stared into the air for a moment, summoning up memory. "Yeeesss. I think that was the name. I hid one night in his tomb, in the mortuary of Husaam al Noori. With his head under my arm. I had no idea—"

"Sharif al Kitab." Najya repeated the name. "I know it too. I'm certain it's the historian that my brother translated. He wrote a chronicle of the Fall of Jerusalem. I have a copy of it at home."

"Oh, I want to read it. So many connections, so much I still don't know."

"Then you will want to know this too." The image keeper reached past her again into the wooden chest and handed her another figure. It was a Frankish knight, fully armored. Over his painted chain mail he wore a pale tabard with a crimson cross running the length and width of it. Only his helmet was missing, so that his hair was visible, long and yellow.

Valerie held it up close to scrutinize it.

Najya laughed nervously. "He looks familiar. It's the eyes, I think. A little like Harry's. Or even, come to think about it, like yours. Is this another one of your ancestors, you suppose?"

Valerie looked toward the image keeper and spoke in a monotone. "It's the knight who killed the infant, isn't it?" Without awaiting an answer, she laid the statue back in his hand. "My father's eyes. They haunt me in nightmares."

"You don't have to let them, dear," Najya comforted her. "He's dead. All of them are long dead. There's only the living to take care of now, Auset and Nefi, and the kas. That's what we should be thinking about now."

The image keeper seemed to agree, and he placed the knight figurine back in its chest. "Yes, and now that you know the story, we will go back. I must finish the work you have given me." He tried to step past her.

Valerie blocked his way. "No," she said quietly. "You've been lying to us."

55

Auto da Fe

The image keeper was affronted. "I have shown you what you wanted to see. There is nothing more. Now, please, let us go out and finish our business."

Valerie held her ground. "This can't be all. It can't be all so bleak that we few are the only believers who sustain an entire underworld of gods. There have got to be more kas some place."

"There are no more kas," he insisted. "Only the ones that you create. All the others are gone."

"No kas? No kas at all?" she repeated. "You forget, I'm an Egyptologist, not some gullible tourist. You took me for a fool. If you'd told a little lie and said you didn't know, I'd have believed you. But I know the names of all the pharaohs. And even if their mummies are crumbling or lost or no longer hold their ka, hundreds of them have likenesses."

He backed up a step, and she pressed on. "Where for example is Hatchepsut? I've seen her statues. I've seen statues of the whole nineteenth dynasty, and of the Ptolemies. Where are Khephren and Menkaure, the pyramid builders, who stand unbroken in the Cairo Museum, and Ramses the Great, who sits gigantic at Abu Simbel? Their kas must all abide some place, and if they do, why not a thousand others?"

Agitated now, she came to the point. "Where are they? Two years into this prophecy and I'm still having to fight to find out things I should have known at the beginning."

The lantern in his hand wavered. "If you take this knowledge upon yourself, you do it at great risk, to yourself and to many others."

"Risk? I've just lost two family members to murder, and Najya and I came within a hair of being shot ourselves a few days ago. So don't tell me about risk. We've earned the right to know the rest of the story."

He laid his hand to the side of his turban, as if he was getting a headache. "May the gods forgive me. I know your lineage and your

---

sacrifices. I will take you to the ones for whom you have made them." He raised his hand to indicate she should move aside to let him get to the door.

Confused, she and Najya stepped back, expecting him to lead them out. Instead he laid another hasp across the inside of the door and hooked a second padlock on it, locking all of them in. Now, the only way to gain entrance from outside was to smash the door.

He raised his hand a second time and brushed them to both sides of the tiny room while he knelt down and set aside the lantern. He rolled back the tattered carpet, exposing an iron ring on a trap door. With a single heave he hauled it up with both hands, and the lantern at his feet revealed a passageway.

Valerie shook her head. "Yet another stone staircase descending into darkness," she sighed. "Why does nothing in this religion go up?" She followed him as he took the lantern and led the way down the steps.

"But then they'd have to call it the 'overworld,' wouldn't they?" Najya remarked behind her, pulling the trap door shut over their heads.

A stone tunnel, as in the tomb she had uncovered two years before, though a bit narrower, descended at a gentle incline for some twenty paces to another door with another padlock. He worked clumsily with the lock for several minutes, thwarted by rust or ineptitude. Finally he yanked the door open toward them and stood back to let them enter.

A vault was laid out like the closet they had just left, but extended significantly farther out in front of them. Here too, ka-dolls and statues, hundreds of them, stood in rows on shelves that reached above the height of a man. But the air was filled with an electricity that had been absent in the other room. And there was something even more unnerving. She saw it first in the closest figures, then realized it was in every one of them. Life shone in their eyes—the unmistakable glow of consciousness in each one.

"I've wandered so often through the souq. I thought I knew every inch of it," Valerie said as she glanced over the colorful display. "But all that time, this chamber was underneath my feet."

"This vault is older than the souq," the image keeper announced succinctly. "When the Anubis priests were gone, the ones who knew the magic of embalming, our ancestors, built this one last tomb—

for all generations. Centuries later the market came, assuring its concealment."

"Are there other vaults like this one? Other places where the ka-souls rest?" Valerie asked.

"No. This is all that is in the Duat, all that is left of our believers," he said. "These sustain the voices of the gods."

"May I?" she asked.

He nodded and she touched the nearest figure. It was warm, as she knew it would be. An Egyptian, Ptolemaic in dress, as were most of the figures around it. "You'll put Yussif and Derek here?"

He nodded. "With the others of your line."

"My line, the line of Rekemheb?" The words felt strange coming from her mouth. What had been an abstract concept had become tangible, something she could see. She glanced around again at the collection of dolls and statues. No, not a collection, for they lived. It was an assembly, rank upon rank of beings who had consciousness as she did. Did they despair, she wondered, or did they set their hopes on her?

"Can you show them to us?" Najya spoke Valerie's next thought. "The children of Rekemheb?"

The image maker looked resigned to controlling the damage that already had been done. He handed Najya the lantern and reached up to the highest shelf. With some effort, he lifted down an alabaster box, half the size of the wooden one that held the knight and the emir. He polished it first with his sleeve and squinted, seemingly annoyed at the layer of gray wax that covered its hasp. "I had forgotten it was sealed," he grumbled. "But I suppose it is correct for you to break it." He handed it to Valerie.

She scraped at the wax imbedded in the bronze hasp with a fingernail for several minutes. Finally it came loose and she opened the lid.

Najya held the lantern over it, illuminating its contents.

Inside the box lay two female figures of exquisite workmanship. They were more dolls than statues, for they had real hair and were clothed in carefully stitched costumes.

Delicately, Valerie lifted out the first of the two.

The image maker took the doll from her and handed it to Najya. "This one is the mother of your lineage," he said. Though made of painted wood, the statue seemed soft, its edges rounded. The real hair that covered the head was thick and black like Najya's and fell to the middle of the doll's back. The figure was swathed in a dark abaya. Slung over one shoulder and laid diagonally across her chest was a brightly colored shawl or infant's sling. It was empty.

"She's lovely, almost sensual." Najya scrutinized the figure under the light.

"And that is the mother of your line," he said as Valerie lifted the second one, red-haired and boyish, from the chest.

She smiled and fingered the androgynous clothing. "I can believe it." She chuckled. "This would be my wardrobe choice too."

Najya held the dark doll next to the red-haired one. "Sister wives, together for centuries in this tiny casket. Do you suppose—?"

"Oh, I'm sure of it. Look at the short hair, the boy's clothing, even the facial expression on this one. And why weren't they put in the same box as their husband instead of only with each other?"

The image keeper cleared his throat and took the figures gently from their hands. "Let us put them back in their chosen place," he said and laid them back in their common bed.

As he slid the alabaster casket back onto its shelf above his head, Valerie looked around again at the multitude of other figures with their softly glowing eyes. "Can they see me?"

"Only if the ka is present," he said. "But they return here only to seek refuge, when the world is inhospitable." He reached overhead again, to a place right next to the chest he had just replaced. "But while we are here, there is one last likeness you will want to see," he said, handing yet another figure to Valerie.

She stared at it as if hypnotized. "So this is what she looked like," she murmured. "I can't remember." She held it closer to the light and ran her finger along the side of the painted face. She touched the tip of the nose, the lips, the hairline. "There isn't a lot of resemblance," she murmured. "Just the hair color and maybe the nose."

"Who is it?" Najya asked.

"My mother." She touched the head of the doll to her lips, feeling its warmth.

"You didn't know her?"

"She died when I was six. I remember her presence, someone strong and warm who held me. But I know her face only from photos." She brooded for a moment. "I wonder why she never came to visit me."

Najya put her arm around Valerie's back. "She might still. You have years ahead of you to look for her."

"That's another story," the image maker said, and Valerie watched as he wrapped the figure in a cloth and set it near the alabaster casket. She felt a sort of comfort knowing her mother was with the others.

Then she stepped as far back as she could against the door to take in the whole collection, motley and multiracial. "Look at them, Najya. Our roots. Our *Umma*. The precious few hundred who've been in hiding, some of them for twenty centuries, while the Aton owns the world."

"If He owns it, He's not taking very good care of it, is He? 'His right hand smites His left,' you said. It can't be what He intended." Najya returned the lantern to their guide.

"You're right. The power struggles, the cycle of martyrdom and vengeance. It's enough to mess up even God."

The image maker looked up suddenly, alarmed. The tomblike room, which was dim beyond the sphere of the lantern light, seemed to come alive. Ka-eyes in groups here and there, to the left and to the right of them, began to glow a shade brighter than before, like coals that had been fanned. The effect was disorienting, as one section pulsed while the other stayed dull, then began to radiate in turn. Soon every shelf was lit, and the mass of eyes glowed in waves.

"Something is wrong. They have all come back." His hand began to shake so that the sphere of light around them trembled.

"What is it?"

"We have got to leave here. The kas must be protected, above all else." The image maker urged them briskly from the vault and sealed the door behind them. Without speaking, he brushed past and hurried ahead of them along the tunnel.

They followed, perturbed at their abrupt dismissal. "Protected from what?" Najya asked him, although he was soon at a distance from them. "Who's going to want to harm a collection of dolls? And how is anyone going to find them?"

The image maker waited at the foot of the stone steps. "I do not know what it is, but the kas only return this way when the One God stirs everywhere at once. They are that way, like the birds startling at an earthquake." He turned and struggled up the steps in his long galabaya, then lifted the trap door over his head.

"What could it be? Do you mean a real earthquake? What could stir the whole world at the same time?" Alarmed now, Valerie scrambled out of the tunnel right behind him, pulling Najya after her.

The image maker dropped the wooden trap swiftly back into place and covered it once again with the carpet. He stood up and jabbed his key at the padlock until it finally slid in and the lock clicked open.

The three of them stepped out into the shop. It was quiet, just as it had been when they left it. Outside, the street was empty, as it had been when they arrived.

"False alarm." Najya shoved her hands into her pockets, as if to show there was nothing they needed to do. "Looks like we got excited about nothing."

The image maker ventured outside and peered in both directions along the empty alley while they waited in the shop. "I bet it was a ploy to get us out of there," Najya grumbled. "Nothing's going on. It looks just the same as when we arrived."

"You mean the kas all came back for nothing?"

"Maybe it was for something good. We just saved Auset and Nefi, after all. What if word spread around the underworld of what had happened, and they all came to acknowledge us."

"You mean like a little ka party, only we didn't recognize it?"

"Why not? I mean we've just been through a lot, but we did win this round. So maybe things really are improving. It could be that science, nature, rationality are beginning to have more power than faith."

"Faith losing its power?" Valerie chewed her lip, uncertain. If that was happening, no one had told Reverend Carter or Yehuda Ibrahim. She stepped outside the shop.

The image maker still stood, perplexed, in the middle of the alley. Suddenly two men sprinted around the corner. A third, who seemed to be an acquaintance, stopped in front of him, breathless.

"Come to Mahdi's shop and see. It is a terrible thing." He waved to them to follow and ran on ahead.

"Mahdi, who's that?" Valerie asked.

The Egyptian shrugged. "Just someone with a coffee shop."

More men rushed along the street now, calling to others to join them. Valerie and Najya followed them to the corner where a crowd had gathered. Valerie tried to peer through the legs of the crowd to the ground, thinking that someone, Mahdi perhaps, had been hurt, but quickly saw everyone was staring upward. She moved back and forth behind the men until she found a space to see between heads. Najya came behind her and rested a hand on her shoulder.

Bolted high on the wall just inside the café doorway, a television played. Someone turned up the sound, but the rumbling from the street was too loud for her to make out the announcer's words. It made no difference; the images spoke for themselves.

She understood now why the ka had fled. She also knew, as the rest of the world did not yet know, that the atrocity was carried out in the name of the Almighty and that in some other name of the Almighty, there would be retribution.

She laid her hand over Najya's, which clutched her shoulder, and leaned back against her for support. Grimly, she watched the two towers burn like sooty flares sending off thick gray smoke against the bright September sky over New York City.

"The power of faith, Najya. Just wait. Soon we'll see more of it."

About the Author

Justine Saracen was a college professor for fifteen years before leaving academic life for classical music management and then writing. Her scholarly book, *Salvation in the Secular*, addressed themes that persisted into later fiction, the evolution of religion, the leitmotifs of fanaticism, and the power of language. In the 1990s she acquired an online following with "The Pappas Journals," "In the Reich," "Lao Ma's Kiss," and "Women in Prison."

More important were research trips to Egypt and Palestine, which gave rise to the Ibis Prophecy, a series that follows a lesbian archeologist through modern, medieval and ancient Egypt. The first novel of the series, *The 100ᵗʰ Generation*, was a finalist in the Queerlit 2005 contest. The sequel, *Vulture's Kiss*, reveals the drama's bloody antecedent in the First Crusades.

Her upcoming project is *The Mephisto Aria*, a lesbian Faust story set in WWII and the world of opera. Justine is a member of the Publishing Triangle in New York City, and currently studying Arabic and Islamic History. You can visit her at her website at http://justine-saracen.tripod.com.

Books Available From Bold Strokes Books

Vulture's Kiss by Justine Saracen. Archeologist Valerie Foret, heir to a terrifying task, returns in a powerful desert adventure set in Egypt and Jerusalem. (978-1-933110-87-5)

Rising Storm by JLee Meyer. The sequel to *First Instinct* takes our heroines on a dangerous journey instead of the honeymoon they'd planned. (978-1-933110-86-8)

Not Single Enough by Grace Lennox. A funny, sexy modern romance about two lonely women who bond over the unexpected and fall in love along the way. (978-1-933110-85-1)

Such a Pretty Face by Gabrielle Goldsby. A sexy, sometimes humorous, sometimes biting contemporary romance that gently exposes the damage to heart and soul when we fail to look beneath the surface for what truly matters. (978-1-933110-84-4)

Second Season by Ali Vali. A romance set in New Orleans amidst betrayal, Hurricane Katrina, and the new beginnings hardship and heartbreak sometimes make possible. (978-1-933110-83-7)

Hearts Aflame by Ronica Black. A poignant, erotic romance between a hard-driving businesswoman and a solitary vet. Packed with adventure and set in the harsh beauty of the Arizona countryside. (978-1-933110-82-0)

Red Light by JD Glass. Tori forges her path as an EMT in the New York City 911 system while discovering what matters most to herself and the woman she loves. (978-1-933110-81-3)

Honor Under Siege by Radclyffe. Secret Service agent Cameron Roberts struggles to protect her lover while searching for a traitor who just may be another woman with a claim on her heart. (978-1-933110-80-6)

Dark Valentine by Jennifer Fulton. Danger and desire fuel a high stakes cat-and-mouse game when an attorney and an endangered witness team up to thwart a killer. (978-1-933110-79-0)

Sequestered Hearts by Erin Dutton. A popular artist suddenly goes into seclusion; a reluctant reporter wants to know why; and a heart locked away yearns to be set free. (978-1-933110-78-3)

Erotic Interludes 5: Road Games eds. Radclyffe and Stacia Seaman. Adventure, "sport," and sex on the road—hot stories of travel adventures and games of seduction. (978-1-933110-77-6)

The Spanish Pearl by Catherine Friend. On a trip to Spain, Kate Vincent is accidentally transported back in time...an epic saga spiced with humor, lust, and danger. (978-1-933110-76-9)

Lady Knight by L-J Baker. Loyalty and honour clash with love and ambition in a medieval world of magic when female knight Riannon meets Lady Eleanor. (978-1-933110-75-2)

Dark Dreamer by Jennifer Fulton. Best-selling horror author, Rowe Devlin falls under the spell of psychic Phoebe Temple. A Dark Vista romance. (978-1-933110-74-5)

Come and Get Me by Julie Cannon. Elliott Foster isn't used to pursuing women, but alluring attorney Lauren Collier makes her change her mind. (978-1-933110-73-8)

Blind Curves by Diane and Jacob Anderson-Minshall. Private eye Yoshi Yakamota comes to the aid of her ex-lover Velvet Erickson in the first Blind Eye mystery. (978-1-933110-72-1)

Dynasty of Rogues by Jane Fletcher. It's hate at first sight for Ranger Riki Sadiq and her new patrol corporal, Tanya Coppelli—except for their undeniable attraction. (978-1-933110-71-4)

Running With the Wind by Nell Stark. Sailing instructor Corrie Marsten has signed off on love until she meets Quinn Davies—one woman she can't ignore. (978-1-933110-70-7)

More than Paradise by Jennifer Fulton. Two women battle danger, risk all, and find in one another an unexpected ally and an unforgettable love. (978-1-933110-69-1)

Flight Risk by Kim Baldwin. For Blayne Keller, being in the wrong place at the wrong time just might turn out to be the best thing that ever happened to her. (978-1-933110-68-4)

Rebel's Quest, Supreme Constellations Book Two by Gun Brooke. On a world torn by war, two women discover a love that defies all boundaries. (978-1-933110-67-7)

Punk and Zen by JD Glass. Angst, sex, love, rock. Trace, Candace, Francesca...Samantha. Losing control—and finding the truth within. BSB Victory Editions. (1-933110-66-X)

Stellium in Scorpio by Andrews & Austin. The passionate reuniting of two powerful women on the glitzy Las Vegas Strip where everything is an illusion and love is a gamble. (1-933110-65-1)

When Dreams Tremble by Radclyffe. Two women whose lives turned out far differently than they'd once imagined discover that sometimes the shape of the future can only be found in the past. (1-933110-64-3)

The Devil Unleashed by Ali Vali. As the heat of violence rises, so does the passion. A Casey Family crime saga. (1-933110-61-9)

Burning Dreams by Susan Smith. The chronicle of the challenges faced by a young drag king and an older woman who share a love "outside the bounds." (1-933110-62-7)

Fresh Tracks by Georgia Beers. Seven women, seven days. A lot can happen when old friends, lovers, and a new girl in town get together in the mountains. (1-933110-63-5)

The Empress and the Acolyte by Jane Fletcher. Jemeryl and Tevi fight to protect the very fabric of their world: time. Lyremouth Chronicles Book Three. (1-933110-60-0)

First Instinct by JLee Meyer. When high-stakes security fraud leads to murder, one woman flees for her life while another risks her heart to protect her. (1-933110-59-7)

Erotic Interludes 4: *Extreme Passions* ed. by Radclyffe and Stacia Seaman. Thirty of today's hottest erotica writers set the pages aflame with love, lust, and steamy liaisons. (1-933110-58-9)

Storms of Change by Radclyffe. In the continuing saga of the Provincetown Tales, duty and love are at odds as Reese and Tory face their greatest challenge. (1-933110-57-0)

Unexpected Ties by Gina L. Dartt. With death before dessert, Kate Shannon and Nikki Harris are swept up in another tale of danger and romance. (1-933110-56-2)

Sleep of Reason by Rose Beecham. While Detective Jude Devine searches for a lost boy, her rocky relationship with Dr. Mercy Westmoreland gets a lot harder. (1-933110-53-8)

Passion's Bright Fury by Radclyffe. Passion strikes without warning when a trauma surgeon and a filmmaker become reluctant allies. (1-933110-54-6)

Broken Wings by L-J Baker. When Rye Woods meets beautiful dryad Flora Withe, her libido, as hidden as her wings, reawakens along with her heart. (1-933110-55-4)

Combust the Sun by Andrews & Austin. A Richfield and Rivers mystery set in L.A. Murder among the stars. (1-933110-52-X)

Of Drag Kings and the Wheel of Fate by Susan Smith. A blind date in a drag club leads to an unlikely romance. (1-933110-51-1)

Tristaine Rises by Cate Culpepper. Brenna, Jesstin, and the Amazons of Tristaine face their greatest challenge for survival. (1-933110-50-3)

Too Close to Touch by Georgia Beers. Kylie O'Brien believes in true love and is willing to wait for it, even though Gretchen, her new boss, is off-limits. (1-933110-47-3)

The 100ᵗʰ Generation by Justine Saracen. Ancient curses, modern-day villains, and an intriguing woman lead archeologist Valerie Foret on the adventure of her life. (1-933110-48-1)

Battle for Tristaine by Cate Culpepper. While Brenna struggles to find her place in the clan, Tristaine is threatened with destruction. Second in the Tristaine series. (1-933110-49-X)

The Traitor and the Chalice by Jane Fletcher. Tevi and Jemeryl risk all in the race to uncover a traitor. The Lyremouth Chronicles Book Two. (1-933110-43-0)

Promising Hearts by Radclyffe. Dr. Vance Phelps arrives in New Hope, Montana, with no hope of happiness—until she meets Mae. (1-933110-44-9)

Carly's Sound by Ali Vali. Poppy Valente and Julia Johnson form a bond of friendship that becomes something far more. A poignant romance about love and renewal. (1-933110-45-7)

Unexpected Sparks by Gina L. Dartt. Kate Shannon's attraction to much younger Nikki Harris is complication enough without a fatal fire that Kate can't ignore. (1-933110-46-5)

Whitewater Rendezvous by Kim Baldwin. Two women on a wilderness kayak adventure discover that true love may be nothing at all like they imagined. (1-933110-38-4)

Erotic Interludes 3: *Lessons in Love* ed. by Radclyffe and Stacia Seaman. Sign on for a class in love…the best lesbian erotica writers take us to "school." (1-9331100-39-2)

Punk Like Me by JD Glass. Twenty-one-year-old Nina has a way with the girls, and she doesn't always play by the rules. (1-933110-40-6)

Coffee Sonata by Gun Brooke. Four women whose lives unexpectedly intersect in a small town by the sea share one thing in common—they all have secrets. (1-933110-41-4)

The Clinic: Tristaine Book One by Cate Culpepper. Brenna, a prison medic, finds herself drawn to Jesstin, a warrior reputed to be descended from ancient Amazons. (1-933110-42-2)

Forever Found by JLee Meyer. Can time, tragedy, and shattered trust destroy a love that seemed destined? Chance reunites childhood friends separated by tragedy. (1-933110-37-6)

Sword of the Guardian by Merry Shannon. Princess Shasta's bold new bodyguard has a secret that could change both of their lives. *He* is actually a *she*. (1-933110-36-8)

Wild Abandon by Ronica Black. Dr. Chandler Brogan and Officer Sarah Monroe are drawn together by their common obsessions—sex, speed, and danger. (1-933110-35-X)

Turn Back Time by Radclyffe. Pearce Rifkin and Wynter Thompson have nothing in common but a shared passion for surgery—and unexpected attraction. (1-933110-34-1)

Chance by Grace Lennox. A sexy, funny, touching story of two women who, in finding themselves, also find one another. (1-933110-31-7)

The Exile and the Sorcerer by Jane Fletcher. First in the Lyremouth Chronicles. Tevi and a shy young sorcerer face monsters, magic, and the challenge of loving. (1-933110-32-5)

A Matter of Trust by Radclyffe. When what should be just business turns into much more, two women struggle to trust the unexpected. (1-933110-33-3)

Sweet Creek by Lee Lynch. A celebration of the enduring nature of love, friendship, and community in the heart-warming lesbian community of Waterfall Falls. (1-933110-29-5)

The Devil Inside by Ali Vali. The head of a New Orleans crime organization falls for a woman who turns her world upside down. (1-933110-30-9)

Grave Silence by Rose Beecham. Detective Jude Devine's investigation of ritual murders is complicated by her torrid affair with pathologist Dr. Mercy Westmoreland. (1-933110-25-2)

Honor Reclaimed by Radclyffe. Secret Service Agent Cameron Roberts and Blair Powell close ranks to find the would-be assassins who nearly claimed Blair's life. (1-933110-18-X)

Honor Bound by Radclyffe. Secret Service Agent Cameron Roberts and Blair Powell face political intrigue, a clandestine threat to Blair's safety, and the seemingly irreconcilable differences that force them ever farther apart. (1-933110-20-1)

Innocent Hearts by Radclyffe. In a wild and unforgiving land, two women learn about love, passion, and the wonders of the heart. (1-933110-21-X)

The Temple at Landfall by Jane Fletcher. An imprinter, one of Celaeno's most revered servants of the Goddess, is also a prisoner to the faith—until a Ranger frees her by claiming her heart. The Celaeno series. (1-933110-27-9)

Protector of the Realm, Supreme Constellations Book One by Gun Brooke. A space adventure filled with suspense and a daring intergalactic romance. (1-933110-26-0)

Force of Nature by Kim Baldwin. From tornados to forest fires, the forces of nature conspire to bring Gable McCoy and Erin Richards close to danger, and closer to each other. (1-933110-23-6)

In Too Deep by Ronica Black. Undercover homicide cop Erin McKenzie tracks a femme fatale who just might be a real killer…with love and danger hot on her heels. (1-933110-17-1)

Erotic Interludes 2: *Stolen Moments* ed. by Radclyffe and Stacia Seaman. Love on the run, in the office, in the shadows…Fast, furious, and almost too hot to handle. (1-933110-16-3)

Course of Action by Gun Brooke. Actress Carolyn Black desperately wants the starring role in an upcoming film produced by Annelie Peterson. Just how far will she go for the dream part of a lifetime? (1-933110-22-8)

Rangers at Roadsend by Jane Fletcher. Sergeant Chip Coppelli has learned to spot trouble coming, and that is exactly what she sees in her new recruit, Katryn Nagata. The Celaeno series. (1-933110-28-7)

Justice Served by Radclyffe. Lieutenant Rebecca Frye and her lover, Dr. Catherine Rawlings, embark on a deadly game of hide-and-seek with an underworld kingpin who traffics in human souls. (1-933110-15-5)

Distant Shores, Silent Thunder by Radclyffe. Dr. Tory King—along with the women who love her—is forced to examine the boundaries of love, friendship, and the ties that transcend time. (1-933110-08-2)

Hunter's Pursuit by Kim Baldwin. A raging blizzard, a mountain hideaway, and a killer-for-hire set a scene for disaster—or desire—when Katarzyna Demetrious rescues a beautiful stranger. (1-933110-09-0)

The Walls of Westernfort by Jane Fletcher. All Temple Guard Natasha Ionadis wants is to serve the Goddess—until she falls in love with one of the rebels she is sworn to destroy. The Celaeno series. (1-933110-24-4)

Erotic Interludes: *Change Of Pace* by Radclyffe. Twenty-five hot-wired encounters guaranteed to spark more than just your imagination. Erotica as you've always dreamed of it. (1-933110-07-4)

Honor Guards by Radclyffe. In a wild flight for their lives, the president's daughter and those who are sworn to protect her wage a desperate struggle for survival. (1-933110-01-5)

Fated Love by Radclyffe. Amidst the chaos and drama of a busy emergency room, two women must contend not only with the fragile nature of life, but also with the irresistible forces of fate. (1-933110-05-8)

Justice in the Shadows by Radclyffe. In a shadow world of secrets and lies, Detective Sergeant Rebecca Frye and her lover, Dr. Catherine Rawlings, join forces in the elusive search for justice. (1-933110-03-1)

shadowland by Radclyffe. In a world on the far edge of desire, two women are drawn together by power, passion, and dark pleasures. An erotic romance. (1-933110-11-2)

Love's Masquerade by Radclyffe. Plunged into the indistinguishable realms of fiction, fantasy, and hidden desires, Auden Frost is forced to question all she believes about the nature of love. (1-933110-14-7)

Love & Honor by Radclyffe. The president's daughter and her lover are faced with difficult choices as they battle a tangled web of Washington intrigue for...love and honor. (1-933110-10-4)

Beyond the Breakwater by Radclyffe. One Provincetown summer, three women learn the true meaning of love, friendship, and family. (1-933110-06-6)

Tomorrow's Promise by Radclyffe. One timeless summer, two very different women discover the power of passion to heal and the promise of hope that only love can bestow. (1-933110-12-0)

Love's Tender Warriors by Radclyffe. Two women who have accepted loneliness as a way of life learn that love is worth fighting for and a battle they cannot afford to lose. (1-933110-02-3)

Love's Melody Lost by Radclyffe. A secretive artist with a haunted past and a young woman escaping a life that has proved to be a lie find their destinies entwined. (1-933110-00-7)

Safe Harbor by Radclyffe. A mysterious newcomer, a reclusive doctor, and a troubled gay teenager learn about love, friendship, and trust during one tumultuous summer in Provincetown. (1-933110-13-9)

Above All, Honor by Radclyffe. Secret Service Agent Cameron Roberts fights her desire for the one woman she can't have—Blair Powell, the daughter of the president of the United States. (1-933110-04-X)